Fourteen and a Quarter

Coined Fiction

To a super "suite" lady, cookies and all! Serena Ivo

SERENA IVO

Some content of this book was inspired by real events and
individuals. To protect privacy, names and identifying details
have been changed.

Published by Serena Ivo. North Charleston, SC.
For permissions and ordering information,
contact Serena Ivo.
www.SerenaIvo.com
SerenaIvo@hotmail.com

First Edition: November 2017. Printed by CreateSpace.

Library of Congress Control Number: 2017916364

ISBN: 0692953914 [paperback]
ISBN-13: 978-0692953914 [paperback]

CONTENTS

DEDICATION

To my eternal companion, My Protector:

Because your belief in me
is greater than what I have in myself,
I persevered and finished.

1

Out Cashed

She felt a thick darkness inside because she, again, perpetuated the lie. She wanted to avoid the purchase, but could not bring herself to reject the counsel of her stylist. William would have treated the refusal as a joke. Did he notice her hesitation over the additional $39 for shampoo?

Darting back to work through bustling sidewalks with a $5 coffee held by a $65 manicure, Brooke felt the fear spreading through her body. Her flight instinct kicked in, and she involuntarily looked for cover. Though the adversary was merely an intangible number, the debt felt alive, a presence stories high, stretching its tentacles toward her to constrict and suffocate. She was breathing hard, almost gasping, but continued to appear powerful and composed to passersby, simply out of habit.

Scanning the street in her mental frenzy, her eye caught the shimmer of a small object on the ground. On impulse, Brooke paced evenly to the spot and saw that it was a quarter. Her consuming need for cash bent her to the ground to pick it up. In her mind, she pictured social peers catching her in Rodeo Drive glam stooping for a germ-laced quarter, and sensing this, her hand hovered over the coin. Gently curling before her view was a stream of smoke drawing her eye to a smoldering cigarette lying two feet away. The scent was wholly diverting. With the nerves of a shoplifter, she assessed the awareness of those walking by, plucked up the butt, and swiftly moved around the corner of the nearest building into a shadowed doorway.

Savoring the drag like it was a massage, she let the nicotine infect her body, soothing away the panic. Three long intervals of peace were pulled off the stick before her mind slowed enough to reason. Brooke examined the charred butt encircled with her lipstick before flicking it to her pumps. She realized her mouth had shared space with a stranger, absorbing stomach flu and cold sores. Wincing, she thought, *What am I doing? Is puffing a ditched cigarette better than picking up a quarter?* A tiny prick of lucidity spiked her thinking. *Where is my judgment?*

The question pointed to the source of her pride, the key to her success. Her judgment of what delineated the classes of society helped her to select qualifying goods, to connect with the sophisticated, to work for the right brands, and to hold conversation that cemented her acceptability. But all those maneuverings required a lined pocketbook. Mantras such as "It takes money to make money" and "Dress for the job you want, not the job you have" propelled the spending that elevated her status. The years of buying her rank in society were coming to account. The rotating credit cards, layered mortgages, and minimum payments ceased treading water.

While nursing the coffee, she groped for answers. There were banal solutions such as declaring bankruptcy, selling the X5, renting a mother-in-law, and strip mall haircuts—wholesale humiliation. She would do nothing that resembled her embarrassing origins. Already entangled in sexual bartering, she saw clearly the allure of gambling…and stealing. Yes, even stealing. Her ponderings led to places darker than the lurking cloud of debt that compounded every second. Yet, no option alarmed her. A public downfall was more appalling than any means to avoid it.

She had emptied her latte minutes ago, but still held the cup to her lips in deliberation. Realistically, most alternatives would result in a situation less survivable than this. Did she want to survive this? Exiting now would ensure leaving the world draped in and surrounded by the best. Her colleagues would remember her urbane dinner parties in her downtown sprawling condo adorned with inspired pieces. A stupefying self-inflicted death would guarantee honors and respect equal to her tastes.

In death, however, the secret could not be controlled. It was prone to discovery. The most tantalizing gossip, laced with speculation and half-truths, would lay waste to her life's work. Her set feasted on the ignominy of others. In order to have the final say over the outcome of her situation, she would have to live it out. To ensure the least amount of injury to her narrative, she must employ the modes of common people. The irony was staggering.

The resolve slowly settled into her core. Taking in measured breaths of the urine-scented air helped her mind to stop debating. The charade was over. As the finality of the decision took hold, the dark sludge inside her melted gradually into emptiness. Letting go of the purpose of the last 13 years of her life created an unfamiliar void, but it felt better than what had been there moments before.

In this newness, Brooke awakened to her surroundings and took in the scene. Herds of business people swiftly moved to their offices and other less directed people sat in the shelter of trees and doorways. The mid-day sun created high contrast shadows and squinting profiles. Luxury cars and impatient taxis paused for red lights. Designer ties flashed their patterns and European handbags bounced to the click of fine heels. It all looked so fantastic. It occurred to her that some of those handsome people also lived the dirty lie. The truth struck her consciousness, and she felt a little less alone.

Twenty feet from her, an overture to this new act was gently strummed on a guitar. A fedora with coinage glinted next to the musician. Acknowledging the sign, she moved calmly from her station and retraced her steps around the corner of the building. To collect the twenty-five cents was, in effect, turning to face the behemoth of debt in her wake.

Her eyes fell upon the spot where the quarter had been. It was gone.

2

Tipped

Marc fumbled through his noon-hour breakfast feeling a bit hungover. He chugged stale water from an abandoned glass on the laminate counter and successfully searched the bread box. Balancing an Asiago bagel on its side, he tried to guide the serrated knife down the middle. In his fatigue, he failed to control the bagel and felt the pop of every point through the flesh of his hand with the second draw of the knife.

Pain seared through his hand, skin and sinew aflame. At first, he tried to squeeze back the tormenting throbs. A deep burgundy color collected on the cutting board, resembling spilt Chianti. Rapt by the blood, he let go of his hand which leaked steadily with every fiery pulse, draining away the falsehood of his identity. The rich, velvet color of his life glistened, a puddle of memories and tradition.

The blood began to fall off the counter to the taupe tile, creating modern art worthy of a canvas: *drip*, Nonna's lasagna; *drip,* backyard bocce games; *drip,* fish feasts for Midnight mass; *drip,* Little Italy dining; *drip,* the flag bumper sticker; *drip,* St. Rosalia in the yard—12 drops, 20 drops, 37 drops—a glorious spray of a phony life at his toes.

"Dude! You're bleeding! Hold up." His roommate, Jeff, entered the kitchen and snatched the dish towel. "Geez, did you cut an artery? Run it under cold water!"

Devoid of emotion, Marc looked up from his feet, and then to the gore that was his hand.

Jeff ushered Marc to the sink and flicked the cold water on. "Maybe you're in shock."

"Yeah, I think I am." Marc let Jeff wash his hand while pink swirled down the sink.

Over the next ten minutes, Jeff assisted Marc in wrapping the hand in excessive gauze. After some unproductive quizzing, Jeff said, "You're looking sick, bro. Really wasted."

"I'm tired. I didn't get much sleep."

"Your knife work sucked. You must be tired." Jeff became serious. "Are you OK, man?"

"The hand is fine. Other than that, I don't know." A debate ensued, and Jeff finally agreed to skip the ER. Marc thanked Jeff and lumbered to his room with the falsehood feeling as heavy as an anvil.

Marc slumped onto the tangled sheets of his bed and replayed in his mind the lunch he had with his mother the previous day. Her revelation triggered a full reassessment of his family. *Mom was so unbelievably insensitive. My parents are liars! And yet, Dad always treats me well. And is it true that Grandpa and Grandma would have rejected me if they had known the truth? I thought they were so cool, and now, it seems that they are jerks. What will Dad's family think? How can it be legal to conceal this from me? Wait, do I have brothers and sisters? Have I dated my sisters? Oh, my God.* The questions and corollaries multiplied like a viral infection, a pandemic annihilating his normalcy.

These emerging riddles were exacerbating the outrage that had plagued him for 24 hours. The anger and worry then congealed into a headache of such potency that it nullified the stinging in Marc's hand. *Porn and a syringe. Sick. Did he do it just for money? How did they get away with it? Of course, the contacts at Mom's government job helped her.* In dour rumination, his eyes wandered around the sparse room of barren walls, electronics, dirty laundry, and weights, and stopped on an object most symbolic of what the truth meant, a Mason jar on his dresser.

His maternal grandfather, an avid coin collector, had given Marc ten 1990 quarters on his tenth birthday, along with a BB gun. The quarters found a home in a Mason jar provided by his mother, and whenever Marc ran across a 1990 quarter, he added it to the jar. With the proliferation of new types of quarters since that year, the hunt for 1990 coins in loose change became a pleasant challenge. The years of picking through coinage had yielded a few hundred dollars in his collection. He intended to use the accumulation for a special purpose. He had plans this summer that required substantial funding, and the jar would have served him well.

But now, to Marc, the quarters had lost their value. The jar of carefully culled coins had become a symbol of his grandparents' conditional adoration, and represented a distorted version of his own life. The practical side of him would have taken the jar to a coin machine and converted it all to cash, ignoring the story behind it. Yet, the jar could be the weighty anvil, the very lie in his hands. Those quarters had to go, and their dismissal must be in a way that was therapeutic.

———————————•————————————

The salt air felt cleansing in his lungs and filled Marc's ears with the sounds of placid low-tide waves and fluttering shore grass. Soft sand spread on either side of him for a mile. At sundown, visibility was diminishing and the details of the spot were hard to see, and therefore, hard to commit to memory. He sat on a log of driftwood overdue to become fuel for a bonfire. His family tree had become the gray, weatherworn wood, taken down by a thunderbolt of reality. Uprooted was the fundamental premise of his identity, the ethnic and cultural side of his genealogy that his paternal family reinforced and celebrated with pride.

Marc knelt down in the cool sand and began to dig with his hands. Wondering how the jar would resurface, he pictured different scenarios: a family building a castle, siblings excavating canals and piling dams, clam diggers on the hunt, or an old man with a metal detector. Perhaps waves would draw up the jar over time and newlyweds would spy it while walking hand-in-hand. If undisturbed for centuries, it could become an archeological discovery reminiscent of the cache of Roman coins found in the ruins of Trier. In any case, the individual who would one day unearth the jar would experience the matchless thrill that only hidden treasure could rouse.

For Marc, however, this occasion in the sand was a burial. He could not emotionally move on if he dwelt on the disappointing fabrications about himself. Life had been good, but what he understood of it was dead. His life and his relationships needed to begin anew. To the sand, the grave, he would entomb the hoax.

The Mason jar packed with nearly one thousand quarters was laid for interment more than two feet beneath the surface, and seemed to beg for some kind of ritual goodbye. Memories of family funerals directed by Father Dimino rolled through Marc's mind for guidance. At minimum, he could sign the cross, since there was no incense or holy water to sanctify the work. Debating which direction of movement would be most intrinsic, left-to-right or right-to-left, bothered him too much to make any gesture. Unceremoniously, he buried the jar and concealed the spot as the remnant glow of the sun dimmed to midnight blue. Were there a marker, the epitaph would have claimed "Born February 20, 1990" under his name of Etruscan origin.

Marc rose and trudged back through the dunes, reflecting on the last time he found a quarter for the jar, now aware that it was his final act of coin collecting.

In a downtown pub with classic rock piping through the speakers, Marc waited for his mother to share her lunch break with him. To pass the time, the familiar menu was his reading material. He noticed the tip on the table from the previous occupants and could not help but check the mint date on the quarters. He scored. Marc took one of the quarters and traded it for another in his pocket.

His mother, Debra, arrived with her I.D. and security tags flapping as she passed through the breezeway. He wished she would remove the lanyard when off the federal campus so she would not look so official. After peeling off her blazer, his prim mother greeted him with a vivacious hello and leaned down to demand a peck on the cheek before she took her seat.

The conversation was entirely predictable with her complaints about office politics and the inexperienced figureheads appointed over her division. Marc shared the typical rundown of his class schedule while deflecting questions about what girl he was dating. His college years were coming to a close, and Debra cheered the news that he had a job interview pending graduation. Then, the conversation took a life-altering turn.

"So, how are you planning to celebrate your graduation?" asked Debra while emptying the sauce cup of dressing over her salad.

"Lots of my friends have backpacked Europe. I'm thinking that would be pretty cool. Jared and I are starting to make plans. He wants to go to Germany and Holland, and I want to go to Italy, of course, maybe Spain."

His mother's penciled eyebrows rose a little. "Europe? Goodness! You haven't yet seen all that the States have to offer: New Orleans, Mount Rushmore, the Everglades, and the Grand Canyon. Why don't you explore America first? That seems to be a better first step, don't you think?"

"Nah, I'm feeling Europe." He bit into his blue cheese burger.

"Listen, sweetie, I'm quite serious. You'll love touring the country so much more. In Europe, you'll have to deal with the languages, and exchanging money, and— Oh! What about all the financial problems and immigrant troubles? There are riots happening in some places!"

"Mom, no. It will be OK. Adam and Russ just came back from Europe and they had no problems. It's going to be fine."

"Are you sure? Really sure? I'd hate for you to have a bad time and waste your money."

"Yes! Mom, you are freaking out over nothing. Chill. I am going to do it, and I will be fine." Marc almost rolled his eyes. He chucked a fry into his mouth.

Debra went quiet and looked far past him like she was having a conversation with herself. It was the same look she got whenever Marc said he hated gyros, or when he wanted his driving permit. "What," he insisted. "What?"

"Marcus, if you are really going to Europe, there's something you need to know."

"Mom, you've got to chill out. What?"

She finished her bite and sat up straight. "Well," she began with awkward formality, "in order to get to Europe, obviously you will need a passport. To get your passport, you will need your birth certificate. And it is possible you may be surprised by what you'll find on the birth certificate."

This is getting weird. Marc's brow furrowed. "What, like, I was born in Kansas or something?"

11

"No." She adjusted her watchband. "Now, Marcus, understand this first. What you are about to learn, know that everything was born out of love, including yourself." The creases in Marc's brow deepened and his stomach tightened. "Your birthday will look a little different."

"What do you mean, 'a little different'?" The burger paused over the plate in his bronze hands as he awaited impact.

"Your birthdate is listed as December 27, 1989." Debra returned to her lunch and forked some salad.

Marc responded slowly, "Which is wrong."

She took time to swallow. "Actually, it is not wrong. That *is* your birthday."

Watching his mother, Marc searched for an indication of a prank in her demeanor. Her posture began to wither. She was not kidding.

"December 27, 1989. That's my birthday. Not February 20, 1990."

"Correct." She smiled, looking a little less tall.

He did not smile. "And why on earth have I celebrated the wrong birthdate my whole life?"

"You were supposed to be born February 20th, but you arrived early."

"That does not explain why we celebrate my due date and not my birthdate." The burger still hovered.

Debra shifted her shoulders, took a few sips of iced tea, and smiled. "When your father and I met, we fell instantly and crazy in love. As you know, your dad is twelve years older than I, and he didn't ever expect to want a family. He was happy being single and enjoyed his dating life, and just wanted to have fun. I came along, and all that changed. We wanted a life together and we wanted a family."

She wiped her mouth with the napkin. After appearing to organize her thoughts, she continued, "As you know, we moved in together and hid it from our parents, well, my parents, because they are so old-fashioned; they would have thrown a fit. It was none of their business anyhow. Because your dad got fixed long before we met, we got some assistance, and by some miracle, it took the first time, which totally surprised us. We decided to get married to prevent my parents from rejecting you and your dad, so we eloped right after we were sure I was pregnant, which would make you a preemie in their eyes had you come on-time. My parents accepted that story, because they are determined to be naïve. Then you actually were a preemie, which is so perfect. So, that part we never fudged, because it's true! It's like it was all meant to be!"

After putting the burger down, Marc silently parsed her story and broke it down to the part that would determine how OK or awful it all was. "You and Dad 'got some assistance,' like Dad got his plumbing reassembled?"

She took an audible breath and tried to sound positive. "We looked into that, and there were many ways where that surgery could fail. If it did work, recovery could take a long time, and your dad was getting older—and so was I, for that matter. Then we looked into sucking the little guys out, and that is prohibitively expensive. In the end, we didn't care how it happened. So, we got a donor, and that's all it took!" Debra resumed eating.

"A donor? Did you go to a sperm bank?" His food seemed suddenly inedible. "I cannot believe what you are saying."

"Honey, your father's name is on the birth certificate. He is your father in all ways except in this one little way. And this stuff is done all the time, I assure you. It is so great because, otherwise, who knows if we could have had children. And you are such a joy to us!"

"So, Dad is not my father." He pressed his lips together.

Debra frowned and nodded emphatically. "Absolutely, he is. Don't say that."

As humiliation and rage began to clash within, Marc consciously went numb and assumed the detachment of a reporter. "So, what do you know of the guy? Anything?"

"We picked the best possible match. The donor was young, 20 or something, and an inch shorter than your dad, five-eight, hazel eyes, dark hair. In fact, everything was the same, really, except he was Greek rather than Italian, which is probably why their coloring was so similar."

"I'm not Italian? Are you kidding me?"

"Technically, no. But you were raised Italian. Nothing can take that away from you."

"Mom, everything is taken away from me! I don't know who the hell I am!"

"Now, you be careful, Marcus. You are the same person you have always been. You have had a superb life, and your father is wonderful—far better than most kids', in my opinion. I will not stand by and allow you to insult me or your father!"

A tornado had burst through the restaurant doors and consumed him only, while his mother watched. Hunched over a nearly untouched meal, Marc clenched his jet black waves with both hands. The lull in conversation hung over the table like a wet towel.

Ignoring his mother's silence, Marc turned to the window, ashen. "So, my no-name, Greek father is, like, 41, out there, somewhere, and I am older than I thought." Marc took the quarter out of his pocket and slid it onto the table. "This is crazy. I can't deal." He stood and unhooked his jacket from the back of the chair.

Debra seized his arm. "Calm down, sweetie. I know this is a surprise, but do not overreact!"

"You are clueless, Mom!" Marc yanked his arm away. "I have to go."

"Honey, just please consider this: when two people fall in love, they want a family. It's natural. Someday, you will understand how we felt."

He glared at her before quitting the table. "And you will never understand how I feel."

3

Invisibility

He saw blood splattered against a face, hands, t-shirt… The face did not look right. No. Not at all. Bike wreck. That was his bike, his contorted face, his blood. Impossibly, Brian was watching himself lie still on the pavement surrounded by panicked people. *Why am I looking down at myself? Wake up! Am I dreaming?* A conscious thought should end the dream, but the scene played on. He had perfect awareness of the sounds and visuals around him, but felt nothing. No pain. Something was terribly wrong. Reality had taken an irrational turn. *If I am dead, why am I thinking? I cannot be dead. How could I know that I'm thinking? What is happening?*

Police, fire, and medics swarmed to handle the traffic disruption, crowd, and the body—his body. No person asked him to get behind the officers. Nobody eyed him at all. Brian watched the movie from different angles. He could come in closer, pull away, and hover above the commotion. His detached and floating consciousness was bewildering.

In consternation, Brian positioned himself over the sidewalk to watch the medics slide his body into the aid car and drive away. He intentionally waited in place to see if his consciousness would follow the body without effort, or would dim. The medics drove out of sight. He heard the fading sirens until the droning of the city overtook them. The public servants methodically restored order to the street. The crowd dissipated. Unnoticed by anyone, Brian remained there fully awake.

He had no shape—no form to look upon to verify that he existed. And yet, his mind was as sound as it was before the collision with the car. He was afraid to leave the area. What was he, if not encased in a body? Was he learning something new about the mind? Maybe there were vital functions ongoing in his body, tethering his mind to it somehow, allowing his cognition to continue until the last spark of life was gone.

Brian waited for the moment when his consciousness would reunite with his mutilated frame and his mind-body connection was restored, but that moment did not come. As long as he waited at the site of the accident, it did not come. Sunlight faded to streetlights, then back to sunlight. Time was distorted. A day had passed, but time was immensely compressed while his mind was idle waiting for the end. The end did not come. When he concluded that reality had become something new for him, time slowed to its usual pace. He moved toward a building to the first large window to see if his consciousness had a reflection. No.

He navigated the city blocks with varying speeds, depending on his wishes. Moving freely in this lucid state, Brian wondered if this was another dimension. He considered assorted theories on what might have happened to him, allowing for some of the myths he had previously rejected as a soundly educated man. He had decided long ago that the idea of a spirit was just the mind and would perish with the body. *What if?*

His body. He wanted to see his body. In a flash, he was in a room, a black room. No, not a room. A small enclosure. A coffin? A morgue. His mangled body lay dead in cold storage, awaiting far-off relatives to deliver it home, he guessed. His life was over, and yet, he was awake. Evidently, he was experiencing an afterlife.

Sadness frosted over his every thought. The gloom and stillness of the refrigerator were too much to bear. He floated out of the refrigerator into the main room of the morgue. Nobody was there, unless he counted as somebody.

Longing for his family then flooded in. When he visualized home, he instantly traversed the 2,118 miles to the mid-century rambler of his youth. There, in the cluttered kitchen, was a dozen members of his family mourning the news of his untimely death. The phone rang intermittently, and his aunt who was a nurse by profession, handled the calls to relieve his parents of the retelling. His balding father stared woodenly out the sliding glass door with a scotch in his hand. His mother's weeping over the table obscured most of her speech, except "too young," "darling," "my baby," and "sweet." His sister and brother sat across from each other in vacant aspect, picking at the tattered tablecloth, avoiding the pitied looks from the rest. Trapped by his shapeless prison, Brian could only view the grief. He was present, but could not soothe. The irreversibility of the circumstances was beyond comprehension.

In the following weeks, Brian made extended visits to his family and friends to witness their sorrow. He monitored the entire process of transporting his body home and the preparations for the funeral. The dated funeral home, darkened by wood paneling, was packed with a couple hundred faces, many long forgotten. It would have made for an incredible party were he alive. Hearing stories of himself, many erroneous and fuzzy, made him question how authentic he had been in life, or if those relationships were genuine. The inaccurate stories and claims of his nearly impeccable character were frustrating to hear, but the hardest to endure was the flood of grief from his parents and siblings. They loved him more than he knew.

Brian visited and revisited those separated from him by death, and it reinforced his sense of total loss. He loved them, but he could not console them or change their situation. They were completely unaware that he was haunting them, and their descent down the rungs of grief haunted him. The point came when leaving those he loved was more desirable than staying near, and Brian returned to the crossroads of his death. Perhaps being in the place of his demise would help him to uncover the key to disappearing entirely, and therefore, finding incorruptible peace.

At the intersection of Mason Avenue and 1st, in the calm of night, Brian mulled the details of his death and the painful times experienced since then. How long would he continue as an amoeba of thoughts with no ability to communicate with people or any other living thing? He did not want this existence. Would suspending thought make him vanish? Using all the concentration he could rally, he tried to stop thinking. His psyche could not abide thoughtlessness with ease. He tried earnestly to suspend thought, several times, for longer and longer periods. The mere awareness of these attempts stimulated his mind. Having never practiced meditation in his life, his novice efforts were futile; thinking repeatedly resumed and he was yet awake. *Is there truly no way to die? Am I immortal?* Morning flooded the streets with life and traffic. Brian quit trying to extinguish himself.

Existing in isolation from other minds and without a body was worse than notions of purgatory, but better than traditional descriptions of hell. All the joys of mortality such as relationships, good food, and athletics had ceased with his death. The once vibrant, young man had become an unbound blob of mental energy incapable of affecting anything. Such a state of existence served no purpose. God definitely did not exist.

Brian guessed he would feel better if he were able, at minimum, to appear in a form he recognized. If he were a spirit, then lore suggested that his form could be human, like the ghosts waltzing in a theme park haunted house ride. Even the cartoonish, sheet-clad version of a spirit could be tolerable. In any case, complete disembodiment was no longer bearable. He yearned for a bodily form if he must live on.

With this thought, he saw hands, torso, legs, and feet—a version of his human body was restored. Or did he will it to be? Or was it always there and he was unable to see it for some reason? This sudden change utterly redefined his existence; he could immediately feel a change in his senses.

As he inspected his appendages in wonder, Brian was forced to reconsider his flat rejection of the theist claim of the existence of the human spirit. The thrill of having a human form cracked his doggedness, and he freed himself to entertain any conjectures on the afterlife he had hitherto heard.

After inspecting his airy fingers, he looked up to see the city full of the usual movement of mortals and vehicles. Yet, the world was new. Spirits like himself were also milling about in the congested sidewalks in great numbers. Skeptically, Brian took in the change of his environment with wide eyes, turning slowly around to confirm that spirits were manifest in every direction. When he was certain that the density of spirit life was not illusory, relief swept over him to know he was not alone in his afterlife. His new form and new environment were rejuvenating to behold. He felt reborn.

For the first time in a long while, Brian walked. As if his body were made of the finest gossamer, his legs strode lightly, his arms swung gently, and his head floated left and right to look around. His diaphanous hands glided over light poles, benches, and tree trunks. Nothing in the material world felt crisp or strong, rather matter had indistinct pressure, like that of breath on skin. Nonetheless, the slight detection of matter was exhilarating. Even with such limitations, he could question, test, analyze, learn, and interact with the world. His senses and cognition had purpose. He could exist with intention, and that bit of control made Brian feel more alive.

Among this marvelous mix of humanity and spirits, he walked the streets like a tourist. Some spirits busied themselves in conversation with each other, while some tried to engage the oblivious living, attempting to participate in mortality. Propped against a building, a middle-aged spirit in a suit read over the shoulder of a man reviewing the editorial page of the Herald. Farther down the block, two finely coiffed female spirits discussed the flared cuffs in a store window. A bewildered, stocky spirit rushed up and spooked Brian, speaking a foreign tongue in a desperate gush. Brian shook his head vigorously, and repeated, "I'm sorry! I don't understand!" until the spirit gave up and moved to the next ear. Speaking audible words caused Brian to blaze with elation. His new existence was much like that of the living.

So far, life in the spirit world and the material world resembled each other, with the varied personalities and behaviors. Enthralled, he enjoyed every spark of life around him. Brian was willing to embrace fully this reality, if he must live on.

He walked past a coffee shop, and the store was so thick with beings, the counter was nearly indiscernible. The familiar craving for a coffee struck him for the first time, and he realized his transparent body echoed the feelings of his living state. The memory of yearning for coffee took hold of him, and he added his presence to the already overflowing café. Lingering for less than an hour, he made small talk with the other spirits, until the sights and smells of the object of his compulsion began to swell to a mild torture. His craving could not be quenched—a consequence of an insubstantial form.

After freeing himself from the shop, he turned and looked for himself in the sizable café window. No reflection. According to eons of lore, invisibility was a coveted power. Many potent things are invisible, like gravity and natural gas. But the tooth fairy is invisible, too. What exactly was he made of? Was he matter at all? The coffee smells could still reach his—nose? mind? memory? However it was that the scent tempted him, he fled down the street to end the affliction.

Brian strode a block looking for his image in every reflective surface while questioning the nature of his constitution. Out of the corner of his eye, he noticed a quarter on the ground and paused. He must make an attempt. Calling on his inner Patrick Swayze, he knelt on the ground, and tried to place his finger on the coin without passing through it. His finger felt the infinitesimal resistance of the quarter giving him confidence that moving it was possible. With intense focus, he visualized power in his finger to slide the coin, but trying over and over, the coin did not budge.

With his finger in the position of pushing the coin, a voice interrupted his concentration. "You cannot do it, you know."

Brian peered up at a middle-aged spirit in Depression-era garb, indicating his demise was met many decades ago or, more recently, on a period movie set. He replied, "What do you mean?"

"You cannot move the coin as claimed in that flick. All you modern spirits try. It's impossible. Don't enslave yourself to the illusion."

"But I can feel the quarter. I really can. There has got to be a way."

"That, sir, would vacate the laws of physics. Time travel is impossible."

"Time travel?" Brian's face screwed up. Time travel was a bizarre topic to raise. "I'm not trying cross time. I am trying to move the coin."

"Sir, to the living world, you are of the past. If you could alter the present, then you will have jumped forward into the future in the eyes of the living, and would affect unfolding events. You are an immortal being with superhuman capabilities, and thus, you have knowledge that could affect the course of the future in irreparable ways."

Brian stood to give the spirit his full attention. The spirit continued, "Myself, I am one hundred thirty-two years old. If I could interact with the living world, the unfolding of the present would be injected with a century of my learning and my bias. The enormity of our power is incalculable. You and I are bound by the inherent laws of the universe, just as the entirety of matter is. We cannot cross time."

"So, you are saying I am made of matter? Then I should be able to push the coin were that true."

"Yes," the spirit nodded. "Your spirit body is of a special matter that is very fine and pure, and unperceivable to the eyes and instruments of the living. A spirit body can sense the material world to some degree. But what you are attempting to do right now can alter the events of the living world, and therefore, you cannot accomplish it." The spirit bid Brian farewell with a tip of his hat and walked off.

The information was too weighty for Brian to absorb completely. Something was amiss in the theory, he felt certain. He resolved that he would—somehow—move an object. Now he had a goal.

The next few months were filled with adventure. Brian tested limits of his spirit body in extreme circumstances. He soared to the tips of mountains, plunged to legendary regions of the ocean, and inspected the mists of the clouds. To address his life-long interests, he viewed famous plays and concerts, trekked through the wilds of the rainforests, and slipped through the narrow passages of the pyramids. The capacities of his spirit body were wonderfully flexible, and needed no bathroom or rest. He could endlessly explore every crevice of the world. Doing so could occupy his curiosities for an eternity.

On the other hand, the limitations of his form were seeds of frustration. Being locked outside the living world was hard to accept when the parade of life was right before Brian's eyes at all times. No living thing regarded him, and frequently, this was maddening. He also carefully avoided situations that would ignite insatiable cravings, like sexuality and stimulating food and drink. The forced abstinence had him feeling far less human.

At least he was able to acquaint himself with other spirits in this state of existence. New bonds, however, were difficult to establish with any lasting strength. The majority of spirits seemed preoccupied, many filled with regret or disappointment. One afternoon, Brian saw a spirit with her head in her hands, crumpled over her knees. Her posture was dramatic and gripping; he was compelled to sit by the woman and ask why she was so upset. She turned to him, abstracted. "I thought I was going to heaven when I died, to see the glories of God. I cannot understand where I am. If this is heaven, then everything I believed about it was wrong. If this is not heaven, then I cannot figure out how to get there. I don't understand what has happened to me."

Brian could not console the poor woman. Courtesy held him back from recommending atheism.

Existential disappointment was everywhere. Similar to the woman on the curb, the self-absorption of spirits was often due to their longing for a different afterlife for which they had prepared. In a distinctive accent, a man in a turban lamented to Brian how he had no tangible body. "If I am not yet perfected in God, then why I am not reincarnated into an infant, or bird, or even a cricket?"

Such questions Brian never faced. Since he had not expected to be conscious after death, he felt better off than the believers. The afterlife was very much a surprise to him.

For reasons unknown, he felt bound to the city of his death, and always returned there in between his travels. One morning, while roaming the city streets, Brian encountered two spirits in gleaming white, as if they had died while singing in a choir. They approached Brian with wide smiles, and a question. The taller of the two asked, "How is your afterlife going, Brian?"

Hearing his name was a thunderclap that seemed to jolt to life something mortal within him. Though he had long yearned to feel so revivified, the sound of his name also caused suspicion. He took a step back and folded his arms. "Fine. Who are you?"

"I am David and this is Vlad. We are missionaries for Jesus Christ. We have good news to share."

Brian gaped at them in disbelief. "With all due respect, guys, let me share a message with you. You are dead, and Jesus ain't here."

Vlad asked, "Do you believe in Jesus Christ?"

"I like Christmas, if that counts."

Vlad nodded kindly. "Jesus Christ will come again to the earth. God promises that you will walk in your earthly body again when Jesus returns."

His own mutilated corpse lying motionless in a morgue came to Brian's mind. "Yikes. I'll pass. Zombie apocalypses—not my thing."

David said, "Whether you accept it or not, your resurrection will happen. What's more, in your resurrected state, you will be judged on how you spent your existence. We are warning everyone to prepare to meet God and repent of their sins."

And how can I, invisible me, sin? I can't do anything. Wow. These guys deny the impotence of the afterlife, thought Brian. "I heard stuff like this before I died. Life is over. Promises of what Jesus would do are provably false. Sorry, guys. It's nice to see some dudes smiling, but I think it's because you do not comprehend reality."

David extended a pleading hand. "Brian, what we are telling you is as certain as the living world. We testify that it is true."

"You mean, you swear to God and hope to die?" Brian quipped.

Vlad smiled wistfully at the joke. "What we say is difficult to understand because you exist in what is called Spirit Prison. You do not yet have access to Paradise which is an existence of light and peace. If you accept our message, you can experience Paradise with us, and joyfully await the day Christ comes and our bodies are restored." Vlad motioned around him. "In Paradise, all of this will make sense. Even life itself."

The notion of spending eternity hoping for a Jesus event sounded pathetic. "You two mean well, but you are talking to a logical man. There are countless spirits around here who thought they knew all about the afterlife and are not too happy with reality. I feel a whole lot better than they do, so I'll just stick with what I know. Good luck to you. I'm sure there are others who will like what you have to say." At that, Brian went on his way. He considered that Paradise could just be a state of mind, for the two peculiar spirits were beaming on the same street he was. *Maybe I needed an attitude adjustment*, he allowed.

More months passed, and Brian grew to accept his condition. He eventually made meaningful connections with a few fellow spirits and continued to explore the world and all its mysteries. He practiced moving small objects to no avail, but never waned in confidence. He also learned to quell his psyche to compress the experience of time. Eternity no longer felt so endless. Of all things, he did not return home to see family or friends. He needed to remain apart from the grief, not for a lack of love, but to maintain emotional stability.

Brian's approach to family was unwavering until one afternoon, his mind filled with the face of his mother. She consumed every thought, and hindered his ability to focus on any other thing. The intensity and constancy of the preoccupation did not falter, and he could not escape it.

Reluctantly, he yielded to the fixation on his mother, and allowed himself to find her in the home he grew up in.

His mother was on the floor of his old bedroom going through his belongings. The bedroom had long been redecorated for guests in impersonal neutrals, but the closets still held the bulk of his possessions. A shoe box was open before her, filled with natural treasures he had collected as a boy: seashells, polished rocks, driftwood, sea glass, pinecones, and fossils. Other boxes lay open of school work and hobbies, labeled by his hand. Comic books were sorted into piles by their hero, according to his system. The room was a casket of the epochs of his life thrown open for him to view, and in the middle of the annals sobbed his mother, on her knees, gripping his baby blanket, and rocking like her stomach hurt. She had aged, and yet, looked like a child. The scene buckled him to his knees. Brian watched in pain, feeling broken for his mother, and mourning the loss of life itself.

He needed to be close to her. He sped to her side, and in the rush, the comic books fluttered.

His mother became rigidly quiet. Her breathing stopped. She stared at the piles of comics. He stared, too.

She gasped for air, and held it again for silence. With hesitation, an older version of his brown eyes looked through him to survey the room for any other movement. Her heart beat loudly. Her voice shook, "Brian?"

Her breath resumed in fits and starts, with tears dripping slowly off her tired face. Brian had to respond, "Mom, I'm here." His voice never reached her ears, but her face changed with the confidence of certainty. Ghostly fingers moved over her cheek to wipe away tears, but they streamed unfazed by his touch.

"Brian, my dear boy." A familiar voice called to him from behind. He warily turned to see the spirit form of his grandmother, Dotty, dressed in white, smiling down at him through half-rims.

"Grandma!" He rose from the side of his mother, who continued to sit motionless in a new serenity. "It's so good to see you. I am amazed that you are here."

"Of course I am here. I yearn to console the heart of my child. Your loss has been a terrible blow to her. Your mother needs comfort so badly. I cannot stay away."

"Seeing you makes me so happy." He threw his arms around her for a quick embrace. "Spirit life is so lonely. Talking to family like this is incredible."

They both regarded his mother who was transfixed by the comics, unconsciously picking at the corner of his faded baby blanket. "Grandma, I was told that spirits cannot move objects. I have tried many times to do so, but I can't. Yet, when I went to Mom, the comic pages moved. I didn't even try. I cannot understand how that happened. I was told that spirit bodies are not able to move things because it breaks the laws of physics."

His grandmother looked at him with the kindness only a wise person could offer. "Yes, Son, spirits cannot interact with the living world. But, today, your mother prayed for a sign of your spirit, and God, in His great mercy, obliged."

Brian paused before responding. God talk was weird. "I don't know what you mean."

"God is both perfectly lawful, and perfectly merciful. His laws ensure that there is order in the universe, and applying those laws with mercy ensures there is joy in the universe."

Brian was stilled by the explanation. They continued to watch his mother in silence. A minute later, his mother bowed her head and whispered, "Thank you, Lord."

Brian felt grateful, too.

4

Outgoing

FRIDAY

Nevaeh chattered on about nonsense at work and took a bite of the baked potato selected from the dollar menu. It lacked salt. She took a paper packet from the ceramic container of seasonings, and dumped the granular contents over its fluffy innards. Nevaeh crinkled her nose at the blandness of the next bite. "Ugh, what is wrong with this potato?" She reached for another packet and resumed the commentary on her photo album. "So, the streets were smelly and grimy, but the beach was gorgeous. Now, turn the page," she directed her coworker.

Sitting across from Nevaeh at the undersized table cluttered with food wrappers was Reggie, turning pages of the photo album of Nevaeh's recent vacation. Reggie managed the front desk of their Internet consulting company, a wiry institution full of youthful peons and conniving administrators ever hunting for venture capital or a buy-out. His stint behind desks in the military made him deft at pushing paper and manipulating schedules for muckety-mucks. Early in their acquaintance, Nevaeh went to the front desk to post a letter, and asked him where the outgoing mail was. Reggie devilishly replied, "He's right here!" She adopted him right then and there as the best kind of office pal.

By the sunlight pouring in from the panoramic windows of the fast food joint, Reggie's finger glided over the page of the photo album and stopped. "Who are these cats?" he asked, thrown, pointing to a picture of finely dressed Africans.

"Oh, them? They are friends at church."

"Brothers? At your church?" His surprise confirmed Nevaeh's suspicion that Reggie thought her crowd was Afro-phobic. Judging by what he knew of her background, Reggie assumed there were no black people woven into her life besides himself. Indeed, Nevaeh came from a town known to be overwhelmingly white. Only a handful of black kids attended her high school. And her church in this region was infrequently attended by inner-city African Americans.

"Yes, there are black people of my faith," she said mindfully nonchalant.

"Hmm. Alright," he consented, trying to not sound doubtful. But the picture could not lie. He continued to thumb through the album as Nevaeh grumbled over her meal.

"I have put so much salt on this potato, and it tastes weird! It's not salty at all!" Nevaeh sat back in her chair and considered returning the potato to the cashier. She took another packet, wondering how ingesting three teaspoons of salt would ultimately make her feel. "I can't believe our company is changing its name again. What a terrible name, too—'Cantaloupe Dog.' Who will ever remember that? I have no idea what it means."

Her coworker shrugged. "Domain names are hard to get. Maybe that's why. I don't know." He closed the album, still working through his disbelief. "Your trip looked pretty cool. I'm glad that you made it back in one piece."

"Yes, safety was not priority one for the catamaran. Anyway, 'Cantaloupe Dog' sounds like a vegan pet store," she said. "Ugh. I'm going to try to salt it again. It's just so--" Pinching the next packet of seasoning, her hand paused over the potato. "I am so stupid! This is sugar. No wonder it wasn't getting salty!"

"Nevi, you nut!" Reggie chortled behind a fist of fingers banded in gold.

Nevaeh laughed through her embarrassment. "I am a total dork. I cannot believe I've been sugaring my baked potato." She smacked her forehead with an open hand and left for the counter to get a fresh spud.

Grinning, Reggie shook his head at his lunch companion, whose unobservant mind frequently lodged herself into muddles. Because Nevaeh was completely unlike him in style, ethnicity, background, interests, and ambitions, their friendship had a quirky vitality that bore no resemblance to the majority of his connections. Much of their relationship was built on Nevaeh's visits to his desk where she vented her dating problems and reported her daily follies. He was a reluctant confidant and advisor, yet they were close enough now that he did not like players to prey on her. For instance, the office snake, Jerod, had recently started messing with Nevaeh's head. Reggie knew that Nevaeh had no basis of experience to detect the complexity of that guy's issues. In such affairs, he warned her when she was at risk, and she heeded him once in a while. Feeling valued by Nevaeh allowed Reggie to forbear her circadian bleating. Her general naiveté also safely shrouded Reggie in her mind exactly as he projected himself, which had been for him a source of freedom.

"So, what are you doing this weekend, Reg?" Nevaeh asked with a replacement tuber in hand.

He snickered and handed her a proper salt packet. "Me and Wesley were going to lay down some tracks, but he texted me before lunch and it sounds like he might be tied up. So, I'm not sure what's going to happen. What about you?"

"I want to go clubbing, but my roommates are going on a hiking trip. Like, I would rather clean toilets all weekend than walk miles uphill to look at trees and squirrels. The parks downtown have those, too. I don't see the point. Can you?"

Reggie smirked at her typical frankness. "There are some nice places out there, but I haven't hiked in years, I admit."

"I don't want to sit around at home. Sounds like you aren't doing anything." Nevaeh beamed rays of sass at him. "I think it's time you and I go dancing!"

Reggie was not prepared to navigate a suggestion to go out with her that night. Besides a weekly lunch, he did not pal around with his coworker eleven years his junior. But no hint of hesitation leaked into his reply. "That's cool."

Reggie snuck in a wad of fries while he wondered how to arrange the evening. "Let's do it."

Nevaeh popped the lid off a broccoli salad. "Nice. Take me to one of your haunts. But it has to have dance music. I have no idea how to dance to rap," she said.

Reggie gave a reasonable nod, and then sucked out the sesame seed wedged by his aureate tooth. "I'll text you a meeting place and we'll kick it."

MONDAY

Nevaeh pushed through the glass double doors of the office and trudged up the modern stairwell of polished concrete and wrought iron. At the top of the half-flight was the main lobby where sat Reggie on a call, the receiver in one hand, and the other occupied by a quarter in a hypnotic weave back and forth through his fingers. She rested her elbows on the counter and returned a crooked grin to his rolling eyes hooded by a white, flat-billed cap.

"Yes, yes. I'll get it to him. He checks his voice mail during the day, so I'm sure he will hear your message. Yes, sir. You got it. Yep. OK. Thanks for calling." Reggie replaced the phone on the hook and said, "Another message for Matt. He's not in yet. But you are, Nevi-girl! I'm glad to see you upright and not groaning up those stairs."

The outing on Friday night had come to an uneasy end. Nevaeh was trying to keep her weight down, and part of this mission was to commit temporarily to a nearly vegetarian diet. At lunch with Reggie on Friday, she had eaten a raw broccoli salad and the infamous potato washed down with a pineapple smoothie. The consequence of such a lunch was a raging case of heartburn, which festered all

Friday afternoon and throughout the night. When she met Reggie downtown to go clubbing, she hoped that the antacids, the pink OTC meds, and a tall glass of milk before leaving her apartment would help her stomach settle. No change was experienced. Instead, her intestines were bloated with gas and gurgles.

The tummy discomfort served to distract from the awkwardness that struck when Reggie escorted her through the doors of a queer nightclub. His choice for their nighttime destination was perplexing. Nevaeh was in no way a lesbian (as he well knew) and Reggie had shown no signs of being anything other than straight (as evidenced, she believed, by his hip-hop wardrobe, swagger, and two naturally conceived children). Her face was too readable to hide the fact that a war of medicine, plant fiber, and shifting bubbles waged inside her. They took a seat along the side the dance floor where she sipped clear soda and he drained a few cocktails. They discussed many things, except the neon question as to whether that nightclub was really Reggie's haunt. They left the club at an early hour. She returned home to stretch out on the couch and puzzle over the events of the night, and did so for the rest of the boring weekend.

She said in hoarse morning voice, not yet exercised for the day, "Yeah, I feel fine now. But it was a rough weekend. Never let me eat broccoli and pineapple in the same meal ever again! I am embarrassed that my stupid lunch ruined our night. Sorry, Reggie."

"Nah, I was worried the problem was worse than what you were saying. You didn't look too good the other night."

She coughed and cleared her throat. "I spent the weekend binging—not on food!—but on DVDs. I devoured an entire British miniseries while I writhed on the couch. So, what did you do for the rest of the weekend?" Nevaeh retrieved her water bottle from her purse to attempt to clear her raspy voice.

Reggie paused to answer in order to take an incoming phone call. After transferring the call to the human resources manager, he answered, "On Saturday, I took Jamarr, Laticia, and their mom to see the new Revengers." Jamarr and Laticia were his children, eight and ten years old, from his marriage that ended years ago. He and his ex-wife partnered amicably to raise their children. "After that, I met Wesley at the studio and did some recording."

Nevaeh brightened, "Maybe, I could watch you guys record some time. Or, would that be awkward, me the only white person in the studio?"

"Wesley is white!" he retorted.

"Wesley is white? Really? I never imagined based on—huh." Instantly, all that she had envisioned from Reggie's rap stories was contorted. Nevaeh could think of only a few white rappers that ever broke solidly onto the hip-hop scene, and one of those had been disbarred from the music world. Reggie was her term of endearment for him, but the man reclining before her was called Reginald by all others. The edginess of "Wesley and Reginald" was all but erased by her bias against white rappers; now, the rap duo sounded to her more like a pair of antique dealers rather than street-knocked hip-hop artists. A moment grinded on while she chewed on these facts.

39

Because she and Reggie had frequent lapses in understanding each other's culture, the two were accustomed to shrugging off fouls. She had no fear that Reggie was offended by her assumptions. "Well, anyhow, watching people create music is extremely cool," Nevaeh said.

"Excuse me!" The heads of both parties turned to Edwin, the HR director, who burst into the lobby and abruptly said, "Reginald, please decline calls for Matthew. He won't be coming in today."

Reggie and Nevaeh cast their eyes over Edwin, normally of professional demeanor, and saw that he was positively bleak. Reggie sat up straight. "Yeah, man. Did something happen?"

Edwin looked out the windows, down at the floor, and back at Reggie. "You know that plane crash last night, Meridian-Air Flight 67?" A leaden pause gripped the lobby as Edwin willed forth the words, "Matthew was on that flight."

Nevaeh gasped. Reggie's low curse followed. No more information was needed. Flight 67 had plunged into the sea just off the coastline. The wreckage was so catastrophic that there was no hope of survivors. Edwin said, "Please send out a meeting request for the entire company to come to the first floor in 30 minutes." He left the lobby.

The news was paralyzing. "Oh, no," Nevaeh whispered.

Reggie shook his head and sunk into his chair, crushed by the gravity of it all. An interval of pure grief ticked by. Then, Nevaeh's sniffling drew Reggie's attention.

He got up, came around the counter, and wrapped his arms around her.

TUESDAY

Matthew was a member of the sales team, a personable extrovert in his twenty-eighth year. Because of his remarkable ability to connect with anyone, he was known by most of the several hundred employees of Cantaloupe Dog. Nevaeh had not been well acquainted with Matthew, but she had enough memories of his infectious laugh bellowing over the din of after-work socials that his loss was impactful. Many bouts of tears had come over her in the last two days, as they had for most of Matthew's coworkers.

A somber cloud hung over the entire company. As if the ghost of Matthew were walking the halls, there was high sensitivity to what was said and what was done. Joking, teasing, and gossiping vanished directly after the collective of employees received the news of his passing on Monday morning. Employees spoke less overall; necessary exchanges were conducted in low registers. Music normally piping out of certain workstations was muted or channeled to headphones. Project meetings were canceled. Employees stayed at their desks to avoid extraneous conversations. Inverse to the reduction of activity in the building, there was an uptick of coffee runs and off-site lunches to escape the gloom.

Nevaeh found the reception desk empty a couple of times that day, but Reggie was at his post mid-afternoon. "This sucks," she mumbled.

"Dark days, Nevi. Dark days."

She sighed heavily. "It's hard not to think about it." He rightly guessed what she meant. The terrible plane crash dominated broadcast news in part because the accident appeared to be due to a mechanical problem caused by poor maintenance of the airplane. Projectiles of accusations, catapulted by the airline, the FAA, and families of the victims, made the reporting particularly corrosive. One's mind could not stanch visualizations of the last few minutes of the flight full of passengers of all ages returning from vacation. Matthew's free, fun, single life, full of promise, was very much like his peers, and thus, his coworkers fairly surmised his final thoughts. The near vertical plunge into the ocean was so sudden and so rapid, experts asserted that g-forces likely rendered the passengers unconscious before the plane hit the surface of the water. All hoped the effect of such physics was experienced by Matthew. After a bit of heavy thinking, Nevaeh added, "Things are so weird here. Everyone is still working through the shock. I cannot stop myself from imagining—" She felt herself welling up. "Poor Matt. So tragic. Have you seen Lola?"

Reggie looked at her inquiringly and shook his head no. He had become a man of even fewer words since the loss of his friend. Nevaeh continued, "She is seriously distraught. I am starting to think she had a thing for Matt." Reggie offered a slight, sage nod. "What about you, Reggie? You've been away from the desk a lot."

He fingered his goatee. "I've been talking with Matt's mom, Cathy. Matt has some things to wrap up, so, I'm helping him to get his business in order, you know, taking on some of the things Cathy can't do for him."

It struck Nevaeh how he spoke of Matthew as if he was alive, and merely occupied for the moment. Speaking of the dead this way felt poignantly hopeful—and loving. She did not doubt that some of the "business" that Reggie was addressing was to empty Matthew's workstation and to handle all client communications incoming from email and telephone. Reggie's peaceful, confident demeanor—projecting Matthew's sense of responsibility—was the ideal manner to present the facts to Matthew's clients. Perhaps Reggie's years in the military, where he likely concluded the business of the fallen, were reflected in his approach to Matthew's matters.

A call came in. Nevaeh said, "I'll catch up with you later. Send my condolences to Cathy."

Reggie pointed his forefinger at her in agreement and answered the phone.

She walked slowly back to her desk passing by dozens of clicking keyboards. But missing from his desk was Jerod. On Friday, he had crossed the border in his beloved rag-top Rabbit to attend an outdoor music festival with Evan, his party buddy that she had heard much about but had never met. She and Jerod were in a fresh flirtation which sometimes feigned a relationship. Because their dynamic felt like dating, she was a little annoyed that Jerod had not communicated with her in his absence. The remoteness of the festival and the international rates on his phone prevented his ability to be in touch while he was gone, Jerod explained before he left. His empty chair indicated that he was still out of town.

Nevaeh passed by a legion of disparate humans housed in one facility: lovely tom-boy, Nari; the alabaster

Stu (walled off by carefully stacked soda cans); Justin, whose marriage featured shameless swinging; Kapila, the daughter of parents who had 4,000 people at their wedding (which she mentioned regularly); Sugi, donning a wardrobe solely of Rush t-shirts; the vegan martyr, Lemont; Susan, who drove a taxi-yellow Hummer; Chanel, in an awkward phase of transitioning; the corpulent gamer, Preston; Jay, the nice Canadian; the modest translator, Tamiko; and Xai, the all-around athlete. The managers fibbed about the skills of the staff, frequently putting the workers into incapacitating contracts. What ensued were waves of crushing pressure and periods of all-nighters that often left employees feeling like the walking dead. On this day, however, the company was abnormally calm in bereavement.

By the countenances of the consultants positioned near the aisle, she could sense that the grief was beginning to lift. Voices could be heard in soft conversation. A few people were out of their seats in leisurely postures. By the next day, the office would be moving forward, completely focused on the demands of clients and deadlines.

Perpendicular to her desk and to all other workstations on the floor was Blaine's, which position jutted his desk into the aisle to force passersby to swerve. He insisted that his desk be so uniquely situated because of his philosophical conviction of Feng Shui, which neutralized all politically incorrect complaints. The other uncomfortable result of his desk arrangement was that his prospect was Nevaeh's profile, causing her to feel watched all the day long. Crowned by flaming red hair and donning the same multi-pocketed parka every day, the programmer clicked his desktop keyboard with austere steadiness. Aside from the traffic disturbances caused by the position of his desk, the unassuming Blaine sought no attention to himself. Nevaeh noticed the addition of a large salt crystal on the corner of his desk. She theorized that Matthew's death inspired the spiritual object to be introduced into Blaine's space.

Nevaeh sat in front of her monitor filled with application windows: a word processor, browsers, and vector and raster design tools. The email inbox was stacked with conversations on change orders and questions over design specifications. Interspersed with the unread subjects were a few personal messages. Though the workload was mounting, she could not resist clicking on the email message from her cousin with the subject line: "Grandma." The contents read:

```
Nevi, have you seen her yet? I'm so sad! I'm
bummed I cannot get there until tomorrow
night. Tell me what you know. Dad is on a
plane right now.
Love, Felice
```

"What?" Nevaeh said unintentionally aloud. A few pairs of eyes glanced up at her to assess the nature of Nevaeh's exclamation. Blaine's was not one of them. She fumbled about her purse to find her phone. It blinked with unheard and unread messages. She had forgotten that the phone was set to silent. She selected the voice mail and played the weeping declaration from her mother that Grandma Molly had experienced a health incident that sent her into rapid systemic failure. The end was near.

Nevaeh put the phone down on her desk, and she rested her head on her chin to think as she re-read Felice's email. *Grandma is dying? No! Not now! This cannot be! I must go to her. It may be too late to see her alive, unless she's not quite on the brink of death. I wonder what happened to her. Is she conscious? Is she in pain? Ugh. Why is this happening now, just after Matt's death? It's too freaky. What cosmic reason could there be?*

The young consultant left the open floor to a darkened, small conference room to call her mother, Darcy. She flicked on the light and jumped at the sight before her. Naj was curled up atop the large conference desk with a fleece jacket over him. "Oh, Naj!" she lightly laughed. "I'm so sorry to wake you. I didn't think anyone was in here."

Squinting back at her was a bed-haired programmer looking disheveled in day-old clothes. "Nevi, hi. I just needed to nap. Sorry. Sorry." He slipped off the desk.

"I am the one that is sorry. Were you here all night?"

Naj raked his hair with his hand, eyes straining to see. "Yes. The Waxon Wear commerce site goes live tomorrow."

"Shoot. I can go somewhere else and let you rest. Really," she said, walking backward.

"No, I need to get up. Too many bugs." Naj tottered around her and moved for the door.

Nevaeh wished him well, and went to one of the swivel chairs scattered on the far side of the table. When she sat down, she spied Bart lying under the table with a sweatshirt on his head secured by a careless arm. Disturbing the naps of the beleaguered programmers felt wrong. Quietly, she stood, slipped out the conference door, and shut off the light.

Beyond the closed door of the conference room, she crossed paths with her department manager, Rachel, a tall thinker with striking black eyes and candid attire. That day's t-shirt read THE BENDS in large mustard letters. "Nevi, how are you doing?"

Nevaeh tipped her head to the side. "I do not know. I'm processing."

Rachel regarded her employee with her characteristic sympathy. "Absolutely. We all are. It is hard to concentrate on deadlines. So, that is why I am checking in with you. How are your projects coming? Will you be ready for the spec review tomorrow?"

The designer's shoulder's dropped. "Rach, I needed to talk to you. Something came up. I am hoping we can move the meeting to another time."

"Can you tell me what's going on? Software issues? Client complaints? Ah, it's something personal."

"Yes," Nevaeh said, with mounting distress. "I just found out my grandmother is dying."

"Oh, Nevi. I am so sorry."

"I would like to go see her tomorrow morning. It is not set in stone yet, but that is what I hope to arrange. I plan to work all evening to get most, if not all of the project documents finished. I apologize that my personal life is getting in the way of work."

"I apologize that work is getting in the way of your personal life!" The manager looked at her employee over the rim of her rhinestone glasses. "Nevi, work *is* your personal life. Everything you do is your personal life. It's all just—life." Nevaeh returned a grateful nod. Rachel then said, "Go to your grandma. The client knows you must be in the meeting and I will see to it that the meeting is moved to Thursday. Let me know if there is anything more I can do."

"Thank you, Rachel."

The women parted ways, and Nevaeh wandered the floor, seeking for a room that was certain to be unoccupied. She chose an empty office that was once home to a manager since hired away by a fiery start-up. There she called her mother, Darcy. After a back-and-forth on Grandma Molly's condition and assessing all the moving parts involved with Nevaeh's project demands, her mother conceded that the following morning would be an optimal time for Nevaeh to come to her grandmother's side. Nevaeh returned to her desk and worked on documents for hours, until the contacts in her eyes were too sticky to continue.

WEDNESDAY

At the assisted living facility, Nevaeh crept into the small bedroom where a petite, huggable nurse was adjusting withering arms and gently rubbing the back of what looked like an already lifeless body. After the woman assured her insensible patient that she would be back soon, Nevaeh approached the bed as the nurse passed out of the threshold.

In a reclined position of the hospital bed, her grandmother rasped breath after slow breath with a slacked jaw and eyes half open and empty. Grandma Molly's state as rehearsed by her mother was confirmed: the sunken eyes were a sign that the patient was "actively dying." The pain medications rendered her unconscious. Nevaeh sat in the chair beside the bed, took her progenitor's age-spotted hand, rubbed an emaciated arm, and offered succoring words. Grandma Molly made no sign that reassured Nevaeh that her presence was heard or felt. Nonetheless, what mattered was being at her grandma's deathbed, because, without doubt, Molly would be by hers were circumstances reversed.

After ten minutes of total quiet, occasionally squeezing a bony hand, Nevaeh spoke into her grandmother's ear to announce herself distinctly. Nothing changed. Molly's eyes were unblinking in their half-open position. The uneven gurgles emitted from her grandma as breath passed in and out were uninterrupted by her words. Nevaeh mouthed discreet pleadings that God would be with them.

At a comfortable moment, Nevaeh's mother and brother entered the room. Grant could not take a seat. The floor creaked as he paced the room in slow motion, while Nevaeh talked quietly with her mother. Darcy was exhausted from a long night of bedside attendance. The systemic collapse of her aged mother had begun the evening before. Since Darcy was the only child of Molly's four children that lived in the vicinity, as the facility's point of contact, she was the first to arrive and bore the task of informing the rest of the family. Molly's other offspring were coming as soon as they could be released from their responsibilities and travel to the remote town. It was unknown if Grandma Molly would last long enough to receive the farewells of all her children.

Nevaeh's fragile emotional condition could not, she sensed, withstand the deluge of mourning that was soon to begin with the arrival of her large family. The clock indicated that she had stayed a respectful amount of time, and she began to put on her jacket to face the rain now pelting the windows. "I am going to go, Mom. Sorry to leave you guys. I have got to get back to work and, well—"

"It's OK, Nevi," Darcy said. "Coming here to say goodbye to Grandma meant a lot. I am glad I was able to see both of my kids at this time. With your father working so much overtime, it would be a lonely few days without you two."

Grant had paused in front of the corkboard on the wall which displayed dozens of photographs of grandchildren pinned in a great spiral around three original photographs of Molly and his grandfather, Walter. Walter had succumbed to cancer three years earlier because he had refused treatment. For Grant, the loss of his grandmother meant losing the last tether to Grandad. While the women quietly talked, he was lost in recollections of the many fishing trips he spent with Walter and his uncles. Such acts of outdoorsmanship that Grandpa Walter encouraged in his male progeny had become infrequent since his health began to fail nearly seven years earlier.

While Nevaeh adjusted the tight sleeves of her coat, the nurse returned and said it was time for more drugs to be administered. Nevaeh stood at this cue and sat onto the air-filled hospice bed. The movement of the bed appeared to startle her grandmother, whose body jumped a little. Nevaeh realized that reflex could not have occurred under total sedation. She searched Molly's face to find it alert, but silent. The old woman's mouth was no longer hanging open. Her eyes were focused on Nevaeh. When their eyes met, the patient's closed lips broadened to a smile, lifting the cheeks.

From behind, a feminine voice gasped, "Oh, look! She's smiling!"

Nevaeh's hand impulsively rested on that smiling cheek sheathed in thin skin. "Hi, Grandma!" Nevaeh greeted with droplets slipping from her eyes.

That spirit who had made thousands of cookies, changed generations of diapers, corrected the grammar of countless sentences, reread bedtime books ad nauseum, nursed those in cribs, bunks, and deathbeds, and grieved the passing of dozens—Molly's spirit radiated an extraordinary message. The message seemed almost unearthly, communicated without words or gestures, yet the power of the spirit of Molly Mae Bowman beamed, "I love you dearly." Astonished, Nevaeh took in the look of pure love from her grandmother.

Nevaeh knew her grandparents loved their grandchildren by acknowledging birthdays and extending frequent invitations to their home and to join them on vacations. But such penetrating adoration never radiated from Molly as it did so forcefully in that moment. The love filled Nevaeh's soul like breath fills the lungs.

Overpowered by the feeling received from her grandmother, Nevaeh's head collapsed onto the invalid's breast to weep. Both of Nevaeh's hands rested on Molly's arms to simulate a hug. Through the blur of consuming sobs, it donned on her that her weight may not be comfortable on the frail soul. She pulled herself up with a face streaming wet. Grandma Molly's face relaxed during the embrace, and a gentle smile returned when their eyes met again for the final time.

"Oh, Grandma!" Nevaeh exclaimed, again placing her hand on Molly's cheek. "I love you, Grandma." Nevaeh pecked the cool skin of the other cheek. She could bear no more.

Nevaeh quickly stood and exited the room as the nurse approached the bed. In the hallway, she found her solemn brother gazing at the floral walls unseeingly and her teary mother ready to curl her arms around Nevaeh. As they cried, Darcy said how amazing and perfect the goodbye with Molly was. The striking nature of Grandma Molly's bestowal of love was that it was personal to Nevaeh and, as evidenced by her mother's reaction, the adoration affected Darcy and Grant, too. The expansiveness of Molly's love bore a transcendent quality; it was love centered on an individual and, at the same time, showered on others just as personally.

Mourning was taking hold in a crippling way and, to stop the landside of emotion, Nevaeh broke the embrace with Darcy and hugged her brother with a heartfelt goodbye. Darcy knew better than to try to stop her daughter from leaving. Solitude was essential for Nevaeh to preserve her mental health. The young woman darted down the hall, out of the facility, and into her car in seconds.

The drive back to work was lengthened by backups caused by the rainy weather, so Nevaeh had extra time for introspection before facing the stresses of work. Thirty minutes into the drive, Nevaeh's heart was further saddened when she received the call from Darcy informing that Grandma Molly had peacefully passed away.

THURSDAY

By Thursday morning, the normal atmosphere of Cantaloupe Dog had fully returned. Mourning for Matthew was now a private matter and the company was operating at its usual, rigorous praxis. Good humor had returned and frustration with minutiae was openly expressed. Reflecting on the death of her grandmother, Nevaeh cried intermittently through Wednesday, and once more when she awoke Thursday morning. But Grandma Molly had lived to an old age, and her departure from life was wrapped in sweetness. The comprehensible grief did not sting nor linger.

Relationships and loss were naturally in the mind, but something out of the ordinary had developed in Nevaeh the previous evening. An unusual tightening sensation centered in her chest spontaneously began. The location of the complaint was disturbing, but she went to bed assuming it would fade overnight. In the morning, the uncomfortable strain remained, though it did not inhibit her movements or energy. She went to work and faced a typical, deadline-driven day.

When returning from lunch, Nevaeh wiggled her eyebrows at Reggie as she passed by the front desk. With his hand, Reggie was molding away the smile provoked by attempts at urban slang he had inspired in the balding, sixty-something, rotund Barry, the business development veep. Barry's lack of self-awareness and driving ambition to be cool to all the "young people" drew out buffoonish behaviors that had everyone biting lips and whispering reports of him in the break room. Barry's posturing would not bother Nevaeh had there not been regular evidence that

Barry comfortably stretched the truth about himself and the company with automaticity. The clincher was when he attempted to lure venture capitalists to invest in their consulting company as a "banking institution." Nevaeh came by this knowledge because Barry had enlisted her to research bank balance sheets on the Internet, which, she later learned, he feigned as the company profile to a group of investors. The only "banking" Cantaloupe Dog did was to bank venture capital money to blow on the flashiest amenities meant to impress more investors.

As she exited the lobby, she heard Reggie say, "Yeah, that is hella dope. Just as you say, Barry."

Nevaeh walked passed the managers' offices flanking the hallway and entered the large open space littered by a sea of desks under industrial lighting. Natural light was blocked from the floor by a border of tall cubicles positioned in front of every window.

The consultant unconsciously rubbed her neckline in response to the persistent tightness in her chest. She was no senior citizen, but maybe she should suspect a cardiac problem. A friend of a friend's husband had recently died at the age of thirty-two from undetected heart issues. Was this tightness something he had experienced before dropping dead? The constriction in her chest seemed to intensify as she questioned its source. The sensation was of an entirely different character than the effects of stress or ingesting hot peppers. She was unconscious to the fact that the more she suspected a heart issue, the more her appearance grew dour.

"Nevi," an accented voice called. "Nevi, do you feel you are OK?"

Nevaeh mentally came to, and saw Tamiko earnestly regarding her in concern. Walking to the desk of the black-haired beauty, she said, "Hey, Tamiko. Yes, it's weird. I feel a little strange, but not really bad or anything. Right here, in my chest, it feels a bit like—"

Speech left Nevaeh when her eyes landed on Tamiko's computer monitor. What she beheld was so offensive, Nevaeh examined the screen carefully to confirm what she was seeing. When she was certain that she was not imagining the heinous projections, Nevaeh demanded in a crazed whisper, "Tamiko! My God, girl! What the heck are you looking at?"

Sweet Tamiko, of such grace and propriety, had graphic pornography squirming on her desktop. With a facial expression that would normally accompany a disgusted tone, Tamiko said dutifully, "The Company has commissioned me to translate this web site into Japanese for a client."

Nevaeh's eyes were now on Tamiko, purposefully avoiding the screen. "You agreed to do this?" Trying to give Tamiko her complete attention, Nevaeh gently rolled her shoulders back to counter-stretch the growing tension in her chest.

No matter the facts or the need, it was obvious that Tamiko was sickened by the assignment. "The client is paying a lot of money to us, and no one else here knows Japanese well enough to carry out the translation."

Nevaeh wanted to grab Tamiko's shoulders and explain how American women would not allow an employer to abuse them in this way. "How can they put a woman on this project? The company is acting like a pimp and you are for hire! Tamiko, you must tell Rajat that you want off the project."

The customs of Tamiko's home country were deeply ingrained. Shirking the work given by employers was virtually unthinkable. "I do not like this project. But it is OK, Nevi. It is just one time. I can do it."

"I do not know how you can. It is disgusting. Horrible! Employees are not even supposed to look at porn at work. This is pure hypocrisy!" Tamiko suddenly looked lost. Nevaeh said, "Hypocrisy. It means—uh—making rules and breaking them at the same time."

Tamiko nodded in defeat. This was a fight she was unwilling to start. Like dozens of others employed at Cantaloupe Dog, the conditions of her visa put her at the beck and call of leadership. Shamefully, she whispered, "This project is embarrassing and ugly. When it is finished, I will be glad." Nevaeh rested her hand on Tamiko's shoulder and the translator meekly pulled her chair back into place. After squeezing her eyes shut as if to clear her resentments, Tamiko glanced at her monitor, positioned her mouse, and commenced typing.

Nevaeh walked on, rolling her shoulders back again. The sensation in her chest seemed to be tugging her frame inward. Furthermore, for the first time, a tingling in her left arm followed by a sharp stab radiated to her fingers. Never before had she experienced such a sting in her arm. Apprehension quickened her pulse. Public service announcements frequently warned of signs of a pending heart attack and she could not deny the possibility anymore. Tentatively, she slipped onto her seat in the dark corner of the floor, hid the applications on her desktop machine, and launched an Internet search for warnings of a heart condition. Many indicators resembled what Nevaeh was experiencing. However, the last thing she wanted to do was draw attention to herself if these symptoms were a psychosomatic result of losing her grandmother the previous day and, of course, the hyperawareness of the brevity of life triggered by Matthew's end. Nevaeh prided herself in being a rational female, and logic told her that since she was not mourning emotively that day, her body was expressing the grief instead.

The task of editing documents and wireframes was thoroughly unappealing when her mind was concerned with her health. Her whole being felt anxious to move. Maybe a walk to the break room would help.

The break room was located three floors down, and Nevaeh opted for the stairs to quell her agitation. At one end of the room were a few coworkers chatting and sipping coffee on the frayed couches. Nevaeh greeted them, took some deep breaths, and then approached the sink within which day-old dirty dishes were dumped. Too many "clean" dishes were precariously stacked next to the overflowing sink. Cabinet doors were ajar with snack bars, tea bags, and coffee supplies unboxed and spilling onto the shelves. To avoid returning to her desk, Nevaeh assumed the task of cleaning up the kitchen. After thoroughly handwashing the dishes, she dried the pile and put away the unmatched mugs and random pieces of plastic and metal silverware. Counters were wiped down and tables cleared of crumpled napkins. Movement felt good. Meanwhile, coworkers occasionally excused themselves to reach into the refrigerator or cupboards, and lounged on the couches to play video games on the widescreen hanging on the far wall.

Regrettably, the constant twinge in her chest still held her attention. She suspected that paying attention to the ache was like pouring water onto a sponge, causing it to enlarge and grow heavier. The kitchen was made tidy and she should return to her desk. If she was having heart trouble, physical rest was imperative, but the notion of sitting down was oddly unappealing. Her whole being wanted to stay moving. The anxious need to move propelled her to find another way to keep afoot.

Back at her desk, Nevaeh perused her document created for the imminent client meeting and decided that it was good enough to print. The document was sent to the main printer located in the copier room embedded within the administrative offices. Monitoring the printer was a suitable reason to stare off in sadness, which she did on Monday and Tuesday in homage to Matthew. Yet, watching the printer photocopy, collate, and staple the papers felt intolerable. To the rhythmic hum of the machine spitting out copies, she cleaned off surfaces of discarded paper and organized the shelf with office supplies of stapler, tape, hole-punch, scissors, and bins of paperclips and other fasteners. Truly, the ache in her chest was having a bizarre, mobilizing effect on her.

Nevaeh sorted through the shallow piles of scrapped papers and misprints scattered about the counter to deposit into the recycling box. Leaping out at her, as if in 3-D, was the name "Matthew Ransom" in a recipient line next to a private email address on a document. Her stomach dropped.

A reluctant curiosity nudged her to slip off the other copies covering the paper in order to examine the entire sheet.

It was a receipt. In her hands was a voucher for a coveted pair of concert tickets to one of the top bands in the world, Psatisfy. Nevaeh's mouth dropped open, as if she had found a diamond in the thumbtacks. The barcodes on the receipt appeared to have the power of entry. A small fortune was paid for the tickets—a prearranged, fantastic future that would not be experienced by the investor. Heartbreaking. She wondered if anyone had access to Matthew's private email account to discover that the purchase was made.

Down the hallway, Nevaeh heard voices in conversation. The smooth, metrical cadence of Reggie could be heard in a professional but intimate exchange with Edwin. In order to catch Reggie's eye, she positioned herself in the doorway and watched the two men walk toward her down the hall. He acknowledged the sight of her with a jut of his chin. When he walked past, she touched his arm and said, "Hey, Reggie."

He paused, "Nevi-girl."

"Could we talk for just a minute? There's something you need to see."

"Sure, sure," he said. Edwin encouraged the two to speak and walked away to his office.

Nevaeh stepped into the copy room with Reggie following in sparkling white sneakers. He asked, "You have me all kinds of curious. Everything alright?"

She found that question difficult to answer, so she opted for neutral. "You know, the same." The receipt for the tickets was held out to him. "You must see this. It is, well, Matt has some unfinished business."

Heavy-lidded eyes under raised brows scanned the sheet of paper. Stark amazement choked his speech. Reflexively, his hand stroked his goatee as if to hold back the curse on the tip of his tongue. Matthew made great fiscal sacrifices and maneuverings to acquire prime seats to see Psatisfy. The date of the concert was fast approaching, and thus, the monetary investment was positively steep. The actual worth of the tickets was not measured by the purchase price, however, but by how difficult it was to acquire them. Of that exertion, Reggie knew Nevaeh had only a superficial understanding.

Reggie cleared his throat. "Man, these are big plans. Very big plans." Biting his lip, he fought for manly composure. "Where did you find this?"

Nevaeh motioned to the counter behind her in process of being organized. "Here, in a pile of misprints. I think Matt might have sent it to the printer, got busy, and forgot about it. I almost tossed it into the recycling box. Thankfully, I saw his name on the paper and examined it."

Reggie nodded his head, still staring at the document in wonder. "I tell you, Matt wants his guest to enjoy this show, and they will. I will be sure of that. I'll let Cathy know when she calls later today." His eyes pulled away from the paper. "Mighty keen oculi you have, Nevi." He began to fold the paper. "Hey, are you holding up alright? I heard about your grandmother. I'm sorry, darling."

Pulling her shoulders back to answer the ache in her chest, she said, "It has been hard, I mean, my grandma dying after all that happened this week. But I am glad I got to say goodbye to her."

"Saying goodbye isn't an opportunity we all have." He waived the receipt. "But I call this pair of tickets a goodbye from Matthew. A very, very *good* bye." They embraced as trusting friends do. He parted with, "You take it easy. I can tell that you need some time."

Nevaeh leaned against the counter and watched Reggie stride out of the room.

Then, for the second time that day, a severe stabbing pain shot down her left arm. Her heartbeat hastened with panic. *Stupid Death,* she thought. *Are you after me now?* Flexing her left hand with foreboding, she noticed her watch. The client meeting was soon to start. There was no time left to mull over her symptoms—or the meaning of life.

The team of Cantaloupe consultants was to meet with a group of healthcare specialists spearheading a new web site venture, "Doctors on Call." The clients were wealthy surgeons with a bright idea on which to experiment with their largess. She walked into the conference room occupied by members of the project team and investors of the start-up. This meeting was the fifth of this kind and everyone was familiar with each other. The discussion commenced after the frenzied database developer darted into the room with a fresh, extra-large coffee in hand.

After the project manager reviewed the progress of the team against the timeline and made adjustments, Nevaeh took control of the meeting. She squelched the niggling in her mind over the events of the copy room and dealt out the document with no-nonsense authority. Together, those collected around the long conference table worked through the pages approving, critiquing, and editing aspects of the design.

Nevaeh's thinking and conversation were sharp for half an hour until a wave of light-headedness swept over her. She lost focus on the discussion and paid quiet, but stern attention to the sensation seizing her. The ability to process what she was hearing briefly disappeared. Was she about to pass out? The single time she had ever lost consciousness was on a blistering day in Mexico City; that episode was preceded by her limbs feeling heavy as lead. In contrast, this instance was an all-absorbing, floaty mindlessness that faded just in time to catch up with the dialogue at the table. After an expansive breath, Nevaeh resumed the conversation seamlessly. Yet, paranoia over having a real health condition competed for her concentration the rest of the meeting.

As was typical with clients who were brainy experts in their fields, but had no Internet business experience, Nevaeh faced change orders that were poorly conceived and even destructive. It was normal for project plans to develop "feature creep." Between meetings, clients had time to think, and their expanding visions of glory and profit would result in such change orders. For the most part, the Cantaloupe team talked the MDs out of expensive, difficult, unworkable, or naïve changes to the project. Having escaped a load of tricky redesign efforts, Nevaeh smiled triumphantly at the doctors and nodded at her project manager to conclude the meeting. She sat back in her chair and took a deep breath in. The extra oxygen expressed her relief and was also craved by her aching chest and worried brain. The odd tension that seemed to emanate from where her heart beat continued through the meeting without end.

Everyone stood to leave the conference room. The group streamed out the door, exchanged farewells, and shook hands. The project manager escorted the clients on a protracted walk toward the front entry of the building. Nevaeh pulled her shoulders back in discomfort and turned the opposite direction to return to her desk.

Again, with force, the lightheaded sensations returned when she entered the vast room that housed her workstation. Her eyes did not see with optimal clarity. Her stride devolved into a shuffle. The stabbing sensation, again, shot down her left arm. Her breath became rapid, as if she had completed a sprint. Independent from her conscious thought, her body was superseding her mind's ability to control it. The list of cardiac symptoms screamed in her mind. There was no doubt that her physical problem was real and not conjured by her imagination. Positioned in the way of her weakening steps down the aisle was Blaine's desk. Gratefully, she fell forward and braced her frame upright on the edge of the table, startling Blaine with her abrupt arrival.

Nevaeh pleaded, "Blaine! I don't feel right. Something's wrong with me." The pallid man's eyes widened. "This is not a joke. If I pass out—call 911. OK?" she said desperately. A burning sensation fired up her spinal cord. Her breathing was erratic and overwhelming. *I'm dying. My heart! I'm dying!* she thought.

Blaine tried to maneuver around his desk in time to catch his coworker buckling to the floor. His wordless rush to Nevaeh's side drew the attention of his neighbors, since he was the last person in the room to move so energetically. The normally silent Blaine yelled out to the room, "Get help, now!" He looked at Nevaeh's blanching face. "Can you hear me, Nevi? Nevi!"

"Yeah," she weakly replied. Were she to black out, Nevaeh deliberately laid down onto her back to avoid knocking her head against something. Her chest moved up and down with frenetic panting and a racing heart.

"Are you in pain? Where does it hurt?"

To these questions, she could barely formulate answers. Her eyes rolled around, out of focus. Her breathing was all-controlling and her mind silently cried: *I am not in pain yet—not yet. When will my heart start to hurt? Dear, God. I'm not ready. I haven't fallen in love. I wanted to marry! I have no children! I should have had Jordan's baby. At least, I would be a mother. Maybe that's why I am dying now—hurt as few people as possible.*

"We're getting help, Nevi. Hang on." Blaine said firmly.

Nevaeh continued to fret in silence: *My family! I love them. I wish I could tell them one more time. I hope they truly know. Grandma! Am I meeting Grandma? Maybe she died before me so that she can meet me when I pass. My heart is still not hurting—not yet. Maybe I'll just go unconscious like Matt and never know how it all ends.*

By this time, her eyes detected that more coworkers were encircling her, and self-consciousness ended her stupor.

Then, a deep voice commanded all bystanders to clear the way.

A demure Japanese accent informed: "She said she did not feel well this morning. She was holding her hand on her chest."

Thick fingers wrapped around one of Nevaeh's wrists to take her pulse. A familiar man with thick, silver hair looked her over and touched her forehead, then touched the skin at the V of her t-shirt, then bent down to press his ear to her chest. It was the cardiac surgeon, Dr. Wilson from the "Doctors on Call" project!

"Hello, Nevi," said the seasoned man of medicine, his face hovering over hers. Hope improved her attention. "What could you be doing on the floor? You were perfectly fine a minute ago! You were not anxious at all. Now, I want you to breathe through your nose. Close your lips! I want you to hold your breath for three slow counts."

The prostrate consultant felt helpless against the involuntary actions of her body. Because she was certain her condition was beyond mind control, she exerted little effort to obey the doctor. But paddles were not being rubbed together and the doctor continued to demand in the kindliest delivery that she pull air through her nostrils. It took several attempts for her to successfully take a full breath through her nose. The doctor then instructed, "Breathe with your diaphragm. Take another deep breath by expanding your stomach and hold it for four seconds. That's right. Let's just do this for a minute or two and see how that feels."

Sirens did not sound and were not roaring closer. Little by little, deep breathing became easier. After a couple of minutes of soothing talk to his patient and their audience, the doctor resumed treatment. "Now, your name? Blaine?

Please help me, Blaine, to get Nevi to sit upright against the side of your desk here. Nevi, you keep taking deep breaths and focus on calming your body."

When it was clear that Nevaeh was not on the brink of death, the crowd dissipated with gracious good wishes and gladness that she was alright. The doctor instructed her to continue to take long, full breaths until her respiration returned to its natural rate. After small talk and fifteen minutes of recovery, the doctor stood and extended his hand to Nevaeh.

"Please, take a seat at your desk, Nevi." Inside of her workstation, she took her chair, and the doctor sat on the edge of her desk. "So, this episode seems to have come out of the blue. I'm going to ask you a few questions so we can make sure you are back to 100%. I understand there's been terrible news for you and the office this week. Have you been worried and losing sleep over these awful losses? Your colleague Matthew and your grandmother, I understand."

Nevaeh meekly replied, "Well, it has been so sad here and, yes, it has been a rough week for me." She leaned forward and said quietly, "Today, though, I have not thought much about Matthew or my grandma. My mind was totally occupied by other matters all day." She shook her head in dismay over her self-absorption.

His brow furrowed. "Please do not take offense, but has your alcohol intake increased this week?"

"No! Not at all. I self-medicate with sugar," she replied.

"I understand that." Dr. Wilson adjusted his position on the table. "I noticed in the meeting that your water bottle was nearly empty. You have been drinking water today. How has your water consumption been this week?"

"I've been drinking water, juice, all kinds of things. I have done what I usually do." She wondered what water had to do with a near-death experience, and cut to the chase. "Sir, is my heart OK?"

The doctor looked curious, and slightly amused, "Oh, yes. My educated guess is that your heart is perfectly fine. I am concerned that you may be suffering dehydration or emotional upset. Both conditions can trigger hyper-ventilation."

"Hyperventilation? Is that the same as shortness of breath? Because I've had other symptoms that point to heart trouble." The doctor pursed his lips doubtfully. "Seriously. There is this tension right here in my chest that is super tight. It aches, and I feel like my shoulders are being pulled in. Since last night, this chest discomfort has bothered me constantly. I have never felt this before in my life. And then three different times today, a sharp, stabbing pain zapped my left arm. And, right before I collapsed, this weird, electric—I don't know—fire shot up my spine to my head."

The doctor nodded, with a flicker of insight in his eye. "Interesting."

Her manager, Rachel, momentarily stopped to ask if Nevaeh felt better and to come to her office when convenient. Before turning away, Rachel slipped onto the desk a coffee mug with an arrangement of Rhododendrons snipped from the office park, and serving as a card, a white sheet of paper folded into quarters propped next to the makeshift vase with the words "For You" in ballpoint.

Dr. Wilson continued, "Tell me, Nevi, have you been resting yourself to keep your heart rate down today?"

"No," Nevaeh answered guiltily, taking away her appreciative eyes from the handmade get-well gifts. "Actually, I've done the exact opposite, which I know is stupid if I am having heart trouble. But I just could not sit still. I felt worse sitting and better on my feet, so," she winced, "I took the stairs and have been moving around—a lot." Behind Dr. Wilson, coworkers in the aisle offered reassuring smiles and privacy by walking on.

"I see," Dr. Wilson said, trying to suppress a grin. "Think now, have you in the past week experienced coughing, a scratchy voice, or even laryngitis?"

Lifting her chin higher, she answered, "Yes! This weekend! I sounded horrible for a couple of days."

"Can I guess that you ate something this weekend that upset your stomach?"

Nevaeh's brows lifted and she said reluctantly, "Yes, I had a really upset stomach on Friday after eating too much raw broccoli and a pineapple smoothie. It ruined my night. Actually, my whole weekend."

"Well, I have good news for you," the doctor said warmly. "I can say with assurance, your symptoms were not a result of cardiac problems. You suffered an acute case of pseudo-dyspnea."

"Pseudo-what? I have never heard of that. Sounds—ah—not good."

"You experienced neither a heart attack nor hyperventilation. You experienced false or imagined shortness of breath. Sometimes, when the nerves in the esophagus are stimulated, it confuses the brain into thinking something is wrong with a vital organ, your heart or lungs, which can cause pseudo-dyspnea. In other words, you have acid reflux, my dear."

"Acid reflux?"

"Heartburn," Dr. Wilson clarified.

Nevaeh gawked at the doctor like he was playing a joke. "Heartburn? That sounds ludicrous. Like, impossible. I ate that meal on Friday. That was nearly a week ago!"

"Hey! Relax! I could be rolling you into surgery right now! Believe me, as a cardiac specialist, rarely am I able to give such good news to a patient," he chuckled. He wrote the diagnosis on a sticky note and handed it to her. "Because pseudo-dyspnea is universally viewed as harmless, I have no concerns about you looking it up on the Internet to alleviate your concerns. My prescription is to stay away from vinaigrettes and raw vegetables for a while." He winked and patted her on the shoulder.

Nevaeh frowned at the sticky note on her finger. Emotions swirled inside, a soup of self-consciousness, relief, and a backlog of mourning. Tears began to collect on her lashes. "I feel so foolish, so embarrassed. I caused a scene in the office with—" she sobbed, "fake hyperventilation!"

Dr. Wilson walked around the end of her desk to leave and said, "Nevi, tears are justified for losing your grandmother and your friend, but not for yourself. Everyone is glad you are alive and healthy. Count your blessings. It's a good day. Your story ended well."

Nevaeh watched the doctor exit her workstation and clear her view of the office floor. Blaine typed away on his keyboard. He sensed Nevaeh's eyes on him and he flashed back a meager smile, which was his version of a hurrah.

Exhibiting no residual concern for the situation, his eyes shifted back to his monitor and his fingers continued to click the keyboard and mouse in an unaffected way. Her gratitude for Blaine grew more, because unlike him, others would soon pile into her workstation to recount the episode. Nevaeh could not bear to discuss the details with anyone. Thankfully, many coworkers located immediately around her desk were, she guessed, in meetings.

The exhausted consultant wiped her eyes with her sleeve and looked at the makeshift bouquet of pink flowers and the crude card made of copier paper with which Rachel beautified her desk. She unfolded the paper and squinted at, not a get-well note, but the receipt for the coveted Psatisfy tickets found in the copier room. Why did Rachel have the tickets and why was she giving them to her? The paper bore no explanation.

Directly, Nevaeh stood and walked to Rachel's office with the sheet in hand. Along the way, coworkers glanced up at her and called out questions about her health. Nevaeh shut down the questioning with brief responses like, "Yes, I'm alright. Totally OK. Sorry, I can't talk right now. I have to meet with Rachel."

Nevaeh successfully dodged being waylaid by lengthy, well-meaning interrogations. Her manager was concluding a phone call when the office door was shut. Rachel smiled up at Nevaeh saying, "Nevi, hello. Sit down. You didn't need that little bit of chaos today. I feel badly for you! Dr. Wilson told me that nothing is wrong with you. If anyone but Dr. Wilson told me that, I would be freaking out and mandating that you take a month off!"

"Hey, I'll take that month off, no matter what!" Nevaeh laughed. "The whole experience was so nutty and sudden. I am thoroughly mortified, but physically, I feel normal now."

"Good," Rachel said. "I want to make sure you have enough time or help with your project. It has been a challenging week, so ask for whatever you need."

Nevaeh shook her head no. "Work is not a problem for me at all. In fact, I find work to be an escape. I am glad I have deadlines and assignments to occupy my brain. I need it." She then held up the receipt for the concert tickets. "You dropped this off at my desk. What were you intending by giving me this?"

"I didn't give you—oh! Was that the card? I thought Reginald wrote you a get-well note. He handed it to me before he left and said to deliver it to you."

"Huh." Nevaeh frowned, completely stumped. Why was Reggie passing the tickets back to her? She reviewed the receipt to find more handwriting or to extract details in the small type to point to the reason. Finding no answer, she said, "I guess I have to ask Reggie. I have no idea why he gave this to me." A sigh came out in with weighty fatigue. "You asked if I need help. Frankly, what I dread is talking to anyone. I am so embarrassed, and so annoyed with myself, and I am still processing everything that has happened this week. I just want to put my head down, and work, and not deal with anybody."

"I understand. I'll walk you back to your desk and manage things to give you a break from interruptions. Just focus on work and leave the rest to me." Rachel went to the door and held it open for Nevaeh, like a nurse guiding her patient through a hospital.

The two women walked back to Nevaeh's desk and Rachel left her with a heartening smile and a thumbs-up. Because Rachel was a compassionate doer, Nevaeh knew she would be buffered from the staff, cocooned in calm for the rest of the day.

Intending to work, she reviewed the dense mass of unread messages in her email inbox. Reggie's name was listed as a sender for a message entitled "FW: May 28." Eagerly, she opened the email hoping it contained an explanation. Its contents took her breath away:

```
Nevi,
I found this in the draft folder in Matthew's
work email. You were meant to find the tickets.
- R

===========================================

From: Matthew Ransom
To:   Nevaeh Mayes
Subject: May 28


Hi Nevi,

I know we do not cross paths much at work and you do
not know me very well, so this message may come as a
surprise to you. I was able to score some tickets to
the Psatisfy concert for Friday night, the 28th. Are
you interested? I figured you might like to go
because I've heard you listening to their music. I
hope you will do me the honor of joining me for a
great night out.

I am going out of town, so I will stop by your des
```

It took all her power to keep the instant flood of tears from devolving into audible sobs. Burying her head into her crossed arms on the desk, she released the deep sadness that quaked her frame.

Possessing the prized tickets to live out Matthew's gift was an awful burden. Matthew spent enough money for the tickets to buy a used car, and yet, was denied the musical experience. The grave silenced his opportunity to show that he carried a torch for her, and it felt insulting to his memory that she had never considered him in a romantic way. There was no joy in the revelation contained in the drafted message—only pain and loss and confusing questions.

While anatomizing the predicament of Matthew's tickets, her tears never ceased. She had cried after the news of Matthew's death, her grandmother's death, and her humiliating collapse from acid reflux. But the tears spilling from her eyes in that moment were of another order. If Matthew had lived to ask her out, and she accepted, her future may have taken turns that could have altered her life forevermore. Matthew Ransom was a nice-looking, friendly, and respected guy. The what-ifs were haunting.

She reviewed the drafted message from Matthew and looked at the receipt over and over hoping that doing so would clarify the past and the future. As for the present, all she could do was weep for him as a sincere offering of thanksgiving for who he had been, and who he wanted to be to her.

To use the tickets felt like dancing on his grave. To give away the tickets felt like stomping on his grave. How was she ever going to attend that spectacular, once-in-a-lifetime concert and feel the thrill and enthusiasm of the crowd? And yet, to not embrace the experience would be the opposite of what Matthew intended. There was only one way she could navigate the experience rightly in Matthew's honor.

She clicked "Reply" on the email, and typed, "Reggie—You are my date. Help me do this."

Some time passed before she could let go of thoughts of Matthew, dry her eyes and runny nose, and turn her mind back to work. Eventually, reluctantly, she closed Matthew's invitation and scanned her incoming email. In Jerod's absence, she had received no texts or calls from him, but there appeared an email entitled, "Miss you." Normally, her heart skipped at any communication from Jerod. Instead, her heart hurt. The gut-wrenching emotions for Matthew could be construed as the palest form of infidelity—if she and Jerod were dating. The mouse hovered over the subject as she shifted uncomfortably in her seat. Finally, she dared to open the message. It read:

```
Hey, I'm still out of town. My car overheated on the
road and forced us to stay a couple of nights in this
bedbug infested motel with wonk wifi.  I'm trying to
answer work email tonight. Let's hang when I get back.
Cook up more of that tortilla soup I can't stop
thinking about, and we will catch up on trash TV
together. Wear red. You look great in red. - Jerod
```

Twice, she analyzed this dispatch devoid of curiosity about her circumstances. There was provoking flattery about her appearance and cooking. There was the suggested homebound hangout. But there was no mention of losing a coworker in a plane crash. These critiques she would fail to make if Matthew's message was not so freshly digested.

One of the two men jumped hurdles and committed funds to prepare a date where she would be publicly on his arm. The other man suggested a clandestine rendezvous, probably at her place, without any exertion or expense on his part.

Instead of palpitations over the prospect of seeing Jerod, she felt—tired.

The cosmos or fate or God or whatever was pelting exhortations at Nevaeh which she was forced to receive in the trenches of life and death. Reggie's continued warnings about Jerod and other past love interests were suddenly understood. She envisioned the empty exchange they would have upon Jerod's return when he would recount, over her tortilla soup, on her couch, his annoyances with his bumpy trip to a music festival with someone other than her, while she would be trying to find words to describe the distressing week she had while he was absent. Why? Because, he would say, she did not know Matt well, her grandma was old, and heartburn is not a health crisis.

If Jerod could not pick up a phone for her, why anticipate that he could commit to her? It took a dead man asking her on a date to open her eyes to the vapid relationship she had with a living man. Whether her health scare was real or imagined, she earnestly faced her own death that day, and saw the hourglass of her life. If she wanted the final moments of her life to be like Grandma Molly's, peacefully reflecting on the love of her progeny, why was she wasting any fraction of her fertile years on Jerod?

Nevaeh deleted Jerod's email message, and serenely awaited a dead man's date.

5

Silver Dollar

Tawny snuck a five-minute breather out of the view of the patrons in the sallow corridor to the loading dock. With the busser out sick, her efforts to clear and wait tables congruently left her spent. Facing the back exit while inclined on the scuffed wall, she glumly examined her right hand. The frequent dips in soapy water from the extra duties led to losing a ring, a souvenir from a road trip with her mother when they explored legendary ghost towns across the Southwest. Hoping for its recovery would only put off the ache.

Her unauthorized break was interrupted by a disconcerting press of hand on her back. A recent regular of the pub smoothly pulled around her side and mirrored her lean on the wall. He was a well-built contractor on a downtown project, with an asymmetrical smile and a dishwater crew cut. For two weeks, he had plied her with audacious flirtation and generous tips, but had not pushed further until that moment. Tawny's pulse raced either from being startled, or because his good looks simmered in that Daniel Craig sort of way. She feigned complete ease, but could not stop her hand from turning her bracelet.

"I'm here to offer my services," he said. His eyes drank her in more tactfully than usual. Flirting with Todd had been a ceaseless game since they first met, but his intense eye contact in that hallway conveyed a different mindset.

To be safe, she ignored the change. "Good. My kitchen outlet blows a fuse when I use the blender."

"Easily done. Or I could just keep you out of the kitchen altogether. You've handled enough dishes today." Evidently, Todd tracked her every move. With any other man, she would find such surveillance disturbing, but instead, she tipped her head for more. He asked, "When are you off?"

"Six," she sighed, "I get to enjoy five more hours of this shift." Reflexively, her thumb rubbed her finger to spin a ring that was no longer there. Her eyes flicked downward at the vacancy, and instantly, she resumed talking. "So, what do you have in mind for tonight?"

"You and I are going take in the sun and have a conversation. I think some fresh air is in order."

The simplicity of the excursion was the perfect conclusion to her day, and the suggestion increased Todd's appeal. Still, she maintained her reserve. "I like the sound of that. I'll meet you here at 7:30."

After a languid head-to-toe scan of the brunette, Todd's eyes stopped on her fidgeting fingers. He tilted off the wall and clasped Tawny's right wrist, then slid his palm into hers as if to pull her in. Alarmed by his advance, her arm firmly resisted until he slipped the missing turquoise band on the correct finger. Feelings of surprise, relief, and unease struck Tawny all at once. The customer knew the lost ring was hers and on which finger she wore it.

What guy notices stuff like that? she thought. The benefaction rendered Tawny incapable of clear communication. "Geez, thank you! How did you—? Where did—?"

"I found it on the ground," Todd explained off-handedly. A peculiar brand of pleasure radiated from him while Tawny made inept attempts to say more. He looked past her, muttering to himself, "Hmm. So that's why." His obscure comment sent her more off-kilter.

"I'll see you tonight," Todd said walking away. He conveyed an impious smile to the dining room while the waitress remained alone to study the Southwestern art of turquoise and silver restored to her finger, and to grapple with the disjointed happiness fluttering through her system.

Tawny's apartment was 20 minutes by bus where she had little time to flip her look. Under low-maintenance constraints, she managed to pull off a high-maintenance presentation. The encounter with Todd that afternoon sent her mind churning. As a waitress, every possible line conceived by men had reached her ears, and she had fallen for a few. There was something so personal in Todd's approach that it did not feel like he was playing. Maybe he was more expertly seductive than the rest, making her a prime sucker. Or, maybe he revealed a sincere connection. She avoided her roommates' questions of who's the guy and will she bring him home. The case felt too muddy to engage her roommates on the matter, and to not answer questions felt like a shield. Truly, she wanted to see what Todd was about. She could save the "I'm stupid" admission for after he lay waste.

Shortly before 7:30 PM, Todd reappeared at the pub casually attired in a fitted shirt with sleeves rolled up, and jeans well-cut for his average height. All traces of his workday were erased by a shower and shave, as were his engaging manners. Expecting to be mortared by an obvious compliment, Tawny was greeted by taut silence coupled with a penetrating lock on her eyes. Her chest burned in response. She inhaled to stifle the sensation; his spicy musk baited her senses while she waited for some hook. Pride straightened her posture, and Tawny raised an eyebrow at him. His only offering was, "Let's go," and mundanely exited the pub as if he was running an errand, with her trailing behind, all at sea. Over the heads of seated customers, the eyes of the wait staff followed them out the door, puzzling over the nature of the outing.

Tawny tried to be offended by his lackluster opening act, but his groomed appearance disarmed her into quiet compliance. Shameful. The handsome need not work hard for women, she conceded. Once past the ogling of the restaurant, however, Todd resumed his normal free flow of frank and attentive speech, punctuated with that fine smile. She wondered if he was enforcing their privacy while in the presence of the staff and regulars, which was illogical since he had openly targeted her with advances when there for lunch. Guys rarely made sense outside of their obvious goals with females. Remembering this, she quieted her mind, resumed the ordinary presumptions of male intentions, and resolved to enjoy his company at arm's length. She hoped her new backbone had calcified in time.

They set out to wander the edges of the park, where enticing emanations lured them to a busy hot dog stand. While waiting in line for the street fare, they covered the basics about each other. Tawny grew up an apartment dweller in the blue-collar suburbs. Todd graduated two years before her from a small high school in an unincorporated part of the state. Both were raised by single mothers: Tawny's parents never married and Todd's parents divorced when he was eleven. Being children of mothers who struggled financially and in their personal lives, they both were effectively independent at a young age. She had just graduated community college and was transferring to the university to become a medical lab technologist. Eight months ago, Todd was made crew lead after years of honing his skills in residential construction.

They carried their meal into the park and found a bench secluded under an aged tree with massive branches arcing downward around them like an umbrella. Under the speckled light of the shade, they ingested drippy, roasted franks, the kind of food Tawny would normally avoid on a first date. The messiness prohibited all pretensions, and kept the mood light.

The flow of conversation was interrupted by crows diving down to a nearby table to bicker over abandoned scraps of a picnic. Todd asked, "Is that what the wait staff does with the food that customers leave on their plates?"

"Oh, sure!" she said with equal sarcasm. "Toddlers leave the best stuff. I love ranch-soaked honeydew and spit-coated French fries," she laughed. "Whoa, they are noisy!"

"Crows are intelligent, you know. Maybe they are critiquing the food *and* discussing the last election," said Todd before biting his second hot dog.

"Crows are definitely cool. I have a stuffed one on my mantle." She sipped her soda.

"A stuffed crow?" Todd looked askance at her pleased profile. "A dead bird. Taxidermy."

"Yes, his name is Neb," she said.

"And you have a stuffed crow because—?"

"Because Bill needed a buddy."

Todd squinted at her. "And who is Bill?"

"My stuffed Mallard. Bill used to belong to my grandpa. I got him after Grandpa died."

"A duck named Bill." He nodded in thought, wiping his mouth with a new napkin. "So, the name Neb must mean something."

He's listening, Tawny thought. "Yes, a neb is a beak."

"Of course," he snickered. "I think I need to meet Neb and Bill."

"That can be arranged. But just a warning! Get on their good side, because they are very protective of me," she lightly warned.

"I know all about the wrath of birds. Don't challenge a crow or bad things happen." Todd raised his left hand; the tip of his pinky was missing.

"Oh, geez! Really?" She grabbed his hand and studied his finger with unexpected zeal.

"Nah. I'm kidding. Perils of the job." She punched his arm as he grinned. "So, is my hand totally repulsive to you or am I still in the game?"

She looked thoughtful. "Is the tip of your finger in a jar of formaldehyde?"

"Definitely not."

"Well, that's too bad. But you are still in the game."

His shoulder leaned into hers. "You're throwing curves, and I like it."

They discussed their respective efforts in school and career. The two topics of study Tawny loved were Greco-Roman mythology for the hedonism, and biology for the freaky labs. He told stories of himself as a child taking apart the toaster and straining his mother's nerves by frequently messing with the outlets. He built his own motorcycle, just to see if he could. Their banter resembled the familiarity of old friends, only doused with sexual tension.

Todd saw the edges of tattoos on Tawny's upper and lower back. "Hmm, there is something tempting here." He peeked at the symbol on her shoulder, and was surprised by what he found. "And what is this?"

"It is whatever *you* think it is." The conversation piece never disappointed.

His eyes narrowed on the ink. "Frankly, I think your scratcher lost control of the needle."

"Keep going."

"It looks like something a shrink would use." Tawny bowed her head once in approval. Todd looked carefully at the inkblot test etched on her shoulder, moving aside the wide strap of her tank top and rubbed the design firmly. He was mischievously quiet.

"The doctor is waiting," she prompted. His touch was a little distracting. "What do you think it looks like?"

"Me, of course."

"Every guy says that," she lied.

"Then everyone agrees: I am immortalized on your shoulder. You must be relieved that I finally asked you out." His reward was a hard shove and her self-conscious laughter.

After disposing of the trash, they moved to the grassy slope adorned with English daisies bordering the shore. They took in the vista while Todd turned the conversation to exploring their dating histories. This topic Tawny had lately begun to resent, but she maintained her aplomb and hoped her reluctance came off as mysterious. Tawny said enough to suggest she was a woman of experience, yet hoped to not appear easy. The reality was that she had long been unrestrained, but had changed course in recent times. It was a thorny case to not have the past indicate terms of the present. And while attempting this balancing act, Tawny questioned herself on where she really stood. Todd was kind. And sexy.

Todd absorbed her recitation with no questions and a ruminative expression. Tawny wished to know the conclusions he drew, but asking would expose her. She indicated that it was his turn.

Todd did not begin until after some calculation. Then, the raw truth of his depthless dating was laid out for her unedited with all the rough edges intact. Todd was not winning her over with his player tendencies, but rather with brazen honesty. His recounting had the air of a confession, rather than bragging of triumphs. Instead of internalizing these revelations as a conspicuous warning, she imprudently shelved the information. Tawny sensed the two of them were in a similar place: the world of dating had lost all its luster.

After an hour of sharing, an easy break in conversation allowed Tawny to sit and soak the warmth of the lowering sun in her black top and slimming jeans. The calm felt nice. The inlet within which they were settled caused the wind to blow in a circular way. Tawny's long chestnut hair shifted around her, rising and falling, rightward or left, depending on the incoming breeze.

Todd boldly took in the beauty of the movement of her hair encircling her rosy features. "You are looking delicious, with your wild Medusa hair," he said. His sinewy forearms rested on his knees as he shredded grass with his fingers. "I wonder: if I kissed Medusa, would I live to tell about it?"

The idea of him wrapping his strength around her frame was frustratingly intriguing. She took the flattery with a sly smile. "Medusa, eh? That's not really a compliment, by the way. But if it's working for you, then hair I am." She tugged a tress and suppressed a giggle.

They heard a mother corralling two preschoolers to the water's edge. "Maybe it's time to be heading off," he slowly suggested.

Pausing first to see if his word choice was intentional, she laughed heartily. "You slay me!"

His face contracted smilingly at the bad joke. "That almost works."

She turned to him, proud. "That was fantastic!" His profile rimmed in golden tones of sundown exhibited angles of a demigod. Tawny had to blink back awe that his rugged looks inspired before their eyes met to glint at each other.

Todd stood and assisted Tawny off the ground. He then entwined his fingers with hers to seek another destination. The cloak of his strong hand made her feel instantly more feminine. It also felt natural, like he held her hand every day. His seduction skills were phenomenal, she judged.

Yet, the more they chatted, it appeared to Tawny that he sincerely accepted her sense of humor, and was not just molding his own desirability like clay. Most people either did not find her wordplay funny, or did not get it at all. Rarely did anyone hit back the way Todd did. Relating to a guy in this manner was distinctive; it awakened the inmost part of her intuition. *He gets me. Something is happening here.*

They decided to seek out some live music and have a few drinks. On a block with a row of nightclubs, they chose one hosting a cover band that was to take stage in an hour. At a table tacky with residue, they continued conversation in a corner made private by faint light. Tawny found Todd's self-possession magnetic, as well as his practical nature that oozed with common sense. He was a steady man and seemed not to ruffle easily, which she supposed would be a counterbalance to her shifting temper.

They covered enough ground that Tawny felt it safe to ask, "So, with your parent's divorce and all, do you see yourself ever settling down and having kids?"

After a moment, Todd answered, "It's not something I've thought much about, but for some reason, with you, having kids sounds interesting. I'm curious to know what you were like when you were little."

Time to test him. "I was a complete brat."

"Liar," he accused.

"Then, I was a compulsive liar."

"I like good stories."

"Nothing sticks to you. You hardly know me. I could be a disaster."

"Believe me. I am crystal clear on what a mess you are. When you come to my place, you'll see I like messes." She rolled her eyes, but Todd's regard had the confidence of knowing a good secret. "Yep, I can picture a mini-you. Her name would be Tulip and she'd dissect bugs, lick French fries, and have a stuffed Pegasus named Muzzle." Tawny's face warmed; she stirred her drink and avoided his amused eyes. "Also," he added in a devilish way, "getting a ring frazzles you. It's worth a few grand to see that again."

Because Todd was an immense flirt, she determined to not take him seriously. Suggesting a proposal is what guys do to keep their bed warm for a few more weeks, not a tactic for first dates. To appear unmoved, she worked the stir stick until he touched her hair to signal he needed her lips. His extended kiss felt like a compliment. Afterward, Todd gazed at her as though he had just solved a problem. Tawny returned her attention to the performance on stage to conceal her feeling completely scrambled. *That kiss was crazy. I'm free-falling into desolation—or into a fairy tale. Stop thinking. Stop feeling.*

Todd smoothly rose from his seat and extended his hand. In similar silence, she accepted his escort to the dance floor. With the mass of jovial bodies, they moved to second-rate renditions under strobes and smoke. Usually by this hour, Tawny would be sloshed and in a vacuous grind with whichever guy was amenable. Because she and Todd had talked so intensely through the evening, she had had little to drink, and resultantly, was quite alert. Nothing obscured the meaning behind their physical interplay. Assured by the ease of his company, Tawny felt the gelling of genuine attachment. They mostly cheered on the band as it rallied the crowd, and embraced for the slow dances. More than once, they melted into a lingering kiss amnesic to the commotion around them. The band took a break, and Todd suggested they return to the table. Tawny excused herself to use the restroom.

In the restroom, Tawny took her time so that she could assess things with Todd. The four hours with him had passed effortlessly. Their spoken and unspoken communications of humor, physicality, downtime, and crowd maneuvering were of the same rhythm. Their natural compatibility would make separating that night counterintuitive. Certain loneliness would trouble her the moment they were to part. She did not want the night to end. She needed to prepare for how she might allow the night to progress. Over the sink, she shook her hands free of excess water and reached for a paper towel.

Fourteen and a Quarter

After drying her hands, Tawny cleared the light shadow of mascara under her eyes with the moist paper. Few improvements were necessary. He was hers; the connection was palpable—physical, biochemical, and matchlessly psychological and emotional. Yet, the doubt fogged her instinct. So many times in the past, in fact, most times her calculations with men were wrong. Promised futures were suddenly absent after a few thickish weeks, or days, of passion. She had been too trusting, or too hopeful, or too drunk.

Uncertainty then overtook her confidence when she recalled the guidance that inspired her recent experimental commitment to abstinence. Months ago, Tawny bemoaned another breakup to her settled cousin, Kimmy, with two kids and a good husband. Tawny knew she was in peril of following the lonely path of her own mother, whose life was a tale of serial tentative attachments to indifferent men. After hearing continued dissatisfaction from her cousin, Kimmy chose not to merely soothe Tawny, but boldly counseled, "Remember this: men will not wait to sleep with their girlfriends, but will wait to sleep with their wives. Play the game differently and you'll find a husband."

She pulled the sable lipstick from her mouth, and blotted with the crumpled towel. The first and only time she withheld against her own desires was with heart-stopping Wayne two months ago. They had a few fervid dates peppered with Tawny's refusals to go all the way. His abrupt sendoff included a shower of insults. The disappointment was sharp, but relatively brief, she admitted to herself. The finale revealed the shallowest side of Wayne, and it was easier to move on. However, she was sure Todd was not the same kind of guy. So, why worry?

Tawny gave up on the experiment. Todd was solid and there was no need to fret. After inserting the lipstick back into her small purse, to prepare for all possibilities, she extracted a quarter out of the day's tips and sought the restroom vending machine housing feminine products. Coins and coition have had a long, intimate relationship. In those far-flung mining towns Tawny had toured on vacation, she learned that ladies of the night employed coins as birth control for their shape and for the spermicidal properties of metal. She was one movement away from using a quarter for the same purpose. After making this unpleasant observation, her fingers dropped the quarter into the chamber for prophylactics, and gripped the lever.

A creaky groan announced the opening of the restroom door, and in bumped two brunettes giggling and looking a little sloppy. Self-consciousness took over, and Tawny pulled her hand back before spinning the dispenser. Retrieving the coin would likewise reveal her designs, so she feigned checking her outfit in the cracked mirror while the restroom swelled with more tipsy women. Had she been intoxicated, shame would not have affected her judgment. But with her wits intact, signifying her intentions was uncomfortable. She left the restroom with less money in her pocketbook and no barrier from assorted consequences of her plans.

Exiting the bathroom, Tawny nearly ran into him. Startled, she looked up at the tall man staring down at her, with hair that fingers craved to run through, sharp green eyes, built to thrill, and clothed in cologne and a clingy shirt.

Emotional whiplash smacked Tawny, now cornered in that dingy hallway, fully detached from her evening and facing a past mistake.

With a tone of mild interest, he said, "Who's the guy? It looks serious." Wayne leaned against the wall with his hands shoved down his jean pockets.

She did not answer him for a second as she reigned in the five different emotional reactions she felt like spouting, and stayed clear. "Hi, Wayne. I'm fine. How are you?"

Wayne read through her paper-thin oblivion. "Really, who's the guy? Your boyfriend? How long?"

"It is none of your business, but things are going well with him," she said, attempting fuzzy honesty.

"Ah, that means he doesn't matter." His Abercrombie form entered the margins of her personal space. Tawny's nerves fired off the message that she was getting exactly what she had wanted from Wayne, yet her brain screamed, *Self-serving jerk!* The internal war rendered her speechless. He inched closer. "Since we stopped seeing each other, you've been on my mind—a lot."

Bluffing confidence, she jutted her chin. "You mean, since you dog-kicked me out of your life."

"Ah, you got it wrong, Tawny," he said with a slight snort. "You dog-kicked me, as I recall. And not just once."

Anger flashed in her eyes. "Interesting perspective, Wayne. Wow. I didn't think I could like you less."

"You are a below average actress." It took effort for her to keep her eyes above his deltoids as he closed the gap. "You're no saint, Tawny. Pretending to be one for me is fascinating. Every part of you says yes, while your lips say no."

The truth of his words stung. Since forced into his chiseled presence, Tawny was suppressing her admiration for this walking fantasy. If she paid full attention to those pulses of attraction, she would morph into fodder for his manipulations. *Seize control.* "What do you want, Wayne? You found me here for a reason. What could you possibly want after calling me every name in the book?"

"I know, I know," he said with a shade of seriousness, "I really have thought a lot about you. Your stubbornness pissed me off, but then I liked it. It's a strange thing."

Wayne was getting into her head. *This exactly what Kimmy was talking about. Wayne is stepping up. He wants more than just a good time. But there's something real between Todd and me. Todd is waiting for me. I've got to get out of here. But Wayne was in my life before Todd, and I did want more from him. And here he stands before me, offering more. No! Be strong! OK, just tell him—*

"Nothing preoccupies a man like false rejection," he cut into her ping-ponging thoughts. "It challenges me to unlock that yes, and I will do it. You're a formidable tease, but two can play that game. Nobody plays like me, and I always win."

I'm such a fool. She put her dignity back on. "Wayne, I will never say yes."

Leaning down, his capable lips loomed close to her face; their proximity unnerved her. "Oh, you do say yes. You have no secrets, girl. It's a big city, but a small town. I'm worth a dozen of the guys you've been with. And you say no to me?" His head rocked driving his point. "Women don't say no to me. Ever." She felt his sleek fingers cradle the nape of her neck, resurrecting temptation. Cologne flooded her nose as his smooth, haunting voice said, "And you want to say yes right now. You can't even look me in the eye."

In spite of the oppressing attraction, Tawny managed to fight the darts of shame he was hurling. "Get the message, Wayne. No!" she retorted, "It's no forever." Backing out of his enclosing net, she said, "A better man is waiting for me. Goodbye."

His slithering taunts snapped at her heels as she dashed away.

Her insides crumpled. Evidently, her determination was a house of cards. Had Wayne kissed her, she might have folded before him, and leveled the success of the night. *I don't know what I am doing.* Tawny took deep breaths and regrouped before turning the corner out of the cave of a hallway. Finding Todd at the table casually reclined in his rigid chair radiating patience and security, she felt rescued.

She sat down. Todd flashed his slanted grin. "Are you OK?"

Tawny unconsciously rubbed her neck. "I'm fine."

"What did he want? He's been watching us all night." Todd took a drink.

She yearned to play dumb, but knew Todd was too perceptive. "He needed reminding that it's over between me and him."

Todd made blasé eye contact with Wayne, who talked with two other men across the club. "So, he wants you back."

Her expression iced over. "He does not want me. He wants it. I refused to sleep with him when we were dating."

"Ouch! I'm sure a guy like him doesn't hear that very often." Todd kept his enjoyment subtle.

"Yes, he believes his ego is impossible to reject." It donned on her that she was confiding in Todd like a trusted friend, forgetting that they were on a date. She checked to see if he was withdrawing having learned this applicable information. Todd, instead, regarded her with reflective wonder.

"You are one curious woman," he said, putting a lock of hair behind her hooped ear. "Lucky for us, curiosity is a driving force in my life. I am certain I'd be dead before I ever had you completely figured out."

His sincerity moved Tawny to demand of Todd an interlude of deep kissing to make clear which man she wanted, and to hint at her aims for the rest of the night. She hoped Wayne was watching, but as the heat increased, she ceased caring.

With their desire intensifying, Todd suggested they depart. He led her by the hand through the crowd shortly after the music threw the audience out of their seats. Todd guided her through the sweaty throng like a bodyguard.

They walked out the alley side door of the bar, and proceeded hand-in-hand to his truck a few blocks away. While walking in the cool of night, they alternated between kissing and talking. Noting their extraordinary compatibility, Tawny weighed her two goals. The short-term goal was to realize the utmost potential of the date. The long-term goal was to find a lasting relationship. There were men in her past she had believed would settle down but did not. Todd had a completely different level of promise than any of them. If she lost Todd by treating him like her past hook-ups, she could regret that choice the rest of her life.

When they reached his truck, Todd wrapped his arms around her for a burning kiss. He was absolutely alive with desire, and made her knees week with his intensity. The sculpted physique she could detect under his clothes became her singular focus. The skin at the base of her back ignited from the grip of his athletic hands that crushed her to him. Besides the physical chemistry, there was a layered connectivity. Todd kissed like he was sending a message to her soul. She allowed herself to be fully lost in the fire until she could no longer ignore her contrary feelings.

When he stopped to unlock the truck, Tawny gently put space between them. Not sensing her inner battle, he urged, "It's open."

Her heart began to race as she verbalized her worry. "Todd, wait a minute."

Under the street lights, she could see his surprise. "Is something wrong?" Her silence prodded him further. "Tawny, talk to me."

Tawny dropped her head into her hands. She reeled with mixed judgment. She explained with reluctance, "I have had a bad run with guys. So, I recently decided to slow things down with men just to, I don't know, try something different."

Todd shifted his weight. "I see."

"Now that I'm with you, I'm starting to think the problem was the type of guy I was dating, not what I was doing." Her wistful eyes rose to meet his.

His voice was even, "I'm guessing you dated guys who were jerks, players, one-track-minded losers, all talk and no substance."

"Yes, exactly."

"And you've imagined me to be a different creature than, say, that guy back in the bar."

"You are entirely different from Wayne."

"Tawny, I am no different from Wayne."

"You are so wrong. He's a scumbag."

"I am a scumbag. I have always been a scumbag. Have no illusions, Tawny."

"That doesn't ring true," she insisted.

He paused in resignation. "Because I don't want to be that to you."

Tawny unfolded her arms and took his maimed hand in hers to caress. "Todd, I am messed up right now. I made this vow to myself on how I would behave, and honestly, it helped me to figure out who Wayne really was. But now—"

His face relaxed a little as he comprehended the situation. "I think I understand what you are afraid of." He squeezed her hand. "We've had an amazing time together. I do not want the night to end now." She nodded as Todd moved close to her and tenderly pled, "I simply want you with me tonight. I won't expect anything to happen. Just stay with me." Her willpower eroded further as his expression of longing washed over.

The time for wishful thinking had passed. "Todd," she said, "I expect everything to happen."

He conceded with a cautious smile.

"This is weird of me, I know. I just—let me ask you this: if I don't go home with you, what happens then?"

Todd withdrew his hand to rub his eyelids and stubble while his other hand clenched keys. Polarized by assurance and doubt, Tawny watched him wrestle with his own will. His next move would be the most enlightening of the night. Disappointed, Todd said, "I go home—alone. Feel miserable all night. Send you text messages about how much it sucks that you aren't with me. I'll down some beers and a two-pound bag of chips and watch reruns of 'That Seventies Show'."

Medusa exposed her neck to the sword. "And then what?"

"What do you mean? You mean, between us?"

She watched him steadily. "Yes."

"We go out again as soon as you can stand it." Todd heard gratitude in her sigh. His escalating respect for her was having a transformative effect on him, and he could sense it. "Tawny, you shouldn't feel this conflicted. I think now that neither of us will feel right if you break the promises you've made to yourself. Geez, part of what knocks me out about you is that you kicked Wayne where it counts. You are no pansy, and that's extremely attractive to me."

"So, is that what I am doing to you right now?" She felt pained, and very much like a pansy.

"Wayne is not nearly the man I am. Let me prove it." Her eyes squeezed shut for a moment to absorb his words. Peace spread in Tawny like a sunrise as she allowed herself to believe him. His respect felt like love. He tilted her glowing face up to his and they kissed for five sweet minutes. He pulled away before he was tempted to try to change her mind. "I'll drive you home."

At her apartment door, Todd parted with, "I'll meet Neb and Bill next time. Right now, I'm going to pick up some Doritos."

Tawny laughed at this. She gazed up at his charming good looks. Yearning and insecurity seeped into the pit that his departure was creating in her soul. "Todd, I just want to say—"

He planted his lips on hers and pulled back. "See you tomorrow. My lunch is at noon. I'll want the Philly." Jogging down the steps, Todd added, "And leave your phone on."

6

Ready, Aim, Shoot

It took twenty minutes to set up the equipment for the photo session. The family-owned neighborhood jewelry shop, Raymond Gems, had finally become serious about its online presence. By recommendation of a mutual friend, the shop hired Kelly to take pictures of some inventory for the launch of a basic Internet shopping experience. Kelly accepted each item with gloved hands and placed it in the small shooting tent on the table. The cubical tent of white fabric housed each ring in succession to be bathed in diffused light. A tiny, additional LED was focused on each subject to enhance the glitter of the gems.

About two dozen platinum and gold rings were captured. Following those, the sales rep assisting Kelly passed the first pendant to her. She focused the camera lens on the sparkling piece. After snapping the photo, the photographer checked the resulting image on the back of the digital camera and realized that the picture did not communicate the size of the pendant. Kelly ungloved her hand and reached to the bottom of her canvas sling bag. With some effort, she blindly detected a quarter and placed it within the shooting tent next to the pendant. The pendant, as she suspected, was nearly the same size of the quarter. The quarter lay tandem to all the pendants that were photographed.

After an hour and a half, Kelly packed her equipment to leave. The salesman that helped her to stage the merchandise asked the typical client questions: When will the pictures be done? How will the store receive the pictures? How did Kelly wish to be paid?

Kelly continued with her packing as she answered, but became meditatively quiet on the last question. "Well," she paused, "would you consider a trade?"

The composed man in a starched shirt smiled. "Occasionally, we do trades. Is there a piece that you have in mind?"

Kelly went to the faux velvet display rack where hung the necklaces she had photographed. "I am drawn to this pendant. Opal is my birthstone, and its shape is so unusual, so retro."

"Yes, isn't it spectacular? That is a custom estate piece we acquired some time ago and are promoting it now because styles from the 1960s are taking hold in fashion. I will talk to my manager and see if a deal can be worked out."

The salesperson left and soon returned to confirm the trade. The necklace was an eye-catching statement, and it complemented the outfits she planned to wear in the next two days. Kelly immediately put on the necklace, and shook the man's hand, shimmering in diamonds. The salesman took one of her bags and opened doors for Kelly. With his escort, she hauled the rest of her cumbersome equipment out the back of the store.

Once the gear was packed into the trunk and the salesman had departed, Kelly slumped into the driver's seat of the Jetta, and took a contemplative swig of her water bottle. The next photo shoot was scheduled for the following morning at a location requiring a daunting four-hour drive. To meet her client, Kelly left the jeweler and drove the entire distance, not fighting fatigue as she anticipated, but in restless fidgets. Her host for the night was an old college friend who offered a fold-out bed to crash on. The girls' night out in the big city subdued Kelly's apprehensions for a little while.

All qualms, however, returned to pester her mind in the morning. Her next client, by the name of Myrna, was known to fill those around her with foreboding. The last conversation she had with Myrna was at ten o'clock, the night before the jewelry shoot. Kelly gathered that Myrna was imbibing heartily, as she was known to do, and in a faint voice slurred over the telephone, "I had a dream that you were there and it all fell apart." When Kelly tried to ask what this statement meant, specifically where "there" was, and what "it" was, the clatter of a poorly restored receiver ended the call.

After morning preparations were concluded, goodbyes between the friends were exchanged. In the Jetta, Kelly exhaled through puffed cheeks, and a moment passed before she could will herself to turn the ignition. After a 30-minute congested drive, she parked across the street of a 1963 split-level in a neighborhood alive with the sounds of preschool children and lawn mowers. The neighborhoods in the region were turning over from the elderly to young families partaking in the local economic boom. Kelly had photographed several such homes of late as a real estate photographer, and these time-capsules were often vacated as-is and sold for staggering prices. The homeowner, Myrna, had bided her time, waiting for such a moment in the market to capitalize on the sale of her house.

Kelly emerged from the car and gripped her trembling hands around the straps of her sling bag. She approached the front of the vacant house and looked about. There was no sign of the client. Working her camera would make the wait constructive, so she returned to the car, mounted the ultra-wide lens to the camera, and commenced the exterior shots while full sun illuminated the front of the house. The sun was bright, but the spring breeze cut through layers of clothing. Kelly tightly rewrapped her thin, decorative scarf to effectively warm her neck.

Several angles of the front of the house had been taken when a five-foot-tall woman in a knee-length cardigan stepped out the front door. "You!" she barked, waving one taloned hand. "You did not follow my instructions! I said to knock on the door when you got here."

Kelly blinked at this unceremonious greeting. She did not recognize the feeble woman, crowned with an oversized French twist pinned like a neat, silver tornado on her head. Her little beady eyes scowled, demanding an explanation. Kelly did not recall such an instruction from

Myrna. Kelly's mouth compressed shut as she gathered her senses. "I apologize," she managed to call back. "I am so sorry. I did not remember you saying that." In spite of the intimidation, Kelly hoped she appeared affronted. Myrna shook her head and turned back into the house. Walking to the front door, Kelly strained to recall if she ever heard Myrna tell her to knock.

As Kelly rounded the wall into the kitchen, Myrna was seated at a spindly chair, tapping her cigarette into the ashtray on the table positioned in the breakfast nook. Myrna took a puff and said while crushing the butt, "I have things I need to do. You don't have much time."

Myrna's self-absorbed nescience to the enormity of the situation finally snapped Kelly out of her reserve and lit her ire. "Why haven't you spoken to me in seventeen years?"

Myrna frowned appreciatively. "Listen, if you and I are ever to have a relationship, your father cannot be a part of it. At eighteen, he joined the army and never looked back. He's been mostly out of my life since then, and now he's out of yours. If it wasn't for your mother making that one visit, I may not have ever met you until now."

Since their last encounter years ago, Myrna had aged to an unrecognizable state. Sitting before Kelly was a crotchety New Englander who was a caricature of an old woman. Gray hair and facial lines from hard liquor, tobacco, and the stress of a high-profile career created around the woman an aura of murk, snark, and smoke. Kelly's last encounter with her grandmother was at the age of eight, arranged on the principle of family bonding by her mother.

Shortly after that visit, Kelly's parents divorced and her mother quickly remarried. No other visits between grandma and grandchild were arranged by the adults in her life. As Kelly's father had so unequivocally cut his mother out of his life, he recently had done likewise with his daughter. Evidently, the Murray family tactic of disowning one's relations had no limits and no mercy.

About a year after her father claimed offense and disappeared, Kelly sent a self-introduction by way of a birthday card to her grandmother retired in the Carolinas. Connecting with Myrna, she hoped, might help her to gain some understanding of the family overall. Myrna wrote back a brief note suggesting that they could meet when next she returned to the city. These first five minutes with her grandmother was an immersive education into the gene pool from which Kelly emerged.

Myrna's decision to sell the old family home was inspired by the bull real estate market. Kelly offered to do the photography for the fliers and online listing. Now, Kelly wondered why she would set herself up for this prickly obligation. Doing so came from the naiveté of growing up with her maternal grandma who was the ideal in terms of what a grandchild wants. Myrna face-slapped the realization that not all grandmas were culled from a chocolatier mold.

Hearing that Myrna had determined to make no personal effort toward her grandchild as a consequence of the failed relationship with her own son, Kelly took it personally, because, of course, Kelly was not her father. She was innocent of all the family drama. Kelly dared to say, "That doesn't explain why you never acknowledged me on holidays or my birthday. My mom sent you boxes of candy at Christmas and our school portraits every year, and you never reached out to us in return."

The thin woman's eyebrows arched high. "Your mother sent me nothing. No candies. Nothing. She's been lying to you."

The astonishing accusation brought Kelly close to the boiling point. "She did send the candies. I saw her box them up and mail them." Kelly's mother was a formal and thoughtful human who made considerate gestures towards others, whether recipients deserved it or not. Every December, Kelly witnessed her mother pack the specialties from a local candy maker and take the package to the post office to be sent to Myrna. To hear Myrna unflinchingly declare her mother a liar was not improving the commencement of the relationship.

"Well, I never got them. So, if she sent candies, they weren't sent to me." At this, Myrna slipped her excessively long nails into her pocketbook and withdrew a pack of cigarettes. "It's not worth talking about. In fact, I forbid that we speak of anything from the past if you and I are going to get along."

Kelly could see this was wisdom, since she was dealing with someone lorded by amnesia, vengeance, intoxicants, or all three. She gripped her camera and snapped, "Agreed. I'll get to work now. This will take a while. Are you staying? Or, will you leave and come back?"

"Oh, I'm staying." Myrna lit the next cigarette and eased back onto the vinyl of the chair.

Kelly retrieved her equipment from the car, including an umbrella and stand, a tripod, and some handheld essentials for the shoot. In the house, she went from room to room, capturing the walls stained yellow from cigarette smoke, windows foggy from broken seals, Formica surfaces, worn carpet, and blue bathroom fixtures. The rental bore all the qualities of an abused bachelor pad. Darkly scuffed walls were riddled with holes from door knobs and fists, which required carefully composed pictures to omit the worst of the damage. No photographs were taken of the scummy shower stalls or the cock-eyed closet doors. Because of trends in home décor, the split-level layout was making a comeback, and Kelly was certain a buyer would be willing to put down half a million for the eyesore. The place would be gutted by the next owner, or just knocked to the ground to build anew.

As she took the photographs, she tried to visualize how the house serving a family of five yielded three offspring with unstable adult lives. Kelly's own memories of the house were faint. She was young enough at the time that her focus was solely on toys and the treehouse that existed in the backyard long ago. The house being mostly empty provided little else to trigger any further recollections.

Her grandmother sat quietly in the kitchen and said nothing while Kelly worked her way through the house. The living room and kitchen were the last spaces to capture. Kelly moved the flash stand and camera into the front room and set up the tripod to where the fireplace was the focal point.

Myrna watched Kelly move the scant furniture in small ways to stage the room and reveal the windows for the best light. "You know what you are doing, kid," Myrna stated from the kitchen table. Though Kelly was certain

Myrna was no photographer, she did not doubt that Myrna's eagle eyes informed her mind. The compliment was real. Connecting personally with Myrna was possible now.

"Thanks, Grandma," Kelly replied. The flash fired several times as she took bracketed images from different angles of the room. As she moved the gear to the kitchen, she ventured to begin a conversation. "So, you said the house has been rented to bachelors for a while. Were they college guys or something?" The condition of the home suggested the inhabitants were men that found keeping house cramped their style.

"Oh, no. Your uncle Dean has been living here with some friends for ten years. Trouble seems to find him, and having the house was good for his stability." Myrna moved her chair slightly to make room for setting up the camera.

As she looked through the viewfinder, and fixed a focal point, Kelly said, "Uncle Dean? I don't think I've ever seen a picture of him."

"Handsome. And so charming. Just the sweetest son imaginable."

"Where did Dean move to?"

Myrna took a drag. "It kills me to say it, but he's serving time in state prison. But most of these things are just misunderstandings, you see. I blame your cousin for the mess he's in, because there is not a bad bone in his body. Such a teddy bear."

Kelly methodically released the shutter several times. "So, a cousin is to blame for his problems. Which cousin?"

"Your busy-body cousin, Rhonda, got him to join AA. That's a cult, you know. People in AA end up doing and saying insane things and calling people out and getting into other peoples' business. So, Dean did AA for a while and stopped talking to me. But he has always struggled in life, and needs my help. So, because we weren't speaking, I couldn't help him, his life went down the tubes. Then, he dropped AA, and like everyone who quits AA, he did crazier things than ever before. He lost everything except the roof over his head which was this house. Next thing we know, the police accused him of robbery. He knows he can come to me for help, so I don't believe a word of it. But my lawyer couldn't get him out of the jam, and now he's in prison. Dean wouldn't be in this mess if Rhonda hadn't got him into that cult. AA is the worst thing that ever happened to Dean and I'll never forgive Rhonda for it."

So, Uncle Dean was the pampered baby boy, Kelly concluded. She had enough life experience to know that Rhonda was trying to save her cousin from the hell of chemical dependency. Clearly, Myrna loved her role as enabler and resented any intervention. Kelly wagered Uncle Dean never paid a day of rent over the decade he lived in the house.

The photo shoot was finished and Kelly started to pack up. Myrna declared, "You're done. Good. Now, we can get out of here and get some lunch. My back is killing me."

Kelly exited the house to put the gear back into the Jetta. As she shut the trunk, the squeaky garage door opened to unveil a gold Lexus with its reverse lights on. Kelly had planned to follow her grandmother to the lunch spot, and make the lengthy drive home directly after the meal. In the moment she opened the Jetta door, Myrna laid on the horn of her Lexus. Kelly looked up to see what or who Myrna was alerting of a collision. There was no sign of any danger. In fact, nobody was around at all. She walked back to the driveway and caught Myrna's frosty glare in the Lexus side mirror. Was Myrna calling Kelly over? Again, Myrna laid on the horn. Kelly obediently shut the Jetta door and walked to her grandmother's car.

"Get in! I said we were going to lunch!" Myrna commanded.

Kelly slipped into the car tentatively. "Sorry, Grandma. I thought I would follow you."

"Not in this city. Our cars would be split up and I'd be waiting for you at the restaurant. I don't have time for that. You ride with me."

Kelly sighed aloud, not caring what impression that left. There was precious little between them to preserve by filtering her thoughts. Myrna cracked the window and lit another cigarette. The passenger, feeling a little sick, could not recall the last time she rode in a car with a smoker. The interior of the car revealed much about Myrna's daily consumption habits. The cup holders, dash compartments, center console, and door panel compartments were stuffed with crushed cigarette packs and empty prescription bottles. With shaky hands, Myrna opened a pill bottle retrieved from her pocketbook. She swallowed a pill, sipped her bottled water, and said, "I have back pain from some jerk rear-ending my car many years ago. The traffic here is one reason why I moved. Maniacs everywhere."

There was plenty of evidence that Myrna quite liked her pain pills. But Kelly said agreeably, "That's a shame. My car was totaled a while ago. It's hard to recover from a car accident. And the traffic here is worse than I have ever experienced. I see why you moved away."

The Lexus backed out of the driveway, crawled to the end of the street, and did not stop at the stop sign, rounding the corner. Assuming it was a California stop, Kelly did not think much about the drive through the neighborhood. The Lexus approached another stop sign that intersected with the two-way arterial. To Kelly's horror, Myrna ignored the sign and drove at a low speed right into traffic to make a left. Cars skidded to a stop in both directions as the Lexus ambled through the lanes to complete the turn.

"Grandma! What on earth are you doing? You're going to get us killed!" Kelly's knuckles were white with tension from holding the door handle to brace herself for impact.

In a voice unperturbed, Myrna answered, "Oh, relax. Believe me, cars will always stop." While Kelly swallowed down the bile in her throat, Myrna began to converse like death was far away. "I'll have Greg, my real estate agent contact you. You give him the pictures. Do you hear me? You are giving Greg Sorensen the pictures." The repetition of the instructions illustrated Myrna's doubt over Kelly's retention for directives.

Gathering enough oxygen, Kelly replied, "Yes, Grandma."

"Greg's an old friend—a hot ticket. He's a weasel, but in the right way for real estate." Such a characterization of the agent made Kelly leery. Myrna continued, "I'm giving your aunt Karen most of the money from the sale. She's having a hard time. Her ex—his name is Rick—he left her and your little cousins. Do you know about Ella and Millie? They are three and five. Anyway, she needs the money. She was a big support when your grandpa died. What a great man, the greatest man that ever lived. She adored her dad. As for your father, he appeared after your grandpa died with a $150 bottle of wine. Karen was so angry with him for missing the funeral, she smashed the bottle on the kitchen table. That was one hell of a mess. Red everywhere." Kelly pictured wine drenching the kitchen she had just photographed with some fascination. By the nonchalance in Myrna's delivery, Kelly suspected this incident was one of the hundreds of scenes fit for film that had occurred in that home. Myrna bred her offspring in her own likeness.

In minutes, Myrna maneuvered the car into a gas station and stopped at a pump. Kelly said, "I've got this, Grandma," and opened the car door to step out.

"No, no, no! Get back in. I've got it handled," Myrna scolded.

Allowing this shaky, frail woman to task herself so needlessly was unthinkable to Kelly. "Oh, I can do it! Truly. You take it easy."

"I told you to get back into the car. Do as I say," her grandmother said.

Kelly shrugged, and reluctantly sat back into the passenger seat. What followed had Kelly wanting to flee the car immediately. The horn blared in long bursts throughout the cover of the gas station. Kelly slid down in her seat and ducked her head, her eyes scanning the lanes of cars for the reaction of the other drivers. All heads were turned to the

Lexus. With a pout of total expectation, Myrna continued to lay on the horn, over and over. Finally, the cashier at the booth stuck his head out the door to look around and see what the problem was. Myrna scowled at the cashier and continued to honk in long blasts. The uniformed cashier cautiously wove between the cars and reached the driver-side window.

Rolling the window down, Myra said, "Put this on premium," and handed the cashier a fifty-dollar bill.

Appearing both insulted and flabbergasted, the man asked, "You want me to fill up your tank?" He looked Kelly over, plainly wondering why a young, able-bodied woman was not performing this service for the elderly driver. He was unable to make eye contact with Kelly because she was shielding her downcast eyes and flushed cheeks with a hand.

"Yes, fill the tank right now. I've got somewhere to go," Myrna said, and punctiliously rolled up the window to end the discussion.

The two women sat quiet in the car while listening to the clinks and thumps occurring in the gas tank. Minutes later, the cashier walked away from the car. Myrna lit another cigarette, cracked the window, and proceeded from the gas station to join cars at the next traffic light.

After the light, the Lexus crawled up the on-ramp preparing to merge with highway traffic. Myrna reached for the dash and turned on her emergency flashers. Kelly supposed that the car would pull over for a mechanical concern. Instead, Myrna merged into the speeding cars at a snail's pace of 30 mph, staying in the far right lane. The car was perfectly fine, but unbiddable Myrna found the edicts of freeway driving not to her liking. Impeding traffic with the leisurely pace had horns wailing. Only supernatural forces kept Kelly from blurting out critiques on Myrna's driving.

Mortification had Kelly yearning to hide under the seat. But something in her DNA accepted the ludicrous pace in seconds. Partly to know how long she must endure the drive, and partly to divert herself, she asked with amazing calm, "Where are we going to lunch, Grandma?"

"Neptune."

"Wow. I've never been there," Kelly said, trying to not sound as astounded as she felt. Neptune was one of the finest restaurants in the city.

Another horn honked at their infuriating pace. "Jackass!" Myrna took another puff. "Your grandfather took me to Neptune for our anniversary every year. Best man in the world."

Kelly was pleased with the choice, and they dialogued lightly as they rolled down the freeway with flashers signaling to all drivers to pass them. Twenty minutes later, the Lexus dawdled down an inner city exit. A huge release of air escaped Kelly that had been held subconsciously through the precarious drive to downtown. Myrna knew her way around the city and soon brought the Lexus to a halt in front of a high-rise building. The two walked to the valet expectant for the keys.

After an upward ride in an elevator, the doors opened to the restaurant near the top of the tower. Myrna announced their arrival at the stately hostess station. She turned to her granddaughter and said, "Now, you are going to meet Bette. Bette's my twin sister. We didn't speak for fifteen years, but recently, we started talking again. And, boy, is she a hot ticket. Rich as Midas."

"You have a twin sister? Oh, man. I—OK. That's cool." Being with Myrna was a head-spinning experience. Kelly's emotions bounced from disappointment, to fear, to anger, to happiness—all in a matter of minutes between these leaps of emotion. Now she was to meet a significant relative that she was not prepared to see, and under conditions that sounded uncertain. Kelly politely excused herself to use the restroom. The restroom resembled a spa, and she wished that she could recline herself on one of the sofas to take a time out from the bizarre day.

After Kelly's moment of recuperation, the two women were guided to a round table within a semi-circle of wrap-around windows, affording a fantastic panoramic view of the city and the bay. The breathtaking scene had Kelly snapping pictures with her phone of the gleaming skyscrapers and noble sailboats on the water. It was unlikely she would ever be seated at such a table again. Myrna commented on the table settings and the staff, and recalled the many meals in Neptune with her dearly departed husband. Kelly found herself laughing at these recollections. Myrna had a surprising sense of humor that was coming out now that she was seated in a place that resurrected warm memories. Her one-liners were as abrupt and eye-popping as anything else she ever said.

Soon, a plump, bejeweled woman with Myrna's face and short, silver hair toddled up to the table with the assistance of the maître d'. Kelly stood up, and Bette shook her hand with a friendly, but reticent hello. The sisters began to speak to each other after the drink order was placed. The conversation seemed superficial, but there was some sort of twin calibrated dialogue with unspoken understanding which effectively reduced how much was verbalized. Kelly understood some of what was shared, but missed a lot of it, too. Watching these borough-bred sisters in brash and cynical conversation was rather enjoyable. One could glean they were raised with the finer things in life, but somehow, Bette secured that lifestyle for a lifetime, whereas Myrna only dabbled in luxury.

Kelly perused the menu and worried over her order. The prices were far beyond her reach, and she did not presume to know what was in the reach of her grandmother. The waitress arrived with worldly polish and without anything in hand to record the order. She pleasantly asked the selections of each sister. When Kelly's turn came, before she could inquire about items that interested her on the menu, Myrna asserted, "She'll have the lobster."

Myrna's assumption that her guest wanted lobster was another bullish act. Adapted now to Myrna's tyranny, Kelly took it in stride. She sipped her drink with a gracious tip of her head to her grandmother for gifting her the most expensive entrée on the menu.

The conversation continued in its cosmopolitan manner. Kelly was told many things, and was asked few questions. The sisters had sized her up with their keen urbanity and decided they knew whatever they wanted to know about Kelly and need not ask much, she guessed. Kelly felt simple.

After the entrées were placed onto the table by a flurry of servers, Kelly admired aloud the beautiful artistry of the chef, and took a picture of her plate for a social media show-and-tell. Both Myrna and Bette ordered enormous steaks. Bette began eating her prime rib immediately, while Myrna ate a bite of bread and took a sip of her cocktail. Kelly noticed that her scarf was in the way of eating and she unwound the yards of silk from her neck. That was the moment the lunch came to a dead stop.

"Is that my necklace?" Myrna ejaculated across the table. Bette's eyes narrowed on Myrna, then on Kelly.

Having totally forgotten about the necklace, Kelly's hand went to her neck and felt for the pendant. Confounded by the forceful question, Kelly said nervously, "No."

"Did you take my necklace?" Myrna asked with heat.

"No, Grandma. How could I?"

"Wait a minute, now," Bette said gently.

The familiar scowl returned to the beady eyes. "I had a necklace just like that, and I can't find it. You think I'm kidding, darling, but I'm not!"

A scene was on the verge of pealing over the din of the exclusive restaurant. The granddaughter gave a quiet, controlled plea. "I just got this necklace yesterday—from a jewelry store!"

"Jewelry store? What jewelry store? Impossible. Have no doubt: that is my necklace."

Bette appeared thoughtful, and rested her utensils. "Let's not spoil our lunch over a trinket."

"I demand to know how she got my necklace!"

Bette asked evenly, "How can you be so sure that is your necklace, Myrna. Really, now. You have not seen your granddaughter in years."

"I swear I got it from a store—yesterday. I did a photo shoot for Raymond Gems in Trenton. The manager gave me this necklace as a trade for the pictures."

Myrna's penetrating stare at Kelly did not flinch as she took another sip of her cocktail. Kelly withered with worry that the exchange would explode in front of the elite and, without doubt, be recorded on multiple phones for Internet infamy. How these accusations could impact Kelly's business reputation was terrifying. Moreover, the tentative relationship between the sisters could be irreversibly damaged if a scene occurred.

This woman, her long-lost grandmother, was delusional.

After critically surveying Kelly for truthfulness, Myrna stated with unnerving calm, "That necklace was custom designed for me as a Mother's Day present from your beloved grandfather. That's my birthstone, and my initials are on the back."

The chain was long enough that Kelly could flip the pendant over and look at it. There, on the back, was an inscription etched in tiny letters: "For M.A.E." Myrna. Anne. Everly.

"Oh, no," Kelly whispered.

"That's right. You think I'm kidding, darling, but I'm not," Myrna repeated. Kelly sat silent, staring at the engraved initials. "Now the question is: did a store really give you that pendant? Or, are you not as sweet as your act?"

This last statement nearly threw Kelly out of her seat to walk out of the restaurant. But, if the clash escalated, her fears over what this lunch could cost her professionally would be realized. Kelly took off the necklace and said, "I would never steal from anyone. I am happy to return this to you, Grandma. The salesman at Raymond Gems told me that it was estate jewelry that the store acquired some time ago. I cannot be certain how they got it, but obviously, it is yours. You should have it back."

"Estate jewelry? Not possible. I haven't sold any of my jewelry to any store. It's a pack of lies."

Bette had been listening to this exchange without any visible expression of judgment until she saw Kelly attempting to handle the situation with grace. Myrna's response to Kelly brought the aunt to the point of choosing sides.

"I can think of one way that store got the necklace." Bette picked up her fork and planted it into the whipped potatoes.

Myrna's eyes did not look at her sister, but instead, rolled to the windows to take in the view. "Really, Bette. I am all ears."

"It's common knowledge that drug addicts will turn to stealing to support their habit."

Whose side was her aunt on? Bette answered Kelly's bewildered look. "No, Kelly, darling. I could not be talking about you. Why, you are the most lucid member of this whole blasted family."

Myrna asked dangerously, "Just what are you suggesting?"

"Isn't my nephew in prison for robbery?" Bette pierced a buttery snow pea.

"Trumped up charges. And what does that have to do with anything?"

Bette said, "I am simply pointing out that maybe your dear Dean took your necklace and sold it to the jewelry store to get drug money."

Though burning with rage, Myrna said with impressive control, "My son is in prison because of the damnable meddling of my niece."

Bette must have expected this response, because she did not skip a beat. "Your son is in prison for robbery. And I am sure of it, because he stole from Rhonda, too."

Myrna was not expecting this, but gathered steam and said, "Perhaps it was retaliation for Rhonda ruining his life! If so, I hope he took it all."

Clutching the napkin in her lap, Kelly watched the volleys between the sisters. Bette turned to Kelly and said, "And this is why we do not gather for holidays in the Murray family. You have been spared, my dear."

"Hey, you leave my granddaughter out of this!" Myrna spat.

Kelly thought, *But wasn't my presence how this all started?*

"No, I think Kelly needs to hear this. You are a sweet girl, Kelly. But do not wreck your life trying to be a Murray. I think you are wonderful. But believe me; you will be much happier if you make this your last visit with your kin. I say this with all the love in my heart: I truly hope to never see you again." With a wide, doting smile, Bette affectionately laid her hand on Kelly's. At this, she stood up to leave the table.

"How dare you say that to my granddaughter? And, here, I thought we came to terms," Myrna said, taking a drink.

"Fifteen years was a good run." Bette took up her pocketbook. "I think we are ready for another fifteen."

"That's right. You go on." Myrna's eyes, again, gazed placidly out the windows.

"Have a *good* life, Kelly," Bette said sincerely, "and never come back." Bette cast a pudgy smile at her great-niece until Kelly began to smile back. When Bette got the sign she wanted, she turned away and left the restaurant.

Silence sat like a block of ice on the table while Myrna sipped her cocktail and looked ponderously at the nearby buildings. With hands coiled in the napkin, Kelly regarded her opulent plate of food, studying the segments of the lobster shell rather scientifically. She finally moved to drink her beverage. With resolve, she continued with the meal intending to make the best of her time at Neptune. She was certain now to never return, for she wished to never revisit this memory again.

Myrna finally muttered, "I had to grow up with her always meddling and judging. Rhonda turned out just like her. You think people can change, but Bette is the exact same person. I don't want her messing with my kids ever again. I cannot believe she tried to put herself between you and me—right in my face! That is downright sick."

Kelly was attempting to consume something of her staggeringly expensive meal. With a piece of shellfish rolling in her mouth, she was able to offer an indifferent, "Hmm," as a response.

They did not stay much longer at the restaurant. The car was called up and Myrna drove in the same obstructive fashion back to the house with nearby drivers blaring their complaints along the way. Kelly was numb from her preposterous afternoon; she was neither embarrassed by the pace of the drive nor concerned with the road rage. Myrna continued to talk about the family and her life, but nothing of what was shared could Kelly recall days later. What lingered instead was a feeling of tremendous loss and what was lost was too complex to itemize. The aftermath would be endured best if it was all left to just a nondescript feeling.

The Lexus pulled into the driveway of the house. Myrna sought another prescription pill. While scrabbling in her pocketbook, she withdrew the necklace. "Here, kid," she said. "You keep it. It looked good on you."

The reversal of Myrna's position about the necklace almost discomposed Kelly with exasperation. Kelly shook her head. "No, Grandma. It means too much to you."

"Exactly. And that's why I want you to keep it."

Over lunch, the pendant had morphed from a custom reward for Kelly's talents into the impetus of the assassination of her character. Somehow, she was expected to receive this object of disdain as a blessing. Myrna was insane. Kelly wished to reject the pendant with a full-bodied outpouring of her offense, but her palm inexplicably opened to receive it. "Thanks, Grandma."

"I know I haven't been there," Myrna said, gazing out the windshield, "But you hear me now—the door is always open."

This olive branch melted Kelly's indignation. "Thank you, Grandma. And thank you for the lunch. It was a beautiful restaurant and an amazing meal." She was earnest.

"Call me when you get home. Four hours is a wicked long drive. It doesn't matter the time. I'll be awake."

"I will."

"Goodbye, kid." At that, Kelly exited the car.

In the Jetta, Kelly arranged her things to depart. Before she drove away, Myrna got out of her car and walked to the front door of the house. A hunch told Kelly to grab her camera. She managed to work it out of her camera bag quickly. As the Jetta rolled slowly past the front of the house, the photographer snapped a picture of the back of her hobbling grandmother, with a silvery French bun tight to her head, and the cardigan blowing about her hips. Blurred in the background was the vacant family home. Kelly sensed it would be the only photograph she would ever take of Myrna.

And it was.

7
Scratch That

"Come on, Jada. Let's get inside and put our stuff down. Stay off the railing, Jada. That's not safe. Good girl. Come inside!" The little girl with springy locks hopped off the railing that edged the walkway and ran down to the open door toward the voice of her mother. The apartment suffocated with oversized furniture and stacks of unfolded laundry and gossip rags. Columns of cardboard boxes and plastic bins indicated a lack of closet space for the unit.

The centerpiece of the room was turned on to emit cartoons. The girl's mother put down the remote. "Sweets, you keep quiet while Mommy gets ready. Riza will be here soon to play with you, OK?"

The child's eyes glanced at the television, and then tracked her mother, who clattered onto the breakfast bar a buckled handbag, oversized key ring, venti coffee, and a handful of quickie-mart purchases. Jada sipped her short hot chocolate. "Why are you leaving, Mommy?"

Her mother answered in singsong, "Oh, you know! Mommy and her friends always go out on Fridays."

"But you were gone last night," the girl accused.

"That's different. It was my manager's birthday party—you know—Kenny, and I had to be there. It was like going to work." *A raucous time*, she thought. The warehouse crew knew how to have fun.

The phone dinged a text. Morgan rummaged through the handbag to message back with her fine nails. Jada opened her girlie pocketbook on the coffee table and extracted a toy smart phone. Morgan smiled at her daughter who had launched the app that pretended to send and speak out text messages. The device was not cheap, but it did subdue the incessant begging for Morgan's cell. Besides, Baby Girl was getting into Mommy's pictures too often. One must have a life, after all.

Moments after sending the text, the warehouse rang. Could she cover the phones on Sunday? Overtime should be out of the question following two nights of clubbing. Fidgeting with the basket of bills on the counter in pouty consideration, she agreed to the overtime. Morgan put down the phone with a sigh. Jada sighed and likewise put her iPhony down.

Morgan laughed. "That's right, Jady, there's too much going on."

"Yeah, too much stuff to do," the little girl said, overacting. She then stood tall. "Mommy, I want to help you get ready."

"OK, girl. You help me. I need lots of help," Morgan called after the little legs darting to her bedroom. "I'll be there in a minute."

After swallowing the last of the mocha, Morgan picked through the pantry for multigrain crackers, and rested on a stool at the breakfast bar to try her luck.

Corny dialogue burbled from the TV while she scooped out the leather coin purse from her bag and selected one of the dozens of quarters inside. She then drew the shiny metallic lottery ticket from the top of the items mounded on the counter. After coworker Renée had scored $200 on a scratch ticket a year ago, Morgan constrained herself to one weekly ticket and had since banked $20 and hit $2 three times. This Friday night routine of picking up a lottery ticket when she stopped to get her party-only cigs was a habit she had come to love. Scratching tickets felt a bit like opening presents.

Chawing on a cracker, she thumbed the Sagittarius horoscope. The phone app reported, "Today, smell the sweet bouquet that is life. Align yourself to endure the highs and lows." Numerals could often be extracted from in the forecast. The word "today" and "to" phonically suggested the number two.

"Mommy! Are you going to dance tonight?"

"Huh? Yes, I think so, Jady."

"OK!" Jada disappeared into her own room.

Morgan examined the ticket entitled "Concentration," subtitled, "Match Two for Two." The game was to scratch only two of the six boxes. If the two numbers matched, then the winner received the revealed dollar amount. The amount could be $2, $20, $200, $2,000, $20,000, and $200,000, or one could win little prizes like a free ticket. Odds of winning claimed to be far above average compared to previous scratch games. Wise selecting would make those odds work for her. Astrologically, the number two was clearly indicated. So, the middle position of the top row would be the first box to scratch.

Taking the edge of the coin, she scraped off the silvery paint coating the box.

"Twenty-thousand," she breathed. Marvelous feelings of power surged through her limbs. *There are good odds in this game*, she thought. *No, there are great odds*, she corrected. Seized with adrenalin, Morgan did a paranoid survey of the room for someone watching her. The only sign of life was the padding of Jada, who evidently had crossed back to her mother's room. The largest amount Morgan could potentially win of any ticket was $200, which was discovered only after losing the game and removing the rest of the silver paint. The ticket at hand was another real chance to win. *More signs. More help*, she mentally pled.

"Really, Gogi! My armpits are bulging with electric hair! Stand back!" The cartoon chatter grabbed her attention. However, it was all weird nonsense as cartoons had widely become and was a ridiculous source for counsel. She sought other signs.

The time on her watch: 7:08 PM. The year the quarter was minted: 1998. The current date: October 9. None of these sources served as counsel. She decided to review the source for her first correct answer. "Align yourself to endure the highs and lows." The ticket's second box on the top row was scratched. That could mean a "high." So the bottom row could be a "low." To align the highs and lows could mean selecting the middle box on the bottom row. Meditating on this theory, she studied the ticket seeking subtle hints of what numbers lie beneath the five darkened boxes. They were impervious. Scratching that bottom box would be an act of faith. Her hand hovered over the box, then gently, carefully, breathlessly rested the quarter on the ticket and scraped away the paint left-to-right.

A number—zero. Her eyes blinked back disbelief. The next numbers: zero–zero–followed by a comma. Her hand stopped. Harassed with hope, her fingers pinched the quarter as a way to literally get a grip. After a suck of air, she scraped the last of the silver paint away, and fixed her eyes on the value $20,000. In fact, stacked was a pair of the value $20,000.

As if struck by a thunderbolt, she felt an intensely warm, goose-pimply flow sweep over her skin and seemingly into her core. She set down the quarter and threw herself off the stool to run in place and clap her hands, eyes squeezed tight. Rolling through her mind was the bounty ahead: knock out the bills, pay back her grandma, vacay in Hawaii, a closet full of shoes, maybe, *maybe* a new car. "Yea!" she yelled. She paced aimlessly. "Yes! Good God, yes! I won! Yes! Ye—"

A nerve-fraying scream rang from across the apartment.

Morgan froze. At the threshold of her bedroom was Jada shrieking over a painful burn over her entire palm. Lying at the girl's feet was a 400°F curling iron that was gripped by the wrong end. Morgan ran to her daughter, scooped up the hysterical girl, and hurtled to the bathroom sink.

Jada thrashed and bawled through the wrangling of her mother who was forcing her crimson hand under the faucet. "I know this is cold, but we have to cool off your skin! Calm down! Oh, I know. I'm sorry! It will feel better in just a second. Keep your hand there just a little longer!"

Soon numbed by the chilly flow of water, Jada ceased screaming and allowed the cooling to continue a few, long minutes.

Damp and emotionally depleted, mother and daughter concluded with a leisurely cuddle in a terry cloth pat down. To mollify Jada's complaints further, Jada was placed onto the toilet lid while Morgan rummaged through the medicine cabinet. "Let's get some ointment on that. I've got just the thing."

Kneeling before her swaddled child, she gently slathered the girl's palm. "Sit still, Jada, this won't hurt. I promise! No, it's true. It will feel better. Trust me." Careful bandaging created a white cotton mitten on Jada's hand.

As the sniveling subsided, the little girl was called to account for what happened. Jada whimpered through her messy hair, "I turned on the curling iron so you can get ready."

"Only Mommy should turn it on! And you did more than turn it on." She lifted the chunk of poorly pressed hair as evidence. "You should never iron your hair, Jada!" Morgan commanded.

"But you do my hair lots of times."

"Only grown-ups can iron hair. You are too young. You could have been severely burned on your head or face. In fact, it is a miracle that you did not burn more than your hand. When Mommy is doing her hair, then I will do yours, OK?"

"OK. Can you put on my tattoo, now?"

"Oh, yes. It's in my pocket. Here." Morgan groped around in her tiny front pocket and withdrew a temporary tattoo purchased at a capsule vending machine. "Where do you want it?"

"Like where yours is." She pointed to her upper arm, the same location where Morgan's wrap around cherry blossom body art drew the eye. In twenty patient seconds, a unicorn was affixed by a wet cloth on Jada's upper arm.

After hanging up the washcloth, Morgan stopped and curiously sniffed the air. "What's that smell?"

She cautiously stepped beyond the bathroom. There lay the smoldering curling iron soundlessly incinerating the cut-rate carpet. She gasped and sprinted to the threshold of her bedroom to snatch up the iron. Morgan kept the expletives to a mumble as she picked at the wide line of charred nylon radiating wisps of smoke. A mini-catastrophe, but the damage deposit might cover it. Then, her good fortune burst into mind. Should all the carpet need replacement, she was situated to handle it. She smiled away the bother. After assessing the condition of the curling iron, she set it back on her vanity in the bedroom. The emergency had passed.

Jada stood over the blackened strip of carpet in a lingerie camisole that Morgan had retired two break-ups ago, now repurposed as her dancing dress. "The floor looks like yucky burnt toast."

"It's OK, sweets. Just, please, do not touch Mommy's curling iron again," Morgan replied, sitting on the tangled sheets atop the bed. Jada nodded, bottom lip protruding. "Come here. Don't be sad. I know your hand hurts, and the carpet is yucky, but I have good news! Something great happened today!" Morgan took Jada's little wrists and said, "Do you know why Mommy was so excited and was jumping up and down? I was so happy because—"

Heavy knocking rattled the front door on its hinges. The little girl's head turned to the sound. "Somebody's hitting the door really loud!"

"Too loud. Just a second." Morgan slipped off the bed and quietly separated the blinds of her bedroom window to see who was at the door. "Ah, crap!" The door banged again.

Morgan hushed her daughter's demand for information. She clamored to the vanity, freshened her lipstick, cupped her bra under the moist, flimsy cotton, finger-combed her hair, profiled right and left to check for even eyebrows and lip liner, then spritzed perfume.

"Make me smell pretty, too, Mommy!" said Jada.

The knocks came again. "OK! Here's a squirt!" Morgan whispered. "Now, be well-behaved, Jada. Don't monkey around when I talk to Mr. Tillman, OK? It's very important! Be good!"

Once in the front room, she turned off the TV, and answered the door with better posture. "It's the super Super! Hello, Mr. Tillman! What can I do for you?"

The heavyset man frowned through his graying six-inch beard and said with eyes void of humor, "It's the ninth. You know exactly why I'm here. Rent is due, and you are still two months behind."

Morgan's hand flipped lengthy hair over her shoulder to unveil her upper body and let the flaxen tresses fall to the middle of her back. Her stance adjusted to exaggerate the curves of her lower half. "You are right. I totally spaced it. But, the great news is: I can pay in cash. In fact, I will have all the money I owe, in cash, in your hands—um—next week," she hoped aloud.

Mr. Tillman eyes compressed into slits as he deciphered her words. As the manager of the complex, he had to employ his instinct for truth detection every month with the various residents. Morgan's eye candy performances, he was aware, got the best of him many times. Morgan had a kid, so he rarely withheld clemency.

His face contracted irritably. "What's that smell? Something is burning."

Morgan's radiant smile lost some luster. Her nose had become accustomed to the odor. "Oh, yes. We had a little accident inside. Everything is OK, though. Nothing is on fire. The place ain't burning down, I promise!"

"I've been on this floor. I didn't hear an alarm. Did the fire alarm go off?"

Morgan found this very astute. "No, it didn't. Huh," she said, momentarily authentic.

"I need to check the alarm. Something went wrong." His renter remained affixed to the threshold, trying to contrive a reason to keep him out of the apartment and free her to her plans. His atomic dose of patience was used up. "You ain't paying me rent *again*," he stressed, "And now, because you won't let me check the fire alarm, you are sure to burn down the whole building and kill the lot of us. I suggest you let me in."

She morphed back into her flirty self in hopes to soften imminent repercussions. "Of course! No problem. Come in!" Lead-footed, he entered the clutter of the apartment. Morgan watched warily as Mr. Tillman turned the corner to the hallway where the alarm was mounted onto the ceiling. He immediately spied the scorched carpet and looked down at Morgan disapprovingly.

"I'm so sorry," Morgan said. "Somehow, the curling iron rolled off the vanity. Thankfully, we found it before anything caught fire. I promise I'll pay for the damage."

Nestled against her mother's thigh, Jada looked up. "Mommy, it didn't roll—" she began to correct until she was soundly hushed.

"Right," Mr. Tillman said, with an eye on Jada's medically wrapped hand. He bent over the burn and poked at it with the calloused tip of his finger. "The carpet's coming out and it will be on your ten-foot tab. I have a feeling that tab will go up in flames, too."

"Hee-hee! You're so funny! Of course I'll pay for it!" Morgan chirped.

He was tall enough to pull the cover off the alarm and assess its functionality. Morgan stroked the crown of her daughter, who winced up at her mother. "Mommy, it smells like the place where you exercise in here. Eww!"

"I just smell your pretty perfume." Morgan insisted, biting her lip. She felt pulled to the counter to secure the lottery ticket, but there were other costly discoveries Mr. Tillman could make if left unattended.

Jada grabbed her nose. "Don't you smell it? It's a really stinky smell!" Mr. Tillman's face became sterner while he pulled at the wires in the alarm. Morgan again shushed her daughter and maneuvered her to step out of the area of the bedrooms. Jada turned back to Mr. Tillman on her way. "Mommy, you were wrong. His crack doesn't show every time. Look!"

Morgan had no time to react, as Mr. Tillman grunted past her shoulder and moved for the open door. "I'm coming back."

Released from his acerbic eye, Morgan exhaled the stress of her thespian efforts while the doorway was darkened again by a petite silhouette.

"Hoy!" Riza called. Jada met Riza at the door with a big hug. "You wrap around me like a lei of sampaguita, little one. Mmm, you smell so good," she said in Filipino accents. The middle-aged woman lived in the complex and worked odd hours for a hotel. As Jada's primary babysitter, Riza assumed a role far beyond that of a neighbor in Jada's life.

"Thanks for coming. I'm kind of under the gun to get out of here," Morgan said, moving toward the counter.

BANG! A broad, russet object smacked the front window and stopped Morgan in her tracks. Riza and Jada were staring at the splayed marks on the pane. "What was that?" Jada asked.

Morgan felt a little sick inside. If her hunch was right, what hammered the window was not a ball or a rock. "It could be a bird," she said, serpentining the oversized couch and coffee table. The three stepped out of the apartment together to see a lump of speckled earth-toned feathers on the walkway. "Oh, it *is* a bird. That's so awful!" Morgan said piteously.

Jada whimpered, "Mommy, is it dead?" Her mother took her hand, not sure what to say.

Riza moved to the mound of plumes. "Oh, the sun is too bright today. The windows are so shiny. Birds get confused." Sweet-talking as she went, the little woman bent down and gently lifted the bird off the concrete. She smiled back at the mother and daughter. "It is alive. It looks at me." Morgan and Jada gathered around Riza to peer down at the inert ball of bird nesting in Riza's palms.

"Oh, it is alive! What a relief. It's just a little stunned," Morgan cheered. For a few minutes, their heads hovered over the bird in a peaceful study of the creature as it gradually revived. Once the bird looked more comfortable, Morgan said to her daughter, "See Jada? See how soft the feathers are? Just take the tip of your finger and lightly touch its back. See? OH!"

The trio of females shrieked. The wild batting of wings pelted the faces of the women as the bird fluttered out of Riza's hands. It darted out of the triangle of heads to tree branches level to the railing. The three laughed at their own fearful reactions thinking that the bird was attacking them.

Morgan said, "That scared me! You, too, Jada? I am so glad the bird is OK. What a weird thing to happen. Look at how hard the bird hit the window. You can see the marks it left." With this, Morgan then walked single-minded back to the apartment door.

Jada trotted to the railing and worried over the bird now recovering on a branch. "It got hurt! We should stay here. It could fall down."

Riza fingered the girl's crown of shiny locks. "The birdie feels better and won't fall down. Let's make dinner for you, little lei," she cajoled. "Oh, child, what is this thing on your hand? Are you hurt, too?"

"Uh-huh. I holded the curler the wrong way."

Tuned out of the dialogue behind her, Morgan glided through the doorjamb and nearly ran into Mr. Tillman who was about to exit. "Sorry! I didn't know you came back."

Riza and Jada were likewise startled to a halt by Mr. Tillman's enormous presence. "It's fixed," he said. Mr. Tillman's eyes narrowed on the sight of Riza.

"That was quick. And that's why you are the super Super!" Morgan said. She attempted to step around his gut and his battered toolbox. Mr. Tillman would not make any accommodation. Instead, he walked forward and had Morgan back-stepping toward Riza at the threshold.

Riza scanned the room. "I smell something burning!"

Mr. Tillman grunted in that telltale fashion and stopped to tower over Riza. "Another delinquent. It's Friday. Where's the rest of your rent?"

"Yes, I promised to pay the rest of the money today. In fact, ah, I think I can give it to you right now." Riza turned her plump grin to Morgan, and asked in an undervoice, "You can pay me now?"

Morgan indeed promised to pay Riza for the last month of babysitting. But this was not the moment she intended to open her pocketbook. "Ah—" Her posture had long since collapsed into an unflattering sag. "Yes. Right. But, as you know, I usually go to the cash machine before coming home at night." Mr. Tillman glared at her from the corners of his eyes. Riza's emerging frown gummed up Morgan's conscience.

Then, a dreadful reveal came from the counter, where Jada had perched herself on the stool, pilfering though Morgan's cavernous knock-off. "I'll get the money for you, Mommy." In a blink, before Morgan could blurt out anything to confuse her daughter, Jada pulled out a fat bank envelope from the purse. Indeed, Jada witnessed the bank run that followed the mini-mart stop.

"Jada, do not go through Mommy's purse! You don't know what that envelope is for!" Morgan reproved.

"But you said that you needed to get Riza lots and lots and lots of money." The babysitter smirked at her little Jasmine lei, who was scrambling down from the stool to deliver the envelope.

At this, Mr. Tillman stepped aside enough to allow Morgan through. She intercepted Jada and took the envelope from her hand. "I will take that. Now, mind your own business and let Mommy talk to the grown-ups." The girl stood in place and watched her mother step back to the adults, who were viewing Morgan with distrust. She looked over the envelope, inside and out, considering how to work the room. For whom would she concoct a story? Before her stood two impatient creditors, but one was also a creditor to the other.

"There. See the money?" said Riza. "I promised that I would give it to you this day. I care for her little girl, you understand."

Mr. Tillman rolled those achromic eyes over to Morgan, whose lips were pursed in contemplation and, in part, in resignation, and dared not look him in the face. She meant to use some of the money that night. She cleared her throat trying to force out an explanation to keep Mr. Tillman's fiscal demands at bay.

Mr. Tillman put his foot down. "You can hand that directly to me." Morgan could not look at either creditor as shame, resentment, and further strategizing slowed her movement to hand him the envelope. "Surprising how you managed to pay this brick to your babysitter today, Shaw."

Her chin popped up. "I have to work to make money, and I cannot work without a babysitter. So, I don't see the surprise at all," came her valiant retort.

"The party Mommy went to last night was work," Jada called from behind them. "But, tonight, her party is not work."

Morgan's eyes flicked at the voice of her precocious daughter, but she would not break. "And I don't apologize for time to recuperate."

"Yes, she is a young woman. So young. And has so many friends," Riza piped in helpfully as she went to use the bathroom.

His own weakness vexed him, and Mr. Tillman would not be manipulated any longer. He said pointing at Morgan's cleavage, "Those spaghetti straps can't bridle me, Shaw. You've flayed me too many times. Since you have all

Serena Ivo

these fine friends, well, I'm sure they will step up and lend you a couch. I'm done here. And so are you. Consider yourself evicted." With the oversized toolbox in hand, Mr. Tillman slowly maneuvered himself between the couch and stacks of storage containers.

Morgan blurted, "No, I will pay you. I can! I will prove it! Wait!" Morgan's sudden sprint for her purse on the counter raised his curiosity enough to halt him at the door. What convenient excuse did she drum up this time? No part of him believed there was a legitimate reason to change his mind.

She looked on the counter for the scratch ticket.

The ticket. Gone. It was just there. She scanned the area around the purse. "Jada, sweets, did you see a scratch ticket here, on the counter?" she asked, sounding a little desperate.

Jada knelt at the coffee table with a pen, writing on one sticky note after another. "Yes, Mommy," she answered through multigrain crackers.

"Where was it?" Morgan demanded.

"It was up there." Jada innocently pointed to where the purse, keys, and cigarettes sat on the counter, and resumed writing.

Frantically picking through the pile on the counter, then through her purse, Morgan repeated, "Where is it? Where is it?" talking to herself.

While writing on a sticky note, Jada said, "I-T," and pulled it off the stack to stick onto the coffee table with five others.

"Jada! Are you sure you didn't move it from here? Did you put it in my bag or take it off the counter?"

"No, Mommy. I seen it right there." A petite finger again pointed to the correct location. "How do you spell 'off'?"

Mr. Tillman's eyes wandered back and forth from the open door to Morgan wildly sorting through another pile of papers on the countertop. She seemed genuinely panicked, and he almost believed it was not an act.

"O-F-F. Mr. Tillman, just… wait… one… second… more." Morgan began looking atop the stools, and then on the ground for the shine of silver.

"There was a fire on the carpet? Thank goodness that—" Riza reentered the room. "Oh, Mr. Tillman! Is Whiskey feeling better?" This question Mr. Tillman ignored.

"Who is Whiskey?" Jada asked.

Riza turned to Jada. "Whiskey is Mr. Tillman's biiiiig, white cat."

"So, that's why he has fur all over his clothes. I wish I had a cat. K-A-T."

"Yes!" Morgan exclaimed. There it was, the ticket, posed vertical along the front of the base of the breakfast bar. It was evidently knocked off the counter. Morgan plucked up the ticket, ran to Mr. Tillman, and held it up to him boastfully on her open palm.

In deadpan, he scrutinized the ticket. With a soft chuckle, he said, "You throw that in front of people to buy more time? You've insulted my intelligence quite enough. Those hot pants are still in the street. You've got a week to get out of here." And he turned on his heel and marched down the walkway.

The verbal blow sent her raging. "To hell with you! This ticket is freakin' real!" she blurted at his back. "You jerk! I'm glad to never see your sorry crack again!"

She took an infuriated breath of air wafting the scent of weed from a neighboring apartment, and lowered the ticket to her eyes. Instantly, her lungs ceased moving and her knees gave way. Collapsing into the doorframe, she stared at the other four values that were once hidden under silver paint. Jada had scratched all the boxes while at the counter, which Morgan let her do every week when a ticket was a loser.

Voided were the luxuries, fun, and even shelter of her future. The easier life she was meant to have flashed like a sorry slideshow in her mind, and plummeted her into a cryptic mourning.

"What happened?" Riza exclaimed at her side. "Did you fall? Let me help you!" She clasped an arm to lift Morgan.

"No. Just leave me be." Tears brimmed in Morgan's eyes. "Please."

Soothingly, Riza placed her hand on Morgan's shoulder. "You are not feeling well, is it?"

Confession was too burdensome to attempt. "I'm feeling OK. Really. I'll get up when I'm ready." The ticket was pressed out of sight into the hollow of Morgan's hand.

"You need food. Let me get you a cookie." Riza rose and walked back to the kitchen. She stopped near the counter and looked down. "Jada, why are you on the floor like that?"

Jada's monotone could be heard from beyond the couch. "Leave me alone. I will get up later. I need a cookie."

8

Two Bits and a Cold-Water Flat

SATURDAY AFTERNOON

Standing idly in the shower, he stared blankly at a hairline crack splitting the grout between the subway tiles while lukewarm water pelted his shoulders. Her proximity, the curse of her nearness, ceaselessly provoked his self-control and he could feel his will to resist weakening. The effort required to combat his longings seemed to expand just beyond his ability to stifle them. His position was one of which every guy of his acquaintance dreamt. But he would declare to all men that his was a glorious hell, an inferno incinerating him from the inside out, and he was sure that he preferred the unrelenting torment to freedom. Cringing as if to stab himself, he plucked the bottle of shampoo from the bath rack and vented the top. Holding the cap to his nose, he inhaled slowly the pungent scent of concentrated coconut and intimations of citrus so that the memory of her golden hair was all that he could see. That scent would fill his face every time he hugged her, or sat beside her, or when a gust flagged her hair in his direction. He supposed it an accurate guess that those locks were coiled in a towel atop her head while she painted her nails, lounging in scant bits of satin under that animal print robe with the ridiculous feathered collar. He loved to pester her about it. He hated why he knew she owned it.

SATURDAY NIGHT

Music reverberated off the forty-foot dome above and the wall against which Caysie positioned herself. Dots of light faintly skittered across all surfaces. She was abandoned for more interesting company. Ashley, the last member of her singleton cohorts, was now dancing with Renaldo, the guy from Chemistry who had been centered in Ashley's scope for many months. Caysie watched the nervous pair mixing with the crush of classmates for half a song when Carsen strode up with his chin scruff and suit jacket slung over his shoulder, repossessing his casual self.

His approach meant no threat. "You look a little lonely over here."

"I'm not now." She sweetly smiled. "It's cool. The girls are exactly where they want to be. I'm happy for them."

"And where do you want to be? Or, should I say, with whom?" he asked.

"You think I would just tell you something like that?"

"What's wrong with telling me? Come on. You can trust me."

"Maybe it's nobody."

"There's always someone." He caught hints of concealment when her lips tightened into a squiggly line. "It's someone I know!"

"Stop it!" she tittered.

"Oh-ho! It's someone I know well!" Her teal-tipped fingers touched her brow. The thought occurred to him that maybe this was his chance. "I can think of only a few guys worthy of you." His kindness coaxed her large eyes to meet his. "You look great, by the way."

"Thanks, Carsen. You do, too. Although, I prefer the jacket on."

If he were to bust out of friend prison, it was time to make a statement. "This strait-jacket makes me mental. But I'll endure it to satisfy your demands." He stretched his arms back into his blazer.

"Yes, much better," she assessed as he pulled at the lapels.

"Is it really that much better?" He then tugged at his uncomfortable collar.

"Every girl in this room would say the same. Guys look good in suits."

To combat the volume of the music, Carsen leaned his head down to her ear bangled with topaz, nestled in a bundle of curls swept to that shoulder. His caramel skin was always scented with fine cologne, awakening her senses. "We're both dressed up and bored over here. I say we go dance and stop holding up this wall."

Caysie regularly put out of her mind how attractive Carsen was. Having been deserted, however, her appreciation of his company intensified with receptiveness. Her brother's friends consistently looked out for her, and thus, Carsen was a safe bet. "Yes, the thought of standing here the rest of the night seems pointless. But I'm a dull dancer compared to you. Are you sure you want to be seen out there with me?"

He wanted to say that there was no other girl in the room whom he would rather escort to the dance floor. Maybe he could talk her into a formal portrait. For sure, he would get a selfie. "You are so gorgeous, nobody will be rating your moves."

"Oh, please!" Her cheeks became a beguiling pink, signaling to the track star that his chance was real.

Towering in pressed black, a fellow student sauntered in from the periphery. "What up," said Riley, who offered a fist for Carsen to pound. In spite of how assured Carsen felt about the blond, Riley's arrival rocked his confidence; an awkward tension settled over the trio.

Caysie rested a heel against the wall and pulled her hands around to the back of her strapless dress of luminous aquamarine. "Carsen is trying to talk me into dancing."

"I promise the wall is structurally sound," he teased.

Riley regarded the two with a colorless expression, not of detachment, but with a mind chock-full of thought.

With a residual smile, she asked, "Riley, where's Jana?"

Riley moved to the girl's side so that Carsen faced them both. "Things are not going too well. She's puking in the bathroom," he said wincingly. "We don't know if it's the flu or food poisoning or what."

"Poor Jana!" Caysie exclaimed. "Who is with her?"

"Kayla. I called Jana's parents, and they are coming to take her home. Jana's really embarrassed and does not want to leave the bathroom. Her dress is covered in sequins and chicken parmesan."

The three expressed heartfelt sympathies for Jana. Due to this unfortunate interruption to the evening, Riley's group was diverted and scattered. While detailing the prom nightmare, Riley received the anticipated call from Jana's parents. He excused himself to guide the adults to the restroom, and meant to return after Jana's family departed.

With his pursuit derailed by bad news, Carsen sensed that Caysie was in no mind to resume where they left off. She smiled and was present, but definitely not sending signals beyond that of friends. With hope still intact, Carsen took her to the dance floor. His head-turning moves made her hoot and clap, which was something to pocket. Her openness, her compliment, and her blushes were fuel enough to continue the chase another day.

At the end of the song, Riley strode circumspectly to the edge of the crowd. He nodded to Carsen and beckoned Caysie with a slight gesture. Carsen expressed gratitude for the dance in a way that only she could hear, and parted the crowd to join other friends.

Walking away from the thumping bass, Riley chuckled over his prom disaster. The details of Jana's exit resembled clandestine human trafficking. The sickly girl worried most that someone would take her picture in that mortifying state and broadcast it for eternal humiliation. That would be unthinkably cruel, agreed Caysie.

"What happened to your posse?" Riley inquired, hands in his pockets. They reached the back of the ballroom amongst the disheveled tables and chairs populated with a handful of outcasts and tired students.

"They've all run off with guys. So, I am as stag as it gets."

"I came here with a date and ended up solo." He kicked away a balloon. "What a night."

She crossed her arms to give herself a mild scold. "I spent a whole lot of money and time on myself just to eat some dinner, apparently."

The young man surveyed her appearance and rolled his head as if releasing tension in his neck. "It is a shame. All that effort. And, your hair, that's no small feat."

"It took an hour at least. I give up." She popped two decorative clips off her crown, methodically worked out the many hidden hairpins that wrangled the side-sweep of her tresses, and pitched them onto a table. Fingering free the strands, her hair was now a mane of tameless waves over her bare shoulders. "Why do I go to these things anyway? It never turns out how I wish. Whether I have a date or not, I end up feeling more alone when it's over. I don't know."

Riley lifted his eyes from the high polish of his shoes and viewed the girl beside him through the black veil of his lengthy bangs. As she dolefully watched the dancers in the distance, party lights illuminated the delicate folds of her dress crossing over her mature form. His gaze held a heartbeat longer than the point of neutrality and briefly drew her attention.

Caysie answered the faint worry on his brow. "I'm OK. Really. I think I just need to go home to my bed and be glad I'm not the one puking." She stepped aside to let a couple pass to the dance floor.

A scowl darkened his angles. "Do you have arrangements for a ride?"

"Not anymore. Brandy left already," she said, unaware of his expression.

The teen checked his phone for the time and messages, and lightened his tone. "Well, it's something to do. Let's go." After collecting their belongings at the coat check, Riley wove through the parking lot with Caysie in his wake. He situated himself into the driver's seat, turning off the radio, and uttering very little. She supposed the outcome of the evening caused his uncharacteristic dejection. After revving the engine and adjusting the dash for heat, his phone hummed. His group of friends was reassembling and suggesting a red-eye movie to finish out the night. He began the reply, paused, and after meditating on the creeping fissure in the windshield, aborted the message and replaced his phone.

The drive from the conference center was a short fifteen minutes, most of it spent in small talk. Caysie was likewise under a cloud of disappointment. All her friends were in the throes of romance, and her night was ending prematurely and dateless. They reached the driveway and he pulled the brake. A forlorn sigh escaped her lips, provoking Riley's concern. "Are you alright?"

Her fingers pulled at the chiffon of her skirt. "I thought I was, but I guess not."

"Being ditched by all your friends is a fairly good reason to be upset."

"Yes, but nobody meant for it to happen," she said. "How could I blame any of them for jumping at their chance?" Riley's eyes flicked. His palm ran through his silken hair. After some introspection, she added, "The truth is, I would rather be in their shoes. I think what's bothering me is that I am never in their shoes."

The motor droned while he took this lamentation in silence. His non-reply was odd. Usually, he was Caysie's greatest support in any emotional turmoil. Her puzzled expression snapped him into speaking. "You and Carsen seemed to be getting on well."

"I guess. I mean, I am not sure. Sometimes guys act interested or they flirt, but it never goes anywhere. I've questioned whether I send off the wrong signals or if it's how I look. Maybe I'm just bad at flirting. I can't figure it out. I'm thinking now that I misread Carsen."

"Oh, no, you were right. He wants you."

"How do you know?"

"Caysie," Riley chastised, "guys know guys. He's been salivating for you all year."

"Did he say something to you?" she asked genuinely surprised.

"He doesn't have to. I just know."

"I had no clue until tonight. But, even then, Carsen didn't do much. So, fine, there's one guy that could be interested. That is, if you are right."

"Geez, Caysie, every guy wants you. Every single one."

"That's absurd."

"It's true. Trust me."

"I know you are trying to make me feel better. But I'm the girl that everyone likes as a friend. That's it. And I have no idea why."

Riley exhaled. Heavily, his hand reached for the ignition and turned off the engine. With a creased brow and sidelong look out the driver's window, his mouth parted as if to speak, and a dreary silence followed.

His quiet, inscrutable discomfort had Caysie focused on his every move. This brooding side of him was surfacing frequently of late, and she wondered with alarm why he was sinking into it again. "Riley? What's wrong?"

He then studied the fractured rubber seal lining the driver-side window. "Caysie," he said, "did it ever occur to you that the reason why no guys ask you out is because of your brother?"

Dumbfounded, she hesitated to answer. "What on earth does that mean?"

"I am saying—perhaps—your situation is by design and not due to any fault of yours." His finger flicked a bit of crumbling seal.

"Are you saying that guys are told to back off?"

"They don't have to be told," he said, thick with gloom. His arctic green eyes slowly rolled up to check her expression. After searching for anything resembling anger in her, he inhaled through his nostrils as his head rocked back onto the seat.

"You don't look right," she said gravely. "What's been going on? What are you saying?"

Gripping the base of the steering wheel, he nonchalantly checked for any sign of life in the house. "If I told you what I mean, then—" At this, he appeared to be taking ill.

She coaxed him tepidly. "Riley, we're best friends. You are making no sense. Talk to me."

"Friends," he muttered, "that's another word for hell!"

The bitter retort came out of nowhere and sideswiped her sensibilities. Caysie could not believe her ears. "Wow, that's—that's—" She swallowed hard. To probe further was a terrifying walk to the edge of a precipice. "I have sensed you've been irritated with me lately. It sounds as though you resent our friendship."

"I am forced to be a friend to you," he said fiercely, glowering at the splintered clapboard on the decrepit garage. She gasped at his condemnation. He then seemed to address another person, maybe himself, with a declaration opposite in meaning from what he just said. "But I don't want to be your friend. No guy alive wants to be your friend."

The lancinating words drained her heart. His sullen profile avoided her eyes rimmed with tears. The car was quiet and cold. After floundering to make sense of him, she gave up. "I can't believe you are hurting me like this."

Feeling falsely accused, he punched the door once with his fist. "Caysie! You claim we are best friends, and yet, after all this time, you don't know the most important thing about me. You have no clue!" His raised voice startled her, as did his Jekyll and Hyde transformation from her buddy to an opponent. The incoherent conversation sent Caysie into a mental scramble for what about Riley she had not yet realized. They spent an inordinate amount of time together in all sorts of situations. He counseled her on everything, including helping her to shop for a prom dress. *Oh. Whoa.*

The prom dress, the earrings, the heels. Then, the tell-tale pattern became apparent. He rarely dated. His prom dates were wholly platonic. In fact, he was curiously asexual when it came to girls. What's more, Caysie—a female—was the closest person to him. Riley regularly commented on her attire, for better or worse, and encouraged her to present herself in certain ways. His influence on her appearance was pervasive. His inattention to dating was glaring. For years, she fished around to extract from him which girls he liked. Perhaps the inquiries were altogether off the mark.

As the facts lined up, the truth became clear. In a sympathetic tone, she asked, "Is it that you're gay?"

Incredulous, he spat, "Geez, no! What would ever make you say that?"

"That's always the thing that people are hiding and afraid to say! I thought, maybe, you were coming out of the closet," she replied all innocence.

At this, Riley snickered at the absurdity and welcomed the relief. "If I were gay, I would have come out a long time ago and gained ultimate popularity. I could have been prom queen." He chuckled off the gloom. "Caysie," he looked at her with a weighty turn of his head. "Come on. If you can't figure it out, then you do not know me at all."

His distinguished countenance, hinting of Cree descent, manfully entreated her blue eyes. He would not relent until she fully understood. A chasm of propriety and history and boundaries were bridged by the lock of Riley's stare. At first, she waited for him to say more. His sincerity, though, had electric mass that sent a burning rush through her chest. If what she was sensing was true, it would unquestionably change everything. Her mouth slightly opened with this understanding.

Once she realized his advances, desire swallowed him whole, for she had never searched his eyes in such a way that drew every throb of yearning to the surface. All the years of reasoning away such a confession crushed his conscience as if to hold him down. But Caysie's constraint, her lack of instant rejection, continued to unlock his passion. Where this was going could very well destroy their lives. And yet, she sat there, watching him, scorched by the heat of him leaning closer to her, as he sought with each passing second to transform into her lover.

In a low voice, he said, "I chose that dress because it exposes your beautiful neck and your shoulders." His eyes rolled along the curve of her nape and glided over her collarbone. "I picked those earrings because they bring out your eyes." His eyes traced her form to her leg where her hand rested pinching the sheer fabric that overlay her satin skirt. He cautiously moved to touch her hand hazarding reproof. Her hand did not withdraw. Tentatively, as if collecting a wounded butterfly, he lifted her slender hand to himself. "It's a crime that I wasn't your date tonight. But you know exactly why. It's a reason that does nothing but torture me every waking minute."

Mute with shock and a trace of fear, her breath came with effort. Flashing through Caysie's mind were the numberless times she shared with Riley, reviewed through the lens of his worshipful adoration, and not the platonic connection she thought they had. Comprehendingly, she whispered, "You like to braid my hair," the pinnacle of evidence.

"I have thought of every way possible to touch you in a form that was—acceptable." A held breath left her, which emboldened him, knowing his words had an effect. He let that fact bathe her memories, and then said, "I don't want to be your friend anymore, Caysie. I don't want to be anything to you except who I really am, a man willing to wreck his life to have you."

With this calamitous, heart-searing confession, tomorrow was bent into a new course. Even if she turned Riley down, life was unalterably redirected. Furthermore, nothing could restore things as they were just minutes before. She was simply choosing what form the change would take. In any case, someone would be devastated. A magnificent tragedy was unfolding before them.

But one could say the tragedy started years ago, and she and Riley were casualties of it. The two of them were bystanders of a long, heartbreaking story. Maybe, they were the happy ending. When this dawned on her, she relaxed infinitesimally.

Riley was empirically handsome (mercifully taking after his mother), and sweet beyond all guys of her acquaintance. The terms of their relationship prevented even the thought of regarding Riley in any other fashion than a faithful confidant and comfortable friend. His secure reliability had her leaning on him for a long list of roles such as chauffeur, tutor, escort, therapist, and personal shopper. She never questioned his indefatigable willingness to serve in these capacities, but she should have. His behavior did not resemble the actions of any other guy she ever heard of. In his pleading, patient eyes, she finally saw clearly what was always there, but never perceived. Riley was devastatingly in love with her, and had been for years.

Her love for him took another form, or so she thought. Why, then, did she become flustered when Riley walked up to her and Carsen? Because entertaining the favor of another boy felt inappropriate somehow. Perhaps her heart was unconsciously reserved for Riley. She finally spoke. "I cannot see how this is going to work."

Her words did not equal rejection. "I have no answers," he said solemnly. "I only know what I am willing and not willing to do."

"Are you willing to wait?" The question was a form of yes.

"All I've done is wait, but your ignorance to my feelings restrained me. Waiting from now on would be a whole lot harder than before." Riley inched closer with her clammy hand lying paralyzed between his. "You are afraid." Her nod came with effort. "I have always been scared, but now, with you here, I don't care about what might happen. It doesn't matter somehow."

Riley could read her thoughts by the minute flits of her eyes and adjustments to her mouth, and he hung on to each manifestation of her awakening. Nevertheless, she ultimately held back. The revelation was explosive, too impactful. Riley had been physically close to her in virtually every setting, but never had his presence felt as overpowering as his proximity in the coupe. Standing next to him the very next day would fray her nerves knowing it could be the instant of discovery. Riley was a proven actor. She was not.

"I think," she took a breath, "I cannot handle things changing so fast. I need time to think—to figure out how to deal with this—if I can at all. You are becoming something completely different to me, and it's a lot to adjust to. You've had all this time to imagine it, and I'm—"

"I am not becoming something different to you," Riley interrupted with the softest intention. "I'm becoming more to you. That's all."

Within his hands, her fingers pressed meekly into his, the first assurance that his dreams were possible. This sign broke him from an insufferable prison of unrequited love, releasing a deluge of feelings and fantasies. Impulsively, he raised her hand to his lips and kissed it with reverence. Moved by his humility, she palmed his smooth, soaring cheekbone. On many occasions, she touched his face to razz him about his five-o'clock shadow, or to clear away a crumb. For the first time, she witnessed the effect her touch had on him and wondered how he ever managed to suppress it. In ardent agony, he pressed her hand to his face, and kissed her wrist. Shifting his frame nearer, his hand glided up her arm and pulled her in. Riley's control was seconds from unravelling. Caysie was confused with amazement, fear, and flutters of sensuality. If she did not stop him, he would careen mindlessly into their mutual demise. She was not ready to live out the consequences.

"Riley!" she begged as his face swept to hers. His racing breath kissed her lips. "Riley," she quietly repeated to sedate him. No explanation was needed. He swallowed back the momentum, and dropped his focus from her crimson mouth to her skin gleaming in the moonlight. Unquenched desire suddenly buried his head into her treasured shoulder within the tangles of her perfumed ringlets. Chills shot through her core as his heated kiss melted into her neck. He recoiled abruptly and collapsed into his seat before she could emphatically push him back.

The enormity of the breach seized them both. Riley cursed under the shield of his hands. Caysie rested her back onto the passenger seat and held herself close.

"I can't walk you to the door," he said despondent. She nodded unoffended. "I have to stay away from you until I can think straight." She nodded again. "I want to say I'm sorry, but I'm not sure I should. I don't know who's to blame for what has happened. But I know this: I'm tired of being angry about everything. I just want to be happy. And I would be happy with you."

Their situation was so complicated now, she could not think of a helpful thing to add. "I should go," Caysie said. She could not thank him, or reassure him, or encourage him, or deny him. Pathetically, she resorted to wondering aloud if she would hear from him the next day. The boy shrugged. She dared not touch him to seal her goodbye, and simply collected her things. Caysie opened the car door, pausing first to see that no one was in sight, and got out. With her exit, Riley hung his head, broken. Everything was broken. "Bye, Riley," she said, and shut the door in grief.

MONDAY MORNING

Caysie stepped out of the house with the bustle of her parents and siblings destined for work, daycare, and school. Her ride was not in view. The only contact from him since prom was received while putting on mascara that morning. She told her mother that she would walk the nine blocks to school. Lie. His text read: ill be in the alley. The teenager pleasantly waved back to the cars as they pulled out of the driveway. When the family vehicles drove past the corner, she turned the opposite way to enter the potholed lane. Anxiety had haunted her all morning, but seeing his car idling in wait kindled panic. Was this right? Was this wrong? Was this illegal? Was this destiny?

Her hand gripped the handle. Would he ravish her? Would he feign nothing happened? Would either version of him feel right?

Caysie slipped into the car and mechanically drew the door shut.

Riley's eyes, shadowed with fatigue, took her in with a fleeting glance, and then squeezed shut. Thirty-one hours of despair had pummeled the youth, leaving him unkempt and drained of his usual verve. Her weekend was tarred with an uncomfortable array of emotions, but she did not bear the burden of the initial confession, or a raging emotional battle suppressed for years. In hushed agitation, she arranged her things and settled sideways in the seat. There was no hello.

They dwelled in somber stillness while the young man prepared his mind for hearing which player would lose the most in this no-win situation. After a discrete check of the mirrors for possible interruptions, he began, "Before prom, I believed I could not feel worse. Those were much happier times, I have discovered." His despair was amplified by the ill-fitting, borrowed clothes that hung on his limbs.

She could cry for him. "It's a mess, Riley." His downcast posture kept her fingers fidgeting. "I heard you were on an Xbox binge this weekend with Darryl."

"Yeah, it's cool how he let me stay there. Kept my mind numb." At this he snorted, "Well, until going to bed. I laid there not knowing when you were rolling over or dreaming. I always thought drywall was this infuriating tease, and now it means you're close." His fingers rubbed his eyes. "I think I am going insane." Every insight into his heart tethered the girl further to him, sinking her incrementally into a fearsome attachment. She listened still. "Caysie, I have to know if you want me. Because if you don't, I can't see you. I mean it. Being near you anymore will be excruciating. Hope carried me before, but if hope was gone, then nothing would be there to keep my heart from being punched every minute. I must know now, how do you feel?"

After carefully parsing her feelings, her dulcet answer came, "I thought about you all day yesterday. I felt empty not talking to you."

He scrutinized her carefully to determine whether she meant it in friendly sympathy or in a consequential manner. Her expression was new to him; her eye contact succored his soul. Liberated, he audibly exhaled years of anguish. In spite of a thousand issues about to hatch, her statement fixed his mind on one thought. "All I want to do is take you home." He eyed the house peeking over the row of fences and trash bins. To act on this wish was terribly unwise, and she knew he was just venting.

Her forced smile veiled her disquiet over the looming temptation. "We must be extremely careful, Riley. Any mistake—well—I cannot imagine the fallout."

"I know. I've had to hold back for so long—" he paused in sober reflection. "Remember hiking the seven-miler, and you and I left the others at the camp to find the alpine lake? You suggested we swim because it was a furnace that day and we were so hot. We were wet and totally alone on that perfect beach. It felt like I was being split in two. Then your friggin' hair was in my face all night in the tent. I was so crazed, I kept chopping firewood to throw my energy somewhere. There have been so many times like that where I could have had you, if you had just known, and it wasn't so wrong."

The example of his trials conjured up many similar instances, and Caysie was astonished at how blind she had been. To her mind, the possibility of Riley having such feelings had been categorically absent. Those memories were now permanently rewritten by his assertion of what could have been. "Why do you get into situations like that with me when it is so hard for you?"

"I cannot stop myself. I crave the misery because it means we're together. It's so twisted. But nothing about our situation is right, and wasn't from the beginning. We were force-fed a bunch of myths."

Caught up in his point-of-view, Caysie felt the weight of his dilemma. She offered, "All along I thought we were having a blast together. I see now that my memories are one-sided. I don't feel responsible for the past, but I cannot provoke your unhappiness anymore. Ten years is enough."

The girl clasped his hand signifying the radical shift of their bond. His thumb stroked her skin; he relished the new meaning of her hand in his—not to help her out of a boat, or goof around with swing dancing, or keep her up on skates. "I must do one more thing before we go to school, but it cannot be done here." Her trust in him kept her curious and calm. The car rolled a few houses down to the ancient detached garage that served as a shed. Stopping there was far from her expectations, and her heart hammered with apprehension. He said, "Only a few minutes, I promise."

Her stomach wove into knots as Riley led her across the property to the side door of the garage. The lock was broken. He stepped aside the open door for her to enter, and shut her into the black. Caysie tracked his movement from his footsteps walking around to face her. Masculine hands tenderly found her neck to cradle her head. Offering a chance to refuse him, his face hovered over hers, aching in wait. His exhilarating touch overrode all prohibitions and taboos, and her heart unconditionally and comprehensively submitted. When her hands grasped his shirt to take him, his mouth found her parted lips.

MONDAY NIGHT

A gaggle of women went out for their first ladies' night to squawk over the job and vent about stresses at home. Laura was a recent hire, thanks to her friend of decades, Rochelle.

The commiserating picked up energy after appetizers arrived and the happy hour drinks were flowing.

"The Jerk says he can't help more with supporting the kids. Trevor and I are going to talk to a lawyer. The guy married a woman making a quarter-mil a year. They can do a helluva lot more," Rochelle threw out. She pinched the last of the bruschetta with an arm encumbered with chunky chain bracelets.

Deana shucked a messy bit of nachos into her mouth with her elaborately painted fingernails commemorating the Super Bowl. "Scott and I are thinking we may go to court, too. That tramp-stamp, muffin-top bimbo Hank married fights with our kids all the time. Goes to show, if a man wants to get his groove on, he sacrifices the kids. The kids come home raging from his place, and it takes days for them to calm down. Then a week later, it starts all over again. Scott says if this keeps up, we are going for the jugular."

Jennifer pursed her lips into a pout. "I think Mitch is screwing me over. He doesn't pay child support at all because he says he's out of work. I am certain he's getting paid under the table for contracting or something. There's no way he could run that pick-up, because, ladies, that ain't no hybrid. Eight miles to the gallon. Besides, how else is he bagging women if he were completely broke?"

"Stupid women are abundant," Maureen said before polishing off her beer.

"Is Mitch even around anymore?" Deana asked Jennifer. "I thought he was long gone."

"Oh no. He's around and reappears conveniently when he's working on some chick. It's uncanny how he wants to see the kids only when he's dating someone new. He uses the kids like pet dogs, just to make him look caring or something." She flipped back a cascade of pin-straight hair to clear the way for a chip laden with salsa.

The ordinarily mild-mannered Sarah interjected, "Well, you all have exes that want to be out of your lives, and I've got a husband who wants his ex *in* our life. Jess wants his sons to have their parents together on holidays and birthdays. Excuse me! I didn't marry *his ex-wife*, but it sure seems like it. I have too many pictures with her standing on the other side of him. I didn't sign up to be on Big Love."

All the women chimed in agreement. Rochelle asked, "How do you guys not fight over that?"

"Oh, we fight about it every time. He doesn't understand how much it upsets me. He thinks I am being selfish for not putting the kids' feelings first. He and his ex-wife blew the marriage up. Why must I do all the penance? I dread holidays now, having to share him with his ex on the most important days of the year. I love Jess, but had I known that this was what life would be like, I'm not sure I would have married him." Her eyes squeezed shut at the honesty that slipped through. "That never leaves this table, ladies." The women covenanted with nods.

Deana turned to the woman who had yet to vent. "Laura, Rochelle seems to think you've avoided the tar pit that we all are stuck in. Tell us about it. I am mighty curious."

After an earful of such difficult reports, Laura sheepishly admitted to the happiness in her life. "I have to say, life is great. The kids get along well, and Riley and I are in a healthy place."

"They do it like rabbits, is what she's saying," Maureen clarified.

Laura shrugged her shoulders with a twinkle in her eye. "It helps that Riley's ex-wife never remarried, and lives far north in Canada. She takes Chip for only two weeks over the summer. She's around so little that it doesn't rock the boat. I think Chip resented her choice to return to her hometown, and switched his loyalties to me."

"Chip is such a sweet kid. His mother's loss is your gain," Rochelle said.

"I just adore him and am so glad he accepted me as a mother. Our lives would be complicated if he had rejected me. I love him like my own. And he is a really good brother to the other kids, so protective and helpful."

"And it's all the more perfect when you hear about Dez. Laura, tell them about your ex."

This grabbed the women's attention. Laura refreshed her smile. "I like who Dez married—Anna. She and I get along great. She even helps us with babysitting the younger ones when we get in a jam."

"Wait!" Sarah blurted. "Your ex-husband's wife babysits your younger kids? Are you serious?"

"I know, it sounds unbelievable. Anna likes children and enjoys helping us out. Dez and I parted on good terms. As Rochelle knows, we were never in love, just good friends that drifted into marriage. So, there were no hard feelings when it ended. I really can't complain about anything between us."

"You are really lucky, Laura. It amazes me every time you talk. You guys are even getting through the teen years without chaos. That is unreal." Deana said.

"It's the Brady Bunch at Laura's house," Maureen quipped.

Surveying her envious coworkers, Laura sounded almost apologetic. "Yes, how things have turned out is such a gift. When Riley and I met, Cici and Chip were both in 2nd grade, and they got along great, so it wasn't hard to combine houses. Cici liked gaining a brother after being an only child. And then, Will and Jack came along. Having more kids was the best decision Riley and I made because it truly anchored our family together."

Maureen shook her head. "Well, good for you guys. I often wonder if it was wise for Sean and me to have had more kids. The older ones resent the younger ones so much. They claim we treat them different, better. It might be true because I was a single parent for so long, working and handling stuff alone. I'm sure I didn't pay them the same attention as I do the younger ones. But that is life. It's not fair and I can't make the past better. They need to grow up and stop sulking over their imperfect childhoods. They should be happy that things are easier now, and they have what we couldn't afford when I was single. Sean is a little rough around the edges, but he's there for them—which is more than I can say for their M.I.A. father." The women agreed, although questioning the existence of her younger children deflated Maureen.

"You are doing your best, Maureen. You always have."

Maureen looked up from the tabletop to meet her friend's eyes. "Thank you, Deana."

The waiter glided over with a maraschino cherry bobbing in an elegant glass and placed it by Jennifer's hand. She shook her head, "I didn't—"

"Compliments of the gentleman in the jean jacket at the bar, miss."

"Ooooh!" The ladies burst into song. Jennifer cautiously peeked back at the man clad in denim who tipped his cap in return, his companions watching the exchange. To her clique at the table, Jennifer flashed an approving eyebrow.

Deana was a boldfaced spy. "I think he's late twenties, Jen."

"Or younger. Being stacked and pushed up works for all ages," said Maureen, sounding tired.

"I need a lift," Sarah groaned, shifting in her shapeless blouse.

Jennifer stirred her drink in open contemplation. "He's pretty cute, and I'm pretty lonely."

Maureen imparted wisdom from the brief stint with husband number two. "You had better find out how old he is, honey. You've got a child and a loser ex. You don't have the energy to mother an overgrown kid."

"I hear what you are saying. Company sounds nice. That's all," assured Jennifer. Maureen bit back additional counsel, and adjusted the placement of her coaster.

"I think Demi Moore has taught us all a lesson," Rochelle thought out loud.

"Well, you can't blame her too much. Come on, now. An underwear model? Have mercy on us all. We'd pounce, too," Deana said. The agreement was even across the circle of women.

Jennifer airily reminded, "Except for Laura, of course. She's got her ripped specimen at home keeping her clock clean."

"Well, Laura has something to offer. She's been keeping tight and perky all these years," Sarah pointed out.

"With no help from Dr. Modify, either!" Rochelle testified.

Laura's hands shielded her embarrassment. "Alright, alright! We can drop it now!"

All the women laughed.

AN UNKNOWN LENGTH OF TIME LATER

Laura was on the usual Saturday quest for laundry. She pilfered through the scattered matter of her children's bedrooms searching for wrinkled balls of socks, jeans, and inside-out t-shirts. The hair falling out of her ponytail tickled her nose each time she bent to lift toys and backpacks. She popped into her teenage son's room and winced at the musty smells and disarray. She made it around the room to his bed and threw back the sheets to find whatever clothes may lie within. Her heart stopped when she discovered a pair of lace-edged pink underwear lying on his mattress. She knew whose it was. She immediately dismissed her first revolting thought. Of course not.

The next explanation was perhaps some kind of distasteful prank. But why? And on whom? Then, of course, the obvious reason was that it was trapped there in the laundry and clung to the sheet from static electricity. The queasy thought came that she needed to test this theory. She pinched the underwear and looked inside. The facts hit hard. Something was wrong. Was Chip using this underwear somehow, for his "needs?" She started feeling a little weak. He would need to be confronted. His father should do it. She dropped the underwear into the basket trying to put it out of her brain. But then, doubt made her turn back to the bed. Scanning the sheets with reluctance, the evidence lay there on the pillow, at least two strands of blond wavy hair. Her hand seized her gaping mouth. Her youngest once told her she saw Chip kissing Cici. She was sure he was mistaken. The two were just whispering to each other, she corrected him.

Her world began to implode.

With wobbly legs, she walked down the hall, passing senior pictures, family portraits full of gleaming smiles, and a candid shot of the four kids with Chip hooking his arm around Cici's neck. She entered the bonus room where her two eldest kids sat chatting. Sickened with foreboding, she stood at the wide entry. They were occupied enough to not sense trouble.

Finally, Laura interrupted, "Chip."

They both looked at their mother. Riley said innocently, "Yeah, Mom?"

After a stiff walk to the coffee table, she feebly said, "I found this in your bed," and dropped Caysie's underwear onto the table. Her children turned to stone. The moment arrived. Laura seethed, "Tell me this instant what has been going on under my roof!"

Riley stood with resolve. "Caysie and I are in love."

Her ears burned like he had screamed into them. "No you are not! You cannot be!" She checked her daughter, who nodded back shamelessly. "Are you telling me that you two have been violating each other in my home?"

"I would never hurt Caysie. Ever," he retorted. "Besides, you and Dad always taught us that if two people love each other, then it's OK. Just be safe. And we are being safe."

Hearing her teachings thrown back at her in this horrendous scenario nearly took her down to the floor. "I never meant the two of you!" she wailed. One hand gripped her chest, the other her mouth. Breakfast was roiling up. Sweat collected all over. Laura looked around the house and envisioned them tainting every space with their bodies. Had they? All the times they were home alone—bedrooms, bathrooms, the hot tub... She clenched her hair with both hands. "It's incest!" she exclaimed.

"In no way is it incest!" Riley rebutted.

"Yes, it is! You are brother and sister!" she shrieked.

"On paper! The relationship is completely contrived."

"How insulting! You are siblings in every sense!"

"We are in no way related. Biologically, things are as valid for us as between you and Dad."

She clawed her face. "Oh geez, don't say such a repulsive thing!"

"Yes, discussing your sex life is repulsive to me, as it should be. But I had to lay the card," Riley said flatly.

Their mother turned toward the window looking like she was going to throw herself out of it. "It's coming apart. There are no words."

"Mom, you've always said that we should never judge love between two consenting adults," Caysie insisted.

Again, she recoiled at hearing the worldly wisdom she had long professed. "Cici, you have been raised by the same parents with your siblings since you were small. Think of your younger brothers. You and Chip are *both* related to Will and Jack. Have you not woken up to that fact? This is insanity!"

Caysie pouted at her mother. "I love my brothers, Mom, but your choice to have children with a second husband is irrelevant to my future."

Laura swung around to face her. "It is the reality of your entire future! None of your family is going away—unless this situation causes your father to leave me." Her face melted further as this possibility leached in. Her two children observed her transformation void of compassion.

"The way I see it, you and Dad created this situation, striving to make us all one happy family. Caysie and I are happy. Well done," said Riley.

Tears pooled as Laura's eyes wandered the room, still appearing to look for some exit from existence. Then, rage percolated upwards from her gut to her eyes. "This disgusting, vile behavior between you and Cici is not my doing. Never, ever did we encourage or suggest a scenario where the two of you would regard each other differently than your siblings. The very idea is insulting to me in the deepest way, and I demand you apologize!"

Riley shook his head no. "Who is really responsible here? I won't apologize when you and Dad basically put into my life every day the hottest girl I know and expect me not to notice that." Caysie's eyes glimmered at the compliment. "Furthermore, you guys have arranged our dates for years."

The tears stopped flowing when the stupefying allegation was cast. "Don't, Chip! I'm warning you to not cross the line! I have not facilitated your *dating*. This sickens me. And it is wholly untrue. And villainous for you to say it!"

Riley, undeterred, pressed on. "Hmm, let's see. Tickets to the movies funded by Laura and Riley. Eating out. Going to baseball games. Weekend camping trips. Water parks. Ski trips—"

At that, she cried out, "NO! Stop! Stop it! How can you say this to me, your *mother*?"

Riley shrugged it off. "If it makes it easier, I'll call you Laura."

Her knees began to buckle. "I'm going to throw up. I caaa—" she gasped, "I can't handle—" She turned and jogged to the bathroom door and gagged into the sink with the next step. The couple watched their mother's body jerk twice over the basin as the gurgling of vomit splattered in. Desperate gasps for recovery echoed in the powder room as she took a seat on the closed toilet. The unreeling of toilet paper followed for her to spit and wipe her mouth.

Next, the sounds of jingling keys and the chatter of little boys wound up the stairwell. Heavy footsteps of leather soles hit the risers as Riley Sr. cheerfully greeted the upper floor. When he reached the top, he sighted his son standing broadly, appearing ready for confrontation. His wife could be heard in the powder room painfully mewling. Caysie sedately sat on the ottoman with determined poise.

"What happened? What is going on?" the father demanded. None of his children spoke. "Laura?"

She wailed into her tissue, "It's Chip and—" She coughed and howled with surging tears like she was about to report a death.

At this, he roared in defense of his wife. "Riley Christopher! What happened? What did you do?"

The unjust indictment threw Caysie off her seat. Taking Riley's hand into both of hers, she wrapped his arm around her waist and positioned her body in front of his as a shield. One hand reached behind her and braced her brother's thigh while his free hand rested on the curve of her neck. Their father could not believe what he was seeing. Was this unnatural affection between them? He spied the pink lace underwear singularly lying on the coffee table. Horror paled his face, and his eyes settled on what he had just discovered to be the conniving, slutty girl he had mistakenly committed to raise as his own, who was evidently perverting the sanctity of his entire family.

THAT NIGHT

Following the domestic meltdown, the damned son stole away with the wretched daughter to escape the turbulence at home. The coupe rolled to a stop in the far corner of a lot. The city park was deserted. Riley yanked the break, and then reached to envelop Caysie within his broad shoulder for her to weep out her heartbreak. His fury was muted for her benefit.

The acid spewed from Riley Sr. against Caysie nearly vaulted father and son into blows. Their father would regard her with curdling disgust from that day forward. Certainly Riley could not abide such maltreatment of Caysie and could never be in the presence of his father again. Their mother, on the other hand, determined that "Chip" was most accountable for Caysie's fall because he was a typical male.

The prospect of Caysie peaceably seeing her biological mother and brothers was so improbable that it caused her chest to ache. Her father, Dez, and step-mother were doubtful allies, and would not likely extend their rescue to Riley. Riley's biological mother was in her own country, and was, to his mind, disinterested in his affairs. The teens faced isolation with high school diplomas and very little money. Things were bleak.

Caysie sagged back into her seat, sniffing from the tears draining in her nose. "We knew this would come to light, but I wasn't ready to face it today. I thought when you moved out next year, we could transition things slowly and bring them along. But now, I'm certain they would have the same reaction no matter how they learned of it. They won't ever accept us. They will try whatever means possible to split us up. Dad is too much in the public eye."

"I don't see them ever respecting our relationship. They don't consider it real at all, like it is just teenage stupidity." The filial connection imposed on them was inexorable, thus their relationship was repellant to the world. Riley continued, "When I think about it, I don't see how we can stay in this city. Everybody, even the cashier at the convenience store, knows who we are, thanks to Dad's conspicuous profession." No community would stay silent over a high school teacher whose own children committed such perversion.

"True. We can't be free here." Caysie wiped her eyes and sniffed again. "The family is coming apart. But I have to say, our parents deserve to experience some of the pain they are oblivious to creating. No kid asks for divorce. No kid wants strangers to suddenly become their parents. No kid wants to pretend to love someone they don't, or pretend to not love someone they do. We must submit and accept all their choices imposed on us. Yet, we must fight to have our choice accepted. When will what we want count for once?"

A hand, snowy and slight, was enfolded by a strong, umber one. "There is a way to force them to accept us, you know."

Depleted of all energy, she exerted no effort to problem solve. "How?"

"Marry me."

Caysie drew a sharp breath. "That certainly forces the issue." The suggestion felt like make-believe. "Do you really want marriage? Or is this retaliation?"

The question peeved him. "You think I would marry the girl I love to retaliate against my parents?" She bit her lip repentantly. "No, of course not. I've already looked into it, and we both have I.D. We go across the border, and in three days, the government will have the final say. Then, you will be my wife—not my buddy, not my roommate, not my girlfriend and, by God, not my sister," he said with loathing.

She considered this tentatively. "I feel we are meant for each other. But that's what all people think when they marry. The stats on teen marriages are not in our favor. Our own parents are on their second marriages."

"Yes, but what couple lives together as friends for a decade before getting serious? I know everything about you, Caysie. I know that eggs make your skin itch, you hate sci-fi, you cannot sharpen a pencil without breaking it six times, and you PMS like a cornered cat. I am confident we'll make it. No doubt."

"It's true that our situation is unusual, to say the least. But," she whimpered, "we have no money and no place to live!" She dabbed her splotchy face flushed from violent crying.

"I'm not worried about getting by. We don't need much." Riley plucked a small shiny object from out of the cup holder, drew close, and looked intensely at her through his obsidian hair. He put the object in her hand and said deliberately, "I will marry you for two bits and a cold-water flat." The two studied the quarter cupped in her palm. "That's how my grandpa proposed to my grandma when times were tight," he explained.

The silver metal was shaped in a perfect circle, a token for a ring. Her conciliatory smile emerged as she acquiesced.

SIX DAYS LATER

Deana sipped her martini, and then coddled the drink with a frown. "Our court date to revise child support is for Thursday. We are bleeding money. Lawyers love divorce."

Jennifer tried to be encouraging. "It's a drag, but at least you've shaken some change out of them. Mitch still keeps that truck gassed up and women at his beck and call on supposedly no income." Her strategic conversation stayed clear of jean-jacket Roy, the man who had commenced their entanglement by ordering a cocktail for her many months ago. She was not ready to be chastised by the circle of women for messing with someone too young, too hot, and too fiscally needy. She could still afford a warm bed.

The personal updates were the usual stream of expositions on their circumstances with soap opera finesse. Maureen finished grumbling over the recent avowal of her sixteen-year-old to move in with his absentee father. Concluding with a deft critique of her naïve son, she turned to the coworker at her left. "And there she sits, all quiet and content, Laura with her Brady Bunch happiness."

Laura returned no smile and sat in absent silence. All eyes appraised their friend who was deeply contemplating a chip detected on the lip of her otherwise perfect glass. Her finger grazed the imperfection to test its keenness. The prolonged dead air stirred concern.

"Laura, are you alright? Has something happened?" Rochelle pried while waving off secondhand smoke.

Laura's mouth opened to begin, but no words found a way out. Her dread visibly mounted as her eyes clamped shut and her color rose. The tenor of the group of women slipped out of blithe commiserating into disquietude. Searching looks shot over the appetizers to detect who, if any, was an insider. All were stumped.

Maureen put her stout hand on Laura's. "Come out with it, girl. What's the trouble?"

Laura spoke in cold spurts. "A week ago, on Wednesday, Chip and Cici called to inform me and Riley that—" she hesitated as the women leaned closer, "because of our complete opposition to them—" at this, expressions turned quizzical as Laura gathered strength, "they left the state and eloped." Rochelle's fork clanged onto her plate. "Evidently, their affair has been going on under our roof for an unknown length of time. So, as of last week, Will and Jack have siblings who are—" she choked, "married, and their parents are seeking divorce. Other than that, all is well at Riley and Laura's."

None of the women moved, except mother hen Maureen. Being a woman of implacable nerves, she immediately organized relief for her table, hailing to the counter, "Mike! Bring us a round of stiff drinks, honey, and three slices of the mud-pie."

9

Drop the Dime

"Rovey, you wicked boy." Liz rubbed his shaven head reflecting the low lights of the club as he escorted Liz back to the table. Rovey was the only man who could partner dance on the tour. His hot dances with the array of women travelers meant nothing. Everyone knew the sun-kissed voyager was having a covert affair with the tour guide, Maggie, for whom he pretended indifference in public to preserve her job. Liz requested Rovey to dance nearly every night, primarily for the thrilling dip at the end. He was not one for subtlety, as his elective baldness indicated. "Dancing with you leaves nothing to the imagination, mister, since you go commando."

"Give it a whirl, love," he replied in a suave fashion. The Australian reservist deemed wearing underwear a nuisance after weeks of survival training in the outback. No matter the weather, Rovey wore the same tattered shirt, shorts, and flip-flops every day, but was mysteriously laundered and showered at all times. Khakis and a button shirt were all he packed, which ensemble appeared once for a theater event on week three of the tour.

Feeling quite alive, Liz sat down next to Carla to catch her breath. Rovey remained on his feet and reached between their companions playing Drop the Dime to retrieve his alcohol. Mickey, Amy, and Freda had a quarter suspended over a glass on a napkin. As they puffed and passed a cigarette, they respectively burned a hole through the napkin. Mickey lost. The coin clattered at the bottom when his hole caused the quarter to tear through the paper. While he guzzled down a full beer, all the women began to wail, "Oh Mickey, you're so fine; you're so fine you blow my mind. Hey Mickey! Hey Mickey!" Mickey cringed after pounding down his glass. Hearing drunken renditions of the Toni Basil hit serenaded to him over and over had him longing to return home to Hong Kong.

The women knew, however, that Mickey loved it as much as he hated it. His tolerance was born out of the bond that all on the tour had developed for each other. The assembly of nearly four dozen young adults had become a family, having spent weeks in the confines of a large coach touring the country. Most of them were Australians on sabbatical. The rest were from parts of the Commonwealth and the States.

After the singing died down, Liz bumped Carla's shoulder to query without words her state of mind, aware that Carla had binged all day on ice cream. Carla answered, "I'm good," as she straightened her miniskirt. Carla flaunted a modern shag crop, a petite nose ring, several tats, and dozens of hooped piercings around her ears. She was all Miami-Dade confidence in presentation, yet had surprised Liz by outing herself as a member of a support group for eating disorders. Her recovery from bulimia was tentative and she trusted Liz for support to avoid purging. Carla confided to Liz's ear, "The ice cream was incredible, by the way. Thirteen scoops of the best hand-churned I could find. Sightseeing in this city is delicious." Liz hooked Carla's pinky with hers and the two locked smiling eyes. Their attention returned to their partying friends. "So, did you pay the toll?" asked Carla.

"Yes, he managed to kiss me below my ear after a fun, little wrestle," Liz said.

"Toggs cornered me earlier, but I got away with one on the cheek. He says no discounts next time," Carla reported, entirely charmed. The "discounts" referred to empty threats by their male travelers to kiss their willing captives full on the mouth.

Liz grinned. "Well, that won't be bad."

Liz looked around at the Aussie guys, five of whom had shaved their heads and called their collective "The Passion Posse." The scheme was devised when the tour had sponsored a themed costume party where all had to come as something starting with the letter P. Liz came as "possessed" and nixed the costume effort altogether. Arriving in pirate garb, The Passion Posse commenced the plunder of womanizing for the rest of the tour. The Posse faithfully lived up to their moniker every day.

Liz nodded as she inspected the men. "You know, there's something refreshing about how blatant Aussie men are. American men are so passive-aggressive. I'm not sure, but I think the Aussie way is starting to work for me."

The two women jumped a little when Victor popped his bald head between them, hanging his arms around their shoulders. "So, you Sheilas have come round to how superior Aussie men are. That's good—that's good. I'm just getting started, my lovelies." Victor was a tall, fit, tan, and model-handsome policeman, whose hip was scarred by a bullet. The women groaned and giggled for having been overheard by the man who truly lived like there was no tomorrow.

Then Natalie, the Canadian on the other side of Carla, drew away Carla's attention with a question. Victor gazed at Liz's profile and nodded with approval. "Look at you, Lizzie-darling! Your lips are far more kissable tonight. I will make a note of that." Liz raised her eyes to the ceiling as her cheeks reddened. He chuckled and kindly squeezed her shoulder before toting his beer to another table.

The influence of Victor was largely responsible for Liz's transformation that evening. The one time they sat together on the coach, Victor declared that Liz wore too much make-up (like all American women, he insisted, especially the Yank newscasters). Australian women wore noticeably little makeup and spent only essential time on their hair. Having such a gorgeous man say she would look prettier without make-up was irresistibly compelling. Liz did not want Victor, but did not mind his admiration. After a few weeks of embracing a more natural appearance, Liz supposed that her habits could change for a lifetime. She was starting to see herself differently through the eyes of these boundless men.

The Aussie guys, including The Passion Posse, never intended harm. The hugging, pecks on the cheek, and full-frontal flirting were just to flatter and tease their agreeable recipients. The tour was to end in 23 days, and the awareness of the impending date had unleashed self-expression beyond what would be comfortable at home. The time limitations caused the women to be likewise more tolerant of male boldness.

When a favorite dance song erupted from the speakers, Liz left Carla (an avowed observer), and bounced to the neighboring table to grab her roommate sitting with a dozen other travelers. Anita, one of the kindest people on the tour, had flawless ebony skin, large shapely eyes, buoyant black hair, and a figure that all admired. The two ladies soaked up the thrill of abandon all around them on the dance floor. During the bridge, two men maneuvered between them, Liz thought, to be their partners. After a few moments, however, Liz found herself separated from Anita, encircled by seven men, shoulder to shoulder, ogling and touching her. Fear struck like lightning, and her comprehension triggered ominous sneers. As she sought to exit the ring of drooling rogues, she was dragged backward by a belt loop on her pants, as if on a leash, and burst out of the circle stumbling to the borders of the dance floor.

Feeling both liberation and dread, Liz spun around to face whose finger was hooked onto her back of her pants. To her relief, it was fellow traveler, Heath. "We are going now," he mandated. His fiancée, Grace, and Anita stood at his side in full agreement. Frivolity in the club was eroding into debauchery. Time to depart.

The coach was to leave in half an hour. Liz and the three South Africans—Heath, Grace and Anita—walked around the streets near the club to experience a summer night in the wakeful city. Restaurants were open. Bars were thumping. Well-dressed and underdressed cliques of women and men padded through the streets. Taxis spurted in and out of traffic seeking passengers. Neon lit the way. They dodged the panhandlers, the mentally ill, and the shady figures haunting the convenience stores. Coming from the predictable suburbs, Liz was captured by the city's exotic personalities, economic diversity, and infectious moxie. Perhaps, she was a city girl.

The foursome circled back to the parked coach to unite with their two dozen cohorts streaming out of the club. A chattering group of fifteen returned from a live musical. Movement down another block caught Liz's eye. The six-legged mass silhouetted in the light of the distant street lamp lumbered toward the coach. Once past the shadow of buildings, Liz perceived that it was Rex and Tall Mike serving as a reluctant pair of bodyguards to Camilla, coaxing her forward, their arms propping upright her petite frame. Her ankles crooked back and forth over her platform heels; her flyaway corkscrew curls bobbed over her shoulders.

When the trio arrived, Rex reported, "That was close. She was crossing the road with some bloke before we caught up to her." Camilla was insensibly docile under the influence and could be herded any direction by anyone. The guys had already uncoupled her from a poor decision in a previous city. Camilla looked up at Rex with lids at half-mast.

"Time to head home, cot case," Rex said.

"Ang on. Where's that tall drink of water?" Camilla slurred.

Tall Mike shook his head in annoyance. "Did the Harry, love." The two men ushered Camilla around the coach where the word "LOWIES" had been written in the dust under the company logo: *Tikiwaka – Tours for the 21-35 yr old.*

The coach was poised to depart at midnight for the scrappy hotel where the travelers could continue to party or to crash into bunks after a long day of sightseeing, shopping, and feasting. Many of the Aussies had phenomenal stamina proven to endure consecutive late nights of heavy drinking, and early mornings followed by full days of tourism. This pattern was encouraged by the unlimited alcohol served on excursions. Liz's closest companions on the tour were far less indulgent. The other calmer set was a handful of Kiwi school teachers who dared not sully their professional reputations with edgy behavior. For the travelers preferring moderation, proximity to the extremists offered rousing vicarious living. Overall, the habits of the group were such that one could expect a long night ahead, and a bevy of stories in the morning.

After the bus was fully boarded, it transported the group back to its temporary home. The party would continue in the basement bar of the hotel, where rounds of drinks with thoroughbred names would be serially imbibed. There was no dance floor, so Liz was not interested in a longer night. The three South Africans thought it prudent to likewise retire.

The hotel, at the edge of downtown, was of minimum quality and enormous. Several tour companies used the hotel as a base. Lodging there was akin to life in a dormitory; the rooms were tiny, unadorned, with communal bathrooms. The expectations of guests were relaxed in terms of noise, attire, and behavior. Hundreds of young people filled the hotel. The common areas became chaotic when the waves of tours came and went.

Anita and Liz finished their bedtime routines, darkened the room, and hunkered down into the bunks. Midway through their gossip, sounds of crazed voices and slamming doors echoed in the hallway. Like a jack-in-the-box, the door flew open. The distinctive silhouette of Tall Mike flashed them, fully stripped. He wished them good-night, and snapped the door closed with the same quickness.

"We must thank him for the unconventional reminder to lock the door," Anita chirped over Liz's cackle. They heard the naked parade continue down the hallway assigned to their tour, popping open door after door for a full city block.

At dawn, over Vegemite on toast, breakfast conversation included an account from the previous night. Rex, not a small man, let loose and swung on the bar chandelier. It seemed like a fish story, but all witnesses in roaring laughter testified that it did happen. Disappointed to have missed this spectacle, Liz wished she had the stamina to experience more of the round-the-clock antics of the tour.

The travelers prepared for leaving the hotel in the usual flurry—scrambling in the bathrooms, clearing out rooms, and hauling baggage down into the lobby. There, they joined a sea of tour groups in the same throes of harried departure. Over the babble of the masses checking out of the hotel, their tour guide, Maggie, strained to instruct her mostly hungover party of 45 on expectations. Liz stood with the South African trio on the furthest edge of the group to glean the directives: leave baggage for the coach to pack, keep essentials on your person, and return by 2:50 PM for departure. There was additional information about a scheduled bridge closure, and significant traffic, and more instructions drowned out by the increasing noise of the lobby. Liz guessed this was the usual request to be punctual or the coach would leave the tardy behind. It was 9:00 in the morning, allowing plenty of time to hit the sites before departure, Liz calculated.

She turned to her companions. "What are you guys planning to do?"

With his exceptional smile, Heath said in his fine accent, "We are going to take a gander at some of the high-end shopping. Come with?" He always extended an invitation, but knew that Liz preferred scouting museums to shopping, especially fantasy shopping.

Liz touched his forearm in gratitude. "Thank you, but I'll pass. I'm going to check out the natural history museum. I hope it's not crowded." She turned to Anita. "See you on the coach." Anita and the other two waved goodbyes and went for the doors opposite Liz's destination.

For the previous two days, the coach had escorted the group to must-see sites in the city, and allotted half of the final day for independent exploration. Liz was accustomed to touring alone, but this city populated by millions felt overwhelming after walking a few of the oversized city blocks. The morning was warm, and hordes of pedestrian commuters and shoppers were efficiently on errand in order to be able to savor air conditioning during the blaze of the day.

Most buildings were twenty floors in height at minimum, making many of the avenues shadowy vales of brick and concrete. Movies that Liz had seen, emphasizing the grimness of urban life, colored her perception of the activity around her. Nobody smiled. Everyone looked past her like she did not exist. Gripping the straps of her backpack, a paranoid feeling nudged that she was being followed by some nefarious character. She peeked back to catch a glimpse of an elegant man ten feet behind her, who had exquisite shoes and a fluffy white Shih Tzu crooked his arm. Feeling very silly, she sought the next sign directing to the museum.

Daring to jaywalk through the angry stop-and-go traffic with a host of others on foot, she reached the stone edifice boasting classic columns and broad, inviting steps. The museum pass was barely affordable, but worth the investment. She browsed with deep satisfaction the dinosaur bones, uncommon gems, and artifacts of native culture. Many pieces in the exhibits were recognizable from coffee table books and magazines. Immersed in a place of such caliber was surreal. For Liz, that was what travel was all about—to see acclaimed places and objects in three dimensions.

Viewing with awe the skeleton of a mammoth, she heard a voice that sounded somewhat familiar. Reflexively, she turned toward the voice to lay eyes on the imperial profile of the actress, Rita Linton-Gray, who was marveling over the twelve-foot-tall fossil with four other friends, family members, or maybe bodyguards. The lucky moment filled Liz with jittery delight. Trying not to outright stare, Liz pretended to read a plaque to catch a few discernable words, and did not move until the Oscar winner with her entourage walked to another exhibit. Suburban life affords no such tales to tell.

The hour had come to leave the unhurried atmosphere of the museum for the feverish tempo of the sidewalk. Once through the rotating door, delicate echoes of the museum were replaced with the deep rumbles of idling motors and strident voices on push-to-talk. Her watch indicated that she could visit another attraction on her way back to the hotel. Resting her pack on a wall, she dug around for her cell. A grim feeling filled her gut as she realized that her phone had been left charging in Carla's room because hers had a dead outlet. Carla had it in safekeeping, she was sure. For a few racing heartbeats, she pictured all the atrocities that could befall her with no chance to rescue herself with a phone call. Then, a herd of second graders clacked up the museum stairs, grounding her in the actual world. The chances of something going terribly wrong were minuscule, she concluded, and she decided to get oriented. Pressing on to the next block, a newsstand offered maps for purchase.

"You are not from here, yes?" said the vendor through a heavy salt-and-pepper mustache.

"I'm on vacation. In fact, I need a city map. Could I have one, please?"

His brow furrowed and he leaned in closer to say in a hush, "You are alone?"

She hesitated to answer truthfully. But his crow's feet and genial tone extracted the answer. "Yes, I am today."

He waited to see if a new arrival would stay long. The customer departed after a quick scan of the headlines. "Young lady, you should not be walking alone. The whole world can see that you are not from the city and bad people look for travelers. You must take the tags off your bag."

Liz waxed curious, but the truth shriveled her insides. She nodded, expressed thanks, and reached to take the map from his hand. He did not let it go until he finished. "Do not open the map outside. Go into a coffee shop. Get a drink. Sit down and look at the map at a table—never on the street. If you need directions, ask people in uniforms. Nobody else."

Her worst fears about this intimidating city were lit by his blunt counsel. At this, he smiled, "And keep your head up. No sad faces. Good luck, child." He released the map to her and accepted the next customer's money for this month's *Mod Man Quarterly* with cheerful regards.

With her back to pedestrians, Liz knelt in the booth to remove the tags from her backpack, and to stuff the map and tags inside it. On her wrist dangled her pocket camera, which she slipped off and deposited into the thigh pocket of her cargo shorts. She rose and wriggled a goodbye with her fingertips to her guardian, who winked back his approval before she turned away. After leaving the newsstand, Liz assumed the disposition of a resident acting socially bored and mentally preoccupied, rather than fascinated with everyone and everything.

A charming coffee shop with wainscoting and lots of beveled glass was found at the end of the block. Mimicking the locals ahead of her in line, she ordered a muffin and the cheapest drink possible with an all-business delivery. She pursued the map with air of reading a magazine at the table furthest from the windows. A low-grade stress came with having to perform for any observers. Comfort would not return until she was situated in a bucket seat on the coach.

Few tourist attractions with affordable entry fees could be found on the handful of routes back to the hotel. The obvious stop was the tower, the tallest skyscraper with a 360° view on the observation deck. The other possibility was the old Orthodox Church that featured some notable art. Maybe she could squeeze in both.

Leaving the cool of the shop for the roasting concrete of the street, she trekked to the tower feeling much less enthusiastic about her day. She held her head up, however, and walked with purpose in the unaffected manners of the locals. The architectural supremacy of the tower could be seen far down the arterial, soaring hundreds of feet above all its neighbors. The sense of its size was distorted by the grand proportions of the city itself, and it took much longer to walk there than anticipated.

Standing before the massive building in the plaza bedecked with hefty planters, contemporary angular sculptures, and a terraced water feature, she paused to consider whether or not to go inside. Nearly all those passing through the doors were smartly dressed and sophisticated. No person was a tourist that she could detect, until in the distance, she spied a small group in shorts and flip-flops making their way to an entrance flagged by modest signage beyond the main set of doors. She tracked the tourists through the security check, across the vast marbled lobby, to the bank of elevators serving those destined for the observation deck. Goosebumps leapt from her skin when the 20-degree drop in temperature smacked her sweat upon entry of the tower.

After purchasing a ticket at admissions, Liz entered the growing line for the elevators with unease. Perhaps the discomfort stemmed from the discrepancy between her tank top summer ensemble and the fashionable attire of those who worked there. Maybe it was the idea of riding an elevator at world-class speeds. Maybe it was all the things that could possibly go wrong when atop one of the tallest buildings in the country.

Those around her were smiling and snapping photos, and she realized that her apprehension was choking the fun out of the experience. By this phase of the tour, she should be a hardened traveler, fearlessly driven to take on the sites. The socializing surrounding her made the choice to summit the tower without a companion starkly lonesome. She leaned out of the line to see if she could eye somebody from the tour. No one recognizable was in line. She hoped to run into a familiar face at the top.

The multiple elevators alternated their rise and fall to the top and to the lobby. Before long, uniformed individuals cowed Liz into an elevator with a dozen others. The doors closed, and the sound system welcomed them to the tower. A recording of facts was spewed into their ears by a baritone with film reel jauntiness. Sixty-three long seconds passed as the elevator shot upwards to ascend over a thousand feet of layered girders, glass, carpet, and cubicles. Jostling against strangers in that steel box jetting to the sky was altogether unnatural, and hence, she itched to get out. There was no ear to whisper to, no phone to rivet on, and no friend with whom to exchange thoughts. The floor numbers flicked overhead where her eyes focused to fretfully spur them on, hoping that they did not stop at a point where doors could not open.

Mercifully, the doors did part at the top story, a large space with interactive displays to present trivia and explain the views of the city. At least a hundred visitors milled about, reading plaques, watching the displays, and lingering by the floor-to-ceiling glass framing the panoramas. Having so many tourists present was reassuring.

To the soundtrack of murmuring voices and digital displays, Liz moved to the windows, where the world was now miniaturized. Distances were phenomenally distorted; the lengthy route from the natural history museum to the tower measured the diameter of her palm. The masses of moving people and traffic were barely discernable from that height. Liz lingered at the mural of glass to locate landmarks, and later, she lightly browsed the displays. Eventually, the stairs to the upper deck enticed her upwards.

On the roof, under the expanse of the sky, the experience was entirely different from indoors. Aside from the boats leaving foamy trails in the bay and the faint moans of horns on diesel engines navigating sea and track, the city was still and peaceful for miles. Wind pelted her face and sounded in her ears, airplanes flew close, and wispy clouds were touchable. The solace of the roof bore no resemblance to the high intensity of the street. Tranquility enveloped Liz as she drank in the scene without the obstruction of window frames and reflections. The chilly air was spiked by sharp gusts, which flagged her wavy hair, tickling her face. Far beyond the bay, clouds heavy with moisture could be seen creeping towards land, ushered by increasing wind.

She rested her elbows on the railing, and contemplated what it was like to travel to the faint cerulean hills in the neighboring state, to cross those emblematic bridges over the water, to see herself through a telescopic lens from the other renowned skyscraper two miles away, or to drop off the edge. Would it feel like flying? Did it take long to reach the ground? Had anyone done that on purpose? She could understand why sad people might jump to their deaths. The bluster of air around her felt amazing, the views were spectacular, and the rooftop was its own brand of quiet. Nothing about this place felt like life below, and it was so close to heaven already. Enlightenment unlocked her mind to how incomprehensibly large the earth was, how infinite space is, and that she was a mere speck of dust to the cosmos. Yet, she was alive. Why was she, this insignificant being, made to live? It must be that she was not insignificant. That paradox humanity has tussled with for eons.

Liz took pictures to record the memory, knowing that none of the images would capture the sensations of her experience on the roof. Furthermore, there was no person with whom to relive all the wonderful details, except the tower itself, which would always know that she had been there. The tower lifted her to a different perspective and opened her mind to deeper thinking. It was an escape from the uneasy world, not to leave life, but to find beautiful reasons to live.

The increasingly chilly atmosphere had incited most visitors to move indoors, leaving the roof nearly vacant. The chance seclusion allowed her to find her lip liner to write on the railing, "LIZ LANE IS HERE." The coming rains would wash the words away, and somehow, that felt right.

The descent to the ground level was straightforward and uneventful. The time was 1:55 PM, an hour to departure. There were no indications at street level that the weather was in flux, which foreknowledge Liz found a tiny bit empowering. The sweltering humidity continued outside the sliding doors of the lobby, belying the forecast as seen from the roof. In spite of her yearnings to return to that limitless perspective, reality beckoned, and she moved directly toward the Greek Orthodox Church one block away. She strode with her head boldly up, face relaxed, feeling aware, but not afraid.

In a contemplative state, she was walking towards the lustrous majestic dome cresting over the trees of the plaza when a gruff voice bellowed out of view, "Hey, Sexy Mama. Where you going? Why are you walking away?" Then, whistles from at least two other individuals joined in. Her reverie broke and dropped her into the coarse quiddity of the street where men were harassing someone—possibly her. She hoped the catcalls were directed to another victim, but her nerves seized anyhow. Running would reveal fear, not strength. She chose to walk faster and ignore the voices.

The shouts sounded closer. "Hey, honey! Shake it for me, girl!" "Wow, look at those legs." "I love me a brunette." Liz stiffened her bearing and locked her head forward.

Again, one of the men hollered, but this time, in a familiar Aussie accent. "Lizzie! Hold up, Liz! We're just messing with ya." She stopped in her tracks, exhaled in relief, and turned to see Rex, Rovey, and Tall Mike walking toward her.

When they reached her, she punched Rex in the arm. "Freaked me out! That was terrifying!"

"Serves you right! Why the heck are you alone? It's not safe here, sweetheart." Liz shrugged off Rex's condemnation. He insisted, "I'm telling you, this city is crawling with scallywags. Rovey was dry as a drover's dog, was offered a coldie, and was trapped in a brothel."

"S'true. Nearly had to sell a kidney to get out of there when I realized where I was. Stick with y'mates," Rovey made plain.

"You need to get off the street, darling. Come with us now. We are going to the hotel for air-con, and throw down a middy before hitting the road," Rex said.

Liz checked her watch. "There's one more stop I want to make, and then I'll head back."

"I wish you wouldn't. I don't like it." Rovey gave her a hard look. "You be careful, Lizzie."

"I promise. I'll see you at the hotel soon." Touched by their brotherly concern for her, she blew them a kiss and waved farewell. The guys waved back and snaked through clogged traffic to the opposite side of the street. With a glowing heart, Liz pressed on to the grounds of the church one hundred yards away.

The ornate carved doors were ajar, and Liz gingerly entered to the squeak of burdened hinges. Before her eyes were walls adorned with gold leaf upon which hung stylized portraits of Jesus Christ and the saints depicted in great acts of mercy and sacrifice. Liz had gone through confirmation as a child, and her family infrequently attended a Presbyterian church. This Christian setting, though, was wholly unfamiliar to her. In the circular layout of the church, seating was almost nonexistent, and the function of the objects in the broad space was not obvious. Several decorated podium-style tables and waist-high candelabras were positioned about the space. A large circular chandelier under the lofty dome hung before an exceptionally ornate golden wall of icons with three doors.

She spied an individual near the front of the church attending to some object; the little woman gestured over her chest, she bowed at times, and she leaned to kiss something. A picture? Liz could not make sense of the order or the purpose the woman's movements. The woman lit a beeswax taper, set it with some other burning candles, and left the church through a side door.

Most walls and pillars had at least one glistening icon of a Christian figure. Wandering the church inspecting the artwork, she hoped to encounter someone who could tell her about the images: what purpose they served, were they originals or copies, and why there were so many. Toward the front of the church, male voices in a foreign tongue could be heard.

On the opposite side of a dividing wall were two Middle Eastern men kneeling on the floor with paint rollers, coating the alabaster wall. They looked up, and Liz cautiously greeted them, sensitive to interrupting their work. "Hello. Sorry to disturb you."

"Oh, it's OK. It's OK," said the taller of the two, topped with dark brown, puffy hair. "Can we help you?"

"I was hoping to find someone to answer a few questions about these paintings."

He translated to the other man whose features were similar to the first. The shorter man nodded courteously to her.

"At the office, you will find the directors of the church. But my friend Betrose can, maybe, also answer your questions." The two men put down their rollers, removed their gloves, and stood up.

Betrose extended his hand to shake hers. She said, "Hi, I am Elizabeth. Nice to meet you, Betrose. Are you Orthodox Christian?"

The tall man intercepted, "Yes, he is. Betrose does not yet know English." Betrose added something as if she could understand. She simply smiled back. The translator added, "My name is Ahmed."

Turning to shake Ahmed's hand, she asked, "May I ask what language you are speaking?"

Ahmed replied, "We come from Syria; we speak Arabic, but sometimes it's different. We do some work for this church."

"Thank you for taking time to talk with me. I'm touring the city and stopped by the church out of curiosity. I've never been in an Orthodox church before. There are so many beautiful things here that I want to learn about. Come this way." She walked them to the place where the woman was seen bowing to an image. "Here's my first question. I saw a woman kissing this painting. Why was she doing that?"

Ahmed talked with Betrose. Betrose came beside Liz and in Arabic, spoke carefully for Ahmed to translate to her. He pressed his hands together as if praying, and moved them forward, away from his chest several times. Ahmed said, "The picture is of Saint Catherine, she is—eh—the mother of this building—eh—the people come and kiss the picture, not her face, her clothes, to say—eh—to worship— eh—no worship—to send their love, their respect for her through the picture. Yes, through the picture, like a telephone."

Liz was surprised that Christians worshipped with paintings. She would never think to kiss a painting herself, but was known to knock on wood regularly. "I think I understand. They use paintings to help communicate their prayers." The men affirmed her summary. "Why are there so many of these paintings?"

Betrose cheerfully replied as Ahmed assisted, "The paintings are windows to heaven. They teach the people stories about God and the scripture. The pictures are like photographs of people who they love."

While speaking of his faith, Betrose's thick, calloused hand laid over his chest puffed with pride. "Thank you, Betrose." She smiled back and scanned the room. There was a large bowl on a stand in the corner. "I have another question. How do they baptize here?"

"Baptize?" Ahmed said, "I do not know the word."

She tried to simplify the terms, "When someone joins this church, do they go underwater? Or is water sprinkled on them?"

Ahmed chuckled, "You want me to ask if they take bath or shower?"

"No!" she laughed. "To join this church, is someone covered in water completely or is water put only on the person's head." Ahmed translated best he could.

Betrose nodded and answered in Ahmed's words, "To join the church, you must be very buried in water, from the head to the foot, and everything. When the person comes out of the water, it is like a birth. It is how babies come to mothers, all wet."

"Baptism by immersion to be reborn," she restated. The enthusiasm of Betrose drew from Liz one more question. In her life, there were Catholics, Evangelicals, and even a Jehovah's Witness. She figured the next answer, but wanted to study further the fascinating translations between these Syrians. Clearly, Ahmed was not Christian.

She could not see an altar or table in the room to determine just how, but she asked, "Does the Orthodox church serve communion?"

Ahmed's eyes squinted as he tried to find words to translate. "Communion? I do not know."

She said directly to Betrose, "Communion? Eucharist?" putting her fingers to her mouth as if to take something in. She hoped the word Eucharist had a similar sound in his tongue. Gesturing no, his shoulders lifted, and he turned to speak with Ahmed.

Ahmed replied, "He does not understand the meaning. It looks like you kiss your fingers."

"Ask if they eat bread and drink wine here."

Ahmed asked the question with mild amusement. Betrose passionately responded with a resounding affirmation. Speaking for Betrose, Ahmed said, "Yes, he knows your meaning. Yes, they take bread and wine every week. The shepherd –er—leader, he serves the bread in the wine from a cup. He gives it to him—all the people—in a spoon."

"Is he saying the bread is *in* the wine? The bread and the wine are not separate?" This was quite unexpected.

The men discussed her question. "He says the bread is in the wine, together, in a cup."

"And the priest, er, leader serves it with a spoon? Like soup?"

Betrose cracked up when he heard Ahmed's rendition. Ahmed said, "He says yes. It is like soup, a little bit."

Liz recoiled inside picturing a hundred people all eating mushy bread from the same spoon. But then, every church did weird stuff that was hard to explain to an outsider.

Interrupting her thoughts, Ahmed asked, "So, miss, are you religious?"

Religious. What a word. She was religious about her reality TV, checking her phone, having her morning cup of Joe, walking her dog, but not much else. She knew that was not what Ahmed was getting at. "Um, I grew up in the Presbyterian Church." *Somewhat,* she thought. But most

Americans say that sort of thing. Ahmed was struggling to comprehend. She added, "Presbyterians are a type of Christian." His face relaxed and smiled. "And you, Ahmed? Are you religious?"

"I am Muslim. That is why I have not heard the special words."

"Cool. You worked very hard to translate all those Christian questions." Ahmed translated what she said, and everyone laughed in agreement.

"Why did you and Betrose come to America? Did you come together?"

Ahmed put his hand on Betrose's shoulder. Betrose knew exactly what the gesture meant. "Betrose and me are old friends and we come to America for the peace." Liz nodded in sympathy. "We work to support our families at home."

Her watch confirmed her hunch that her limited time in the church was finished. "Well, I wish you both much success. It's been a great pleasure getting to know you. Thank you for taking the time to talk with me."

She urged Ahmed and Betrose to pose for a quick photograph. As she held her camera up, someone in the room offered to take the picture. A few yards behind her stood a white-bearded man in sturdy European sandals with a DSLR telephoto lens protruding off his barrel chest, his rosy-faced wife beside him. Liz happily accepted and wedged herself between the guys hanging their arms over each other's shoulders. When they posed for the camera, an elevating sensation tingled through her body. Between the three of them, harmony cut across languages and religion to create a moving, ecumenical experience. The feeling might be joy.

Following the portrait, they all shook hands goodbye, and the men excused themselves to return to their work. After reviewing the map once more, she left the church feeling profound hope for the world, which overpowered all the evidences of darkness on the street that otherwise would disturb her. Before rounding the corner of the block, she looked back at the noble tower, and the humble church at its feet, to seal into her memory the unobstructed view of these two places that had altered her view of humanity in a consequential way. It was clear why this city had the reputation for indelibly marking one's soul.

In a brisk stride, Liz weaved her way back to the hotel. She crossed the threshold of the lobby at 2:52 PM and sought the dozens of familiar faces on her tour. Her eyes roved the room bustling with hundreds of incoming and exiting travelers, her steps carefully avoiding the mounds of baggage congesting the floor, pardoning herself to tourist after sweaty tourist. Her gut began to quake, just a little, when she failed to spot a member of her tour. Two Tikiwaka coaches were parked in the bus lane beyond another set of doors and she figured that her group was loading. Outside the building, she discovered that one coach had just arrived, while the other was completely empty. The facts ignited alarm. Her tour may be gone.

Back inside, she rushed to the end of one of the eight lines at the elongated check-in desk. Liz felt increasing worry as the line haltingly inched forward with yawning hotel guests. If the coach left, what was she to do?

A hardened clerk headed her line at the reception desk. Liz said, "My name is Liz Lane. I'm on the Tikiwaka Tour *Roving America* which was supposed to leave at 2:50. I don't see any of my tour here. Did they change the departure time?"

The employee, weary from non-stop problem-solving performed for disorganized young people, repeated "Roving America" while referring to a paper out of Liz's view. "It arrived Tuesday the 2nd. Your guide is Maggie?"

Liz was rubbing her temples. "Yes."

"That tour left a half-hour ago, kid."

Liz's knees nearly buckled. "No! I was told to be here at 2:50! Why did it leave so early? That can't be right!"

The woman showed no sympathy. "It says here the departure time was 2:15. It left on time."

Liz's mouth hung open. Her breath was trapped in her throat. Perspiration broke out all over. "What do I do?" she squeaked.

"Don't you have a phone?" the woman retorted.

Liz knew how insane this would sound. "I don't have it with me."

The only indication of the woman's opinion was eyebrows raised high, waiting for the punch line. Liz's eyes sank to the surface of the counter. The woman resumed without emotion. "You can try to catch the tour in another town, or you can fly home. Or, stay here and see more of the city. Some people do that."

Liz felt profoundly dense for mishearing the time. She wanted to fume that the coach was not held for her, but she had been amply warned about the consequences of tardiness the entire tour. The woman detected the desire in

Liz to exact blame. "There's a bridge closure this weekend. All the tours are coming in and out of the city on time. It is what it is. Tough luck."

Reminded of the bridge closure, Liz was forced to accept reality; the tour was not to blame. Her inattention to Maggie's instruction was the reason. Feeling very low, she weakly asked, "How do I catch up with the tour?"

The woman sucked in some of the warm air to gain enough composure to help Liz. She flipped through a binder of timetables and searched a page with her boney finger. The woman looked up with no sign that her fossilized heart had cracked. "You have to catch the train to Greenville. The tour stays there tonight. It's back on the road tomorrow for another eight hours."

The solution seemed attainable. "Thank you very much." Liz sniveled away the postnasal drip of unshed tears. "Do you, by chance, have a timetable for the trains?"

The woman had anticipated this question and generously did not act more put out. In her straight-faced manner, she flipped to a different tab in the binder to find the rail timetables, and offered Liz the answer. "Only two trains go to Greenville each day: one leaves in the morning and one in the afternoon. The afternoon leaves at 3:55. It's a three-hour ride with one transfer. You've got to high-tail it out of here, kid, and get to the station."

Liz tried to compute how she would accomplish this with a tight budget and little knowledge of navigating the city. The woman already wise to Liz's naiveté pulled up the laminated copy of a city map on her desk and pointed on the map as she spoke. "You need to get to Union Station which is here. The hotel is here. Now, have you taken the subway?" Liz shook a forlorn no. "Then you don't know what to do. If you end up on the wrong line, you're toast. Just walk it. You'll die a little 'cause it's hotter than Hades out there, but you won't get lost. It's a direct route. Just stay on 3rd. I'll contact your tour and tell them to expect you at the station." Liz swallowed and nodded acceptance. "Now, get out of here."

Liz earnestly thanked the receptionist. When she turned away toward the multitude of travelers, assuming to sprint, the woman warned, "And don't run because those shoes aren't Len Matteos and you ain't catchin' a cab. You'll look like a stupid tourist. Next!"

Well chastened, Liz bolted for the doors and obediently slowed to speed walking once out on the sidewalk. This time on the street, she was neither a wide-eyed innocent nor a world-wise participant. Rather, she was a desperate fool on the cusp of Tikiwaka ignominy. With a pace slowed only by "Don't Walk" in red, Liz marched straight up the avenue, barely flinching to see the places and faces around her, completely withdrawn, thinking only of making the train on time. She was heedless of the living statues of gold and silver, the pigeons, the violinist, the beggars, and the stands of knock-off goods. The gusts of wind and darkening skies drew no notice. The hundreds of passersby would think her a seasoned citizen with such force of spirit and disregard for the city itself, carried forward by a visibly locked jaw.

It may have been two miles covered before the façade of Union Station came into view. Her heart scuttled when she saw the unbecoming industrial building, in great need of cleaning. The sight of commuters under similar pressure to meet a train quickened her pace to a jog. Rain began to spit from the gathering clouds above. Running fit the context of the scene.

Aboard an escalator plunging into the bowels of the train station, lower, lower, bumped by black-clad youth chasing each other and by suited commuters cutting through the steady stream of unaffected, forward stares, she felt the intensity of the city compound as the long escalators descended below ground. Arriving on the level of the station with a wall full of ticket windows, she maneuvered away from the bottleneck of the escalators to the hub of the space. The low concrete ceiling surprised her senses. She had presumed most train stations featured soaring, airy ceilings and windows with rows of mullions, but this place was compressed, hot, and cast in the green glow of artificial lighting.

The arms of the station fanned out like a tiled asterisk. Bodies crisscrossed in all directions, determined and impatient. She moved around the urgent foot traffic and anchored one of the ticketing lines. The roar of the trains and the muffled announcements over the intercom amplified the noise in her mind rather than drowned it out. In such a turbulent environment, could she acquire the ticket and board the train on time? Then what? Find a flight home. The tour company would not coordinate another connection.

Every line seemed to move faster than hers. Unhappy complaints shouted through the ticket window indicated that time would further burn. When the lead customer finally stormed off, her line moved forward with evenness until her turn. She stated her destination, and the purchase of the ticket went quietly until the attendant gave brief directions through the glass. Liz asked, "What?" twice. The woman answered, but Liz could not hear. The peeved pout of the attendant forced out Liz's thanks.

Walking back into the commotion, she examined her ticket for the platform and departure time for her train. The information was clear on the ticket, but the station signage was not. She looked at the placards above her head—some pointing away to the branching ells, some pointing up escalators, some pointing down—the information was incomprehensible in her panicked state. The station was so vast and crowded that only the veterans knew how to navigate it. She reexamined the time; the clock on the wall was a minute faster than her watch. The train would be gone before she could grasp where to go. Irritated expressions of "excuse me" and other censure bit her ears, insinuating that she, the green outsider, was impeding the flow of the city. Embarrassment worsened her emotional state. The tour guide, the coach driver, her travelling companions—all would be baffled at her, and annoyed that she inconvenienced the tour. So stupid. The shame.

Her eyes kept skimming over the signs, when a presence, head-to-toe in navy blue, filled her peripheral vision. "Can I help you, miss?" the observant, stocky cop asked.

Fireworks of hope burst within her. "Please! I don't know where to get my train!" she said, pinching her ticket.

He took the ticket, and with a millisecond glance at the strip of paper, he grabbed her arm and pulled her forward. "Come on!"

He darted towards one of the hallways. She tried to follow. The backpack hindered her agility, and he paused to peel the load off her back. "We can make it. Let's go!"

Freed from the weight, she perused him down the long passage, jogging around a blind corner. The police escort parted the human traffic with orders to gangway. The lengthy corridor opened to multiple platforms. She saw in the distance a train filling with passengers, and sensed it was their target. After taking a final peek back to ensure Liz was with him, the officer dashed for the vacating platform and hopped through the threshold of a car's sliding doors, knocking her backpack through the interior of the train. He reached behind to put a hand on her shoulder, and guided her to an open seat while the calls for departure echoed. He rested the backpack onto her lap, flashed a benevolent smile at her, and worked his way through the density of bodies to the door.

Sweat dotted her brow. Her gratitude was overwhelming. "How can I ever thank you?" Liz called out to her ministering angel. The spectacle had all passengers attentive to the exchange between her disheveled, panting self and the officer.

The cop turned back to her before stepping onto the platform and yelled, "Don't ever forget me."

The doors closed. The train rolled away.

When the tower came crashing down the following week, the officer's words replayed in her memory as a request for immortality, which served to uplift her on days when she needed purpose.

10

Air Pressure

"You worry too much," Logan complained. "I know cars."

"A belt is holding up the exhaust. There is no traction on the tires," his sister pointed out, again.

"There is traction. Don and I checked the tires and they are fine."

"I saw Washington's head. We are driving a thousand miles on slicks."

Logan sucked in extra air to pull back his rejoinder. The young man wisely guessed that Mercedes' worry was not over the condition of the car, but rather over the reason for driving it. "Sade, I know your safety class said to use a quarter to check tread, but that's a manufacturer shtick to sell more tires. A penny is the standard, and the tires are fine. Come on. Let's stay positive. Don would not put us on the road in something he didn't trust."

Mercedes conceded with silence. She turned her head to the passenger window and dimmed into a trance as the endless acres of grape vines darted by, row upon row, with large piles of dehydrating grapes at their bases. To see millions of raisins under the sun, open for the taking, undisturbed by anyone, there was a slight shift to wonder within Mercedes for the seconds she wove the thought together. The lightness passed as swiftly as it came, and the sullen realities of the frailty of life returned.

In a Nova with no air conditioning, the brother and sister withered under the 115°F heat of central California. Windows remained rolled up since the air burned skin blowing in at 85 mph. The air flowing from the floor vents at their ankles and from the petite triangle vent windows circulated the otherwise stifling atmosphere of the car, but no less drained them of all energy. The monstrous engine under the hood earned the respect of everyone who appreciated cars. But such a machine produced a deafening roar, particularly since the car had no muffler, over which it was difficult to talk without raising one's voice. Were it not for the overhead shade of the car, Mercedes surmised she would be just like those raisins, immobile and shriveling under the broiling sun.

Far in the distance, high above the pavement, yellow arches formed through the heat warping the atmosphere and hailed relief to the travelers. In the refrigerator of a dining room, they downed their third soft-serve cone of the day and used the restroom of the fast food joint. Ten minutes later, the bellowing Nova ascended the on-ramp to resume the eighteen-hour drive.

Familial obligation had inspired the trip. As a consequence of challenging occupations in his past, Uncle Don had scarred lungs and faced late-in-life lung disease. Despite the wide ranges in life expectancy proposed by various doctors, the feeling among family members was, by the look of him, he would not last the fall. The siblings made the midsummer drive to a small, far-flung country town in the lower reaches of California's breadbasket to pay their respects to his cognizant corpse—a talking, wheezing, bony shadow of the one-time adventurer. He was never a playful or an attentive relative, but he made gestures toward his nieces and nephews that indicated his fondness. One such act was the bequeathing of his rusty Nova to his car-loving nephew. The siblings had anticipated this gift, and took one-way flights to visit their uncle, knowing that the drive home would be in the undistinguished, beloved vehicle. Logan had eyed the Nova for many years with obvious longing, and Uncle Don knew it was time to set the vehicle free from its carport coffin and bequeath it one who was determined to give it a new life.

To his niece, Uncle Don gave his old acoustic guitar. He had often played it by campfires at infrequent family reunions and holidays. Mercedes was not a musician, but she did request that Don play the instrument for her. As thanks for the years of her ear, he had rested the guitar into its case and packed it into the trunk of the Nova, minutes before the two departed. During the decline of Don's health, the neck had become curved from resting too long on a wall, causing the wires to hit the frets. Even if Mercedes did invest to restore the six-string, she could not say to what purpose. In any condition, it would remain as quiet as her uncle would be in a few months.

Witnessing Uncle Don purposefully rid himself of the objects that expressed his life, imbued the farewell with morbidity. Uncle Don was not sad, but the siblings took these gifts with reluctance. Forcing him to keep these objects would not sustain his life, but the exchange seemed to commence his funeral. Both wanted to cry with sorrow rather than joy, to have the Nova and guitar. Instead, they managed to reflect the business mind of Don, following his usual stoic lead.

From the rolling, thunderous car, the niece and nephew waved dolefully to their uncle standing sentinel in his oneness, tethered to his burden of oxygen, tanked and wheeled at his side. The tears and the reminiscing bubbled out within the confines of the car as the Nova entered the long, dusty gravel lane that traveled an eighth of a mile to the rambler. They took one last long look at the sprawling farm that was once lush with life. The drought and the water laws had sapped the income from the farm, and forced their uncle into an early retirement. With his lungs in free fall, Uncle Don quit the agricultural grind, and sought a buyer. No more family memories would be made there.

Mercedes and Logan were quiet much of the drive, listening to the fuzzy emissions of the ancient radio. The Nova sped northward up the freeway, moving out of the flat, arid farmlands, into the greenery of the Sacramento area, then over the inclines of the Siskiyou Pass. They stopped for lunch and dinner at forgettable dives and pressed on through Oregon. The environment became more familiar as the road wove through evergreens under clouded skies. Windows were rolled down to take in the crisp air, tinted with moisture. With four hours to go, they crossed the vast Columbia River and caught a glimpse of the grey, asymmetrical peak of Mt. St. Helens as they hummed up the interstate. The sinking sun was setting an orange glow over the flat terrain of Centralia. Summers in Washington State were tolerable, and often heavenly. The pronounced change in conditions made the three days of incessant perspiring on Uncle Don's farm seems like weeks ago.

The typical congestion of Western Washington greeted the grill of the Nova when they entered the Puget Sound area. Bumper-to-bumper traffic clustered around Olympia, Tacoma, and Seattle. It was in the dark of night when they broke free from the Seattle traffic, and resumed a swift pace to their destination of Everett, forty minutes yet away.

It was at that point that the windows were rolled up. A homecoming rain blew in from the coast. The drop in temperatures was precipitous, and thunder rumbled by as the cold and warm air clashed in the sky. Logan felt around for the wipers and set the squeaky arms to task. Mercedes was stirred awake by the pinging of rain on the hollow car that managed to sound through the blare of the engine. "I see signs that we are almost home," she sighed. "I cannot wait to get out of this car."

"I'm glad the entire drive was not like this. The wipers are so old, they are nearly worthless," Logan said. The wipers moved the water into arcs rather than clearing the windshield for visibility. The traffic was widely spread apart on the freeway at the late hour, so the two felt relatively at ease despite the deluge. The headlights worked well, and the car showed no signs of fatigue as it barreled vigorously up the freeway.

Flashing briefly and indistinctly, distorted by the smeared rain on the glass, it almost looked like two white lights in the distance were streaking across the siblings' lane of the freeway. Mercedes was too groggy for the instant variation in the scattering of red tail lights to alarm her, but her brother's breath was caught when his brain in bullet-fast calculation detected eminent danger. For less than a second, the headlights of the Nova illuminated the passenger door of a white car. There was no time to break. The cars were too close. No time for screaming. The wheel was gripped. The cars collided. All went black.

One, two, three, four, five, six vehicles crushed against each other, vaulting metal and glass over the ink-black freeway. The siblings were found slumped in the front seats, blood spattered and dripping from cuts, their breathing uneven. The first responders extricated the two young adults from under the cache of construction materials that had flung from the back of a truck, riddled the windows, and penetrated the interior of the car. Metal flashing was gouged into Logan's abdomen and it required the uttermost expertise to recover the young man and send him to the hospital in a viable condition. His sister was less harmed, but no less unconscious of the calamity. No whirling sirens, shouting, pouring rain, or bright lights stirred the siblings. The two were ferried to the trauma center incognizant of the proficient hands applying medical equipment to their bodies.

Six days passed before Logan's eyes fluttered open to the sight of a masked nurse smiling down at him. The hospital room was unfriendly in its rigid whiteness and cold stainless steel, but the warmth of the nurse welcoming him back to life overrode the sterility of the room.

"What happened?" Logan managed to whisper.

"You survived a car accident."

Logan closed his eyes to remember. The freeze-framed image that came to mind was the broad side of a white car in mid-spin. His eyes popped open wildly. "Mercedes?"

"She's just fine. She fared better than you. She was battered and bruised, but she's up walking and feeling better."

"Thank God," he exhaled. "Can I see her?"

"Yes," answered the nurse. "She asked to be the first to see you. Your mother is here, but she understands that Mercedes should see you first." Logan wrinkled his brow at this. The nurse continued in response, "You almost did not make it, sir. You are under strong painkillers, so you cannot know that your abdomen was perforated in the accident. You lost your liver, sir, and have undergone a transplant. You are one of the luckiest fellas in intensive care this week."

Logan wondered if the drugs were affecting his comprehension. "I got a transplant? Seriously?"

The nurse laid her gloved hand on his arm to calm him. "Your sister will come in as soon as we get her robed and masked. It won't be long."

As Logan waited for his sister, he attempted to raise his hand to touch his stomach. But they were resting on the blankets and strung up by tubes to the various dangling pouches about him. He was too exhausted to sense time.

His sister did arrive, fully covered in germ-free layers. Tears were cresting and creeping down her cheeks behind the mask. "Logan!" she wept, "I am so glad you are awake. We thought we were going to lose you."

"Did I really get a transplant?"

At this, the young woman's voice cracked into audible crying. She suppressed her urge to unload in sobs, and collected herself. "Logan, I am here to share something with you. It's a letter."

"A letter? To me? From whom?"

"Just listen," she said, and peered down at the hotel letterhead encased in sanitary plastic.

To Logan and Mercedes,

Do not be sad for me, kids. I know this is difficult for you. I hope to explain things in a way that you might feel the joy that I do.

I did not think of fatherhood until I was certain my health was ending my life. I feel no regret, but I am conscious of not having experienced something that most men do. When I heard that you needed help to live, I was sure of my responsibility. What I have gained in this action is the fulfillment akin to fatherhood. From my own flesh and blood, I give life. To think that this failing body could sustain life is marvelous to me. I live through my worthy nephew as fathers live through their children. Saving your life will bring more generations of our family into this beautiful, wondrous earth. My last breaths are filled with purpose. I need no more days in this world.

Do not worry about Ol' Ruby. Decades ago, I souped her up with that roll cage. How glad I am that she protected you in the accident. Remove her "organs" and she can live through another Nova in need of parts. She and I leave this life protecting and serving. My joy is full.

Live on.
Uncle Don

11

Rodent Love

"In the last two nights, I've gotten maybe a total of seven hours of sleep. I could divorce you for dragging me here at this hour." Serenity was holding her arm in an achy kink to avoid someone's double-wide stroller crammed between two rows of knees.

Chase was impervious. "Sleep is overrated. I told you, we need to be here an hour before it opens to get a spot in the garage, load the tram, and clear security. Besides, the heat hits at about 11:00, so it's critical to get through the gate as early as possible."

"What an unsexy start to our honeymoon. We should be in our birthday suits until 1:00, and then, maybe, think about coming here after room service." Two sets of parents sent glares their direction at Serenity's indifference to privacy.

Chase brushed off her comment. "Our honeymoon started eons ago in that department. The Crash! Oh, yeah! It's a monster! Check it out! A three-hundred-foot drop! We're going there first thing."

"That? No way. It cannot be the first ride. I'll be nauseous the rest of the day. Oh, pills. Shoot. Do you have water?"

"No. Look!" Chase thumped her arm with the back of his hand. "There's Vampire Empire, that new 4-D ride that is blowing people's minds."

The unremarkable backside of the building did not divert Serenity. "I can't believe we forgot water," she said eyeing a sweaty, oversized rider taking a long pull of his water bottle.

The open-air tram stopped, and the couple ducked out with the hundred others struggling with daypacks and fussy kids. En masse, the riders left the tram area and clamored for the gates located 200 yards away.

The phone stuffed deep in Chase's pocket jingled a peppy similitude of a movie anthem, and he answered it sounding very close to giddy, "Yeah! OK, you're there. Hang on. We just got off the tram. We'll be in there in two minutes. We just passed the fountain. Oh, hey, I see you. Whoa! Neon! Nice! OK. Bye."

The new husband swerved ahead of his wife and picked up pace. "Come on!" he goaded. A new layer of annoyance put Serenity at risk of falling into peevishness. Even so, the promised fun in the cheeriest place on earth should not be dashed by the enthusiasm of her husband, she decided. He stopped at a group of people, all but one sharing his height, each sporting green neon shirts printed with a black rat silhouette in front, and words on the back side reading "The Hardy Party." As a thank-you for the Hardy sponsorship of the majority of the wedding expenses, Chase had welcomed his family to join the newlyweds on their honeymoon. Serenity had obliged, for few gestures could reciprocate as meaningfully to the Hardys as this invitation. The groom doled out hugs to the circle, then turned back to Serenity with his hand making a brusque summons.

The eldest and shortest female of the group, Sheryl, completely filled out her full-sized t-shirt bearing her name. Rat-shaped jewelry dangled from within her blonde, fluffy, feathered hair coaxed by hot-rollers. A sequined lanyard was the dazzling vaunt of her years attending Sidney Adventures Theme Park. She threw her thick arms around Serenity and squished her to her ample bosom. "There's the beautiful bride! Did you sleep well? Here's your shirt, darling. You are so petite; I hope it's not too big. Rook, hand me the lanyard. Where'd I put the earrings? Oh, here, in my pocket. These are for you, kiddo. Look! We match! And how cute is this? A little rat tail with some bows. It hooks to your shirt in the back. See mine? Don't you just love it? I got one for everyone with their names embroidered. You guys! Put them back on! My word, it's hot. I'm pitting out already. Serenity, there's the restroom so you can change. We'll get a spot in line. Brad, hand me the mister."

Serenity thanked her mother-in-law and walked to the restrooms as the commanding voice of her father-in-law, Gary, issued directives to the most efficient line according to the insiders' blog his second-born, Rook, had reviewed.

After changing into the shirt and popping a pill to prevent motion sickness, Serenity exited the restroom and sighted her husband's family in overstated green with the other thousands simultaneously encroaching on the gates. The bickering among the siblings was detectable over the squabble of the enormous crowd. She had not completely recovered from the early alarm and spastic rush to leave the hotel on the first day of her honeymoon, but her mood seemed far better than the contentious siblings arguing over the first object of the day. Today was her first real taste of the renowned Hardy passion for Sidney Adventures.

The closer the family came to entering their Mecca, the more unrecognizable her husband became. "It's a stupid idea. I'm not waiting another minute to ride The Crash. It's the best ride here."

"No, man! Vampire Empire. It just opened. If we are going to ride it more than once, then we have to get Rat Passes. Rook and James can do that. You, Reny, and the rest get in line at Vampire and hold a place. We'll meet you there after we get the passes." A Rat Pass enabled the possessor to enter an exclusive line to board an attraction within minutes rather than hours.

"No! We head straight to the back of the park for The Crash and beat the crowds who do the rides at the front of the park in the morning. The line for it will be insane if we wait. Crash first."

Serenity piped in, "I'm not sure I can do The Crash yet, Chase."

"What's that?" Chase looked like he forgot she had come with them. "Oh, you'll be fine!"

"Listen to your shackles, man. Vampire. We've got to get the Rat Passes this morning. I'm riding that more than once. Everyone says it's sick."

The strategizing continued like a tennis match over the park entrance procedures. With epitomic cordiality, the park employee smiled at them freshly bleached teeth as she scanned the passes of the debaters within which the new wife was wedged. "Thank you, Serenity!" said the gatekeeper, the first of perfect strangers invited by her t-shirt to greet her like an acquaintance.

Once all were inside the park, Sheryl and Gary considered options for a snack. Maybe the Hardy Party needed a little pick-me-up. The heads of the family left for a corner store yards away on Avenue America, the initial setting of the park that mimicked the central street of a quintessential Midwestern town from a forgotten era. Meanwhile, Serenity's attention ping-ponged between the four siblings, whose bickering canopied overhead.

Jamie, the youngest of the four at a fresh nineteen, had just dyed her hair black to rid herself of the burden of blond. The males of the pack vied for her vote, and she offered plenty of heat. "The Vampire Empire line is already clogged. We've done The Crash lots of times. We have to go now to the Wartsmead Castle in Wizzarlund! We won't be able to do the broom ride there if we wait till this afternoon!"

Gary and Sheryl's return disrupted the argument. "OK, kiddos! Here's some licorice tails. Brad, pass them out. And I bought new pins for the lanyards! Honey, can you hand me the other bag? Look at these, guys. I had to have them: Sidney signature earmuffs! On sale! Won't that be fun for winter? Have you guys decided where we are going first?"

As the purchases circled around, throngs of people passed them by, and the siblings accused each other of damming progress to the rides. Gary had suffered the disunity long enough. "OK, now, settle down. I think the newlyweds should pick the first stop. It's their honeymoon after all. What's it going to be?"

"That's right," Chase agreed, "Crash it is." The siblings groaned in unison.

"Reny, is that where you want to go, honey?" Sheryl asked, reading Serenity correctly.

"I will seriously puke if I ride that now," replied the grateful daughter-in-law.

Sheryl addressed the audible pouting from her son. "Chase! Hush! Be good to your bride! We can wait a little; you know we'll ride The Crash today. Let's make sure Reny's alright. Sweets, where do you wish to go?"

Feeling very much like the thorn in everyone's side, hoping to make at least someone happy, she selected the option that was all the rage. Knowing that it was some kind of fully-enclosed cinema experience, the attraction appeared to be a safer choice to avoid nausea than the rollercoasters in the park. "Vampire Empire sounds interesting. I would be OK with that."

"Yeah, baby!" Brad pumped a bulky arm. The decision muted further debate and launched a half-mile of powerwalking to the touted ride. The mood of the family swung into an eager anticipation, and for Serenity, ended the toppling dominoes of irritants since her early rise. This was the turning point of the day, and Serenity was committed to mirroring the peppiness of the park and embracing the experience.

The darting collective of neon green maneuvered past strollers and tottering grandparents left behind by the masses of youth and the able-bodied sprinting for the popular rides. Half skipping to keep up with the long strides of the family, Serenity hoped that there would be some time over the next three days to browse the interiors of the charming facades of the varied shops along Avenue America. The smells of caramel, popcorn, and cotton candy wafted from the confectionery. The park workers on the street were dressed in classic whites and gingham posing as shopkeepers, a postman, an organ grinder, and a flower vendor. A trolley wobbled by full of patrons attempting their third day. The street felt like a movie set, but beckoned none of the Hardys except the newest member.

Their crowd maneuvering brought them to a district that simulated the rural Northwest. A contrived logging town sat on the bank of a manmade river, which body of water featured a leisurely ride on a barge for fifty riders per circuit. Vendors offered elk burgers, salmon filets, and side dishes rich in berries. Noises from the gun gallery and the ATV track mixed with country tunes performed by plaid-clad musicians inside a rustic barn. Soaring pines laced with artificial moss framed the concrete pathways leading to the various attractions.

As they moved through the center of the "town," the siblings began to point up to the top floor of a façade of a two-storied mercantile. Ignorant to what could be noteworthy of such a location, Serenity pulled on Chase's arm and interrupted him mid-sentence. "What are you guys pointing at?"

Chase spoke in oddly hushed tones, "Oh, that's Tavern 22. It's this exclusive restaurant that you have to know certain Sidney employees to gain access. See that gray steel side door that doesn't look like anything? That's the entrance. The food is stupid expensive, like two hundred bucks per person. We are so going there. We just need to get our in."

Serenity gathered that the "we" referred to his co-conspirators, and tried to not take it personally. To penetrate such a Sidney mystery had yet to become her dream.

The group arrived at the cattle gates guiding the line for Vampire Empire, and it was at this point that the strategists divvied up the responsibilities of who would get the Rat Passes and who would hold a place in line. The method would ensure two rides on the attraction that day. The wait for the ride was already an hour and a half, and the Rat Pass line was an estimated 30 minutes. The group split up, and Serenity remained at her husband's side with his parents. While the four slowly inched forward up the line, Chase thumbed his smart phone non-stop, proposing further maneuverings for the day as he checked the wait times for rides and evaluated food options. Gary wiped his vanishing hairline as he critiqued the schemes, nixing anything that sounded like fluff. Sheryl speculated often on the exact temperature and interjected strong opinions on the next meal. Employing her skills as a receptionist, Sheryl entertained Serenity with happy and harmless chitchat with a brand of warmth that always left recipients feeling valued.

Much to everyone's surprise, in short of half an hour, Rook, Brad, and Jamie could be seen pardoning themselves up the cattle gates threaded through the artificial woodland. Fisting an inordinate number of Rat Passes in her hand, Jamie trumpeted the blessed encounter with a large group which gave them their Rat Passes precisely for that time slot because, to the Hardy's good fortune, many of the would-be riders had come down with a debilitating case of the runs and needed to vacate the park. The Hardys immediately abandoned the regular line, and negotiated a blanket of ferns to the cattle gates for Rat Pass holders. In minutes, they had bounded past hundreds of the unlucky, and were soon snapping belts across their laps. Serenity could not help but feel the thrill of the windfall, and was high-fiving with everyone. Chase and Serenity shared a moment of hugging and laughing. This was what Sidney Adventures was all about. This was magical!

The movie attraction was not a stationary cinema experience as expected, but rather it surprised with a swift electromagnetic vehicle that climbed, dove, spun and retreated. On giant screens, the senses were bombarded with realistic visuals of speeding through woodlands, gliding over gray cold beaches, and climbing unreachable places. Assorted fragrances filled their noses such as briny sea wind, luscious evergreen, and a hit of wet dog. The most bewildering effects were the kinetic elements of misting rain from above, the sweltering heat of fire, frigid blasts on their stony cold seats, and the splattering of "blood." The simulator was a technical masterpiece, and was unspeakably thrilling. The Hardys applauded the ride at its end, and piled out with bouncy quickness, leaving behind a slumped Serenity at the back of the car. Jamie, being second to last to exit, saw her sister-in-law's gray countenance and hailed back the departing group already recounting the moment the ride inexplicably made their skin glitter.

"Crap!" Chase blurted, "This ain't good. James, help me get her out." The brother and sister coaxed a nauseated and unsteady Serenity out of the car and escorted her out of the building where they plopped her on the nearest bench. In a slumberous slouch across the planks, Serenity produced faint, woozy groans. Chase knew better than to express hope that Serenity would recover in a few minutes. Still fresh in his memory was that turbulent jet ride last summer when his bride regurgitated an entire personal pan pizza into a paper bag. Not pretty. "We should get her in the shade to recover. She'll need a little time. Let's take her to The Fishing Derby to cool off and rest."

The Hardy Party was on hiatus. Unless...

"Hey, Mom!" Chase went on, "Would you get in line for food while she holds the table? She can't do The Troller. If we use the one-rider line, I think the rest of us could do that in the meantime. Reny, you're looking a little green. Feeling pretty bad, eh? I know you want to lie here, but we need to get out of the sun. Here's my hat. I'm going to pack you to a restaurant and you can just chill, there. OK? I'll take that moan as a yes. Guys, help me get her on my back."

Chase backpacked his listless load to the open-air restaurant that had growing lines in front of an understaffed counter. Sidney Adventures was known for decent, pricey food served at a perplexingly slow pace. In the nick of time, Serenity stretched out on a bench in The Fishing Derby, which effectively snatched the table away from a large family, uniformed in tie-dye, zooming across the sprawling counter restaurant to claim it. The Hardys were relieved to dump their belongings onto the seats and have Serenity remain as an occupant. Sheryl wished the others a good time and assumed the last place in the order line which had lengthened far beyond the expansive shelter.

The Troller injected the riders full of adrenalin with a knotty ride that crisscrossed over the river, threaded the trees, and curved behind a man-made waterfall. Within an hour, the siblings and their father returned to a table full of food, and Sheryl's welcome of eager questions.

Chase was pleased to see Serenity upright, quietly ingesting crackers and sips of lemon-lime soda. "Reny! You're up! We just did The Troller. No doubt, you would have hurled after that one. Nothing but corners and G's. It's cool that you could hold the table, though. Rook, did you check the wait for The Crash? Hour and a half? Perfect. Reny will be alright by then. Let's eat quick and get out of here." Serenity was feeling foggy-headed enough to accept the plan with a droopy shrug. In haste, the crew downed their meal and departed the restaurant.

For the first time that day, Chase trekked beside Serenity at a reasonable pace in guilty awareness of her less-than-optimal morning. After adding themselves to the line for The Crash, the siblings and Gary launched into a profoundly specific comparison of world-class coasters to the notorious one they were about to ride. Chase defended the status of The Crash as the top coaster while Serenity silently analyzed the flower beds where there appeared to be edible mixed greens. Ever mindful of social inclusion, Sheryl managed to veer the discussion into a full review of the wedding and reception. On that subject, Serenity contributed, and could feel the smallest return of the man she wed two days before.

Finally, the long pilgrimage to the front of the ride ended. They boarded the inverted electromagnetic coaster in orderly fashion with hoots and hollers from the Hardy pack. Serenity's seat was on the edge of the row next to Chase, Jamie, and Brad. The ride attendant checked that harnesses were secure and delivered over the intercom the usual list of safety rules with airline attendant plasticity.

With a piqued smile, Serenity said to her husband, "You owe me big after this. Big. I dread this as much as you dread a baby shower."

"Apples and oranges. Hey! No hands, guys! Spread 'em! That's how we do it!"

Enough time had passed that Serenity was confident that the motion-sickness pills were in effect. The infectious buzz of her husband inspired her to end the wimpy chapter of her day. "You're on. In fact, I'll top that. Legs locked!"

Chase pumped his fists and rallied, "Yes! That's my girl! Let's do this thing! Woo-hoo!"

His siblings likewise cheered the commencement of the ride. Without a jerk, the train darted forward and reached 60 mph in two ferocious seconds. The skin on their cheeks stretched back uncomfortably as the coaster climbed a few hundred feet to a staggering height. The whole Hardy clan was yelping in anticipation of the drop. The coaster slowed at the top and then dove down a terrifying incline the length of a football field, and then threw the occupants into wild twists, inversions, hills, and barrel rolls. Serenity forced her arms and legs to defy g-forces at full extension. The brothers were roaring war cries for battle. The coaster flipped through an art deco cityscape, wrapping around towering faux buildings and the coiffured gardens of a large city park. At some indeterminate millisecond, a fiery sensation lit Serenity's toe, which was mildly distracting when all other aspects of her person were under the duress of the physics of the ride. The train slowed to a graceful halt.

Chase belted praises for the ride. "Oh yeah! That was epic!"

Serenity's attention began to collect to her right foot which was growing acidly hot in the toe. After reclaiming her flip-flops, she limped off the ride to a bench out of the way of the exiting masses. The sight of her foot upon close examination was nothing short of appalling. "Oh, my gosh. Oh, my gosh!" Serenity swallowed. "My toe! My toe! Oh no!"

Chase stood above her, restoring his cap back onto his head, elbow to elbow with his exuberant siblings. "What, baby? Your toe hurts? Need a Band-Aid?"

"Band-Aid? My toe is gone! It's gone!"

"It's gone?" Chase's head tipped to view her foot. "Oh, whoa. That's weird. When did that happen?"

231

"Just now! On the ride! It happened on the ride!" The rest of the family leaned in and looked at her foot clutched in her hand. What they saw was her big toe with the tip severed off flat, exactly at the end of her toenail. It was not bleeding, but was crimson, as if seared off with a red-hot knife.

Assorted responses piped in from the Hardy Party. "That's wicked looking, man." "Poor, Reny! What a horrible thing to have happened!" "It's not bleeding. That's kind of cool." "Oh, sweetie. Are you in a lot of pain? Can I get you an aspirin? Maybe there's Neosporin at the gift shop." "Move your head. I can't focus the phone." "How did she do that, anyway?" "Stop bumping me. I can't get the shot." "Here, honey. There's aloe in my lip gloss." "Can she walk? We've got to use our Rat Passes right now."

Chase stood up at this call to leave, and eyeballed the passes in Rook's hand to return to Vampire Empire. His loyalties were split in two with his wife in near hysterics and his siblings insisting that the group meet their reservation.

Gary was never one to treat a female like a girl. "Ah, she's tough. She can walk it off. Right, James?"

Jamie was accustomed to meeting her father's coaching standards for toughness. She had "walked off" many an injury, but taking his side would be deadly in sister-in-law protocol. "I don't know, Dad," she replied with a worried face.

"Sure, baby! You can walk it off. It's not a huge deal. It's not bleeding."

"Chase! How could you say that! My toe is gone!" Serenity shouted.

Gary touched Chase's arm to signal that they were leaving. The newlyweds needed time to themselves, evidently. Chase implored his father to give him another minute. Gary resisted the pleas, and with a not-so-subtle push of his hand on a couple of backs, moved the rest of the Hardy Party to return to Vampire Empire.

Watching his family walk away further agitated Chase into sorting out the situation with his new wife, who was crying convulsively over her mangled toe. "How could this have happened?" Chase asked kneeling in front of her.

"I don't know! On one of the corners, I felt this stinging feeling and that's all!"

"How did you have your legs?"

"Like this." She spread her arms apart in a V shape.

"You mean your legs were past the side of the coaster?"

"Yes, and—"

"Reny! You are supposed to keep your hands and feet inside the coaster! Not hanging off the side!"

"My feet were dangling! There's no car to put them in!"

"But your feet were past the side of the coaster! Why would you do that?"

"Chase! Nothing should have hit my foot! That ride is poorly designed!"

"No, Reny!" Chase hollered. "It's totally your fault! You should not have put your foot outside the line of the seats! I can't believe you did that!"

"Don't blame me! I did nothing wrong! Anyone could do what I did! Anyone could lose their toe! We should sue Sidney Adventures. They destroyed my toe!"

"Your toe is not destroyed. It's fine! Only the tip is gone. You can still walk."

"It's deformed! I can never wear sandals again!"

"It's hardly noticeable. My feet aren't perfect and I still wear sandals."

Serenity scowled at Chase's left foot, which had malformed, yellowed, curling toenails from years of untreated toenail fungus. "Your foot is disgusting and everyone wishes you'd cover it up!"

"Everyone is used to it and nobody gives a rip."

Her ire bubbled over. "Your foot grosses me out. And now my foot grosses me out. And you don't care at all!"

Realizing their exchange had become a scene, Chase begged softly with open hands. "Baby, we've got to leave or we are going to miss the time slot for our Rat Passes. Your foot looks OK. I promise!"

"I don't care about that ride! We must tell The Crash attendants that my toe was cut off by that stupid coaster and is somewhere on the ground. I want my toe back!"

Chase sensed that reasoning with her would only continue to escalate the argument. "OK. Listen, I'll talk to someone." She let go of her wrath and began to sob at his first true act of support for her in the predicament. "You sit here. Just calm down, please, Reny. We'll work it out."

Chase shot up and jogged back to speak with one of the attendants. She toggled between her downsized toe and

Chase deliberating with the attendant who eyed her during the exchange. Chase returned to report, "I don't know that there's much to be done. We have no way of proving how your toe looked before the ride. And you don't know how it happened, or where it happened on the ride."

"Of course he would say that! I want to go to the lost and found and report it! They'll find it and prove me right!"

It took everything in Chase to bite back the accusation that she was delusional, and his voice was drenched in exasperation. "What are you going to say? 'I'm missing the top of my toe. Give me a fan deck and I'll find a paint color that matches it. It's shriveled like a raisin and it's laying somewhere under The Crash. And, by the way, I'll sue you when you give it back to me.'" Serenity gave in to reason and wailed at the truth. "Anyway, a bird probably ate it by now." Serenity wailed again into her hands. Chase smacked his head at his miscalculation. "Forget that! I'm sure nothing ate it." A text dinged on Chase's phone. He checked it. The family was cruising up the Rat Pass line. "Reny, we are not in Sidney Adventures that long and it's our honeymoon. If we hurry, we can ride Vampire and get back to having a good time. Your foot doesn't look that bad, I promise!"

"I can't even walk, Chase! How can I run? I can't even stand, my toe burns so bad!"

Chase stuffed the rat tail hanging from his shirt into his back pocket. "I'll carry you. On my back, please!"

Glowering still, she climbed on Chase's back and he jogged her through many acres of the muggy amusement park. Anxious to get in line, his increasing impoliteness signified to Serenity that her husband was morphing back into the Sidney-obsessed foreigner the closer he got to Vampire Empire. In between commands to the people he skirted around, under his breath he added, "Geriatrics blocking the way. Get that kid on a leash! Strollers should be on the right. Don't these people drive?" Serenity sensed that his momentary sympathy for her was to meet his own selfish ends. Maybe the two should take a break from each other.

Unwilling to contend with Chase while he was under the Sidney influence, she commanded, "Stop, Chase. I don't feel like going on another ride right now. Put me down and leave me here. You go ahead."

"Oh, really?" Chase seemed eager to be relieved of his equine duty. "OK, then, if you want."

He deposited Serenity on a bench when they entered the plaza in the heart of the amusement park. It was a beautiful location and less crowded because the lack of rides in that area. He kissed her forehead in thanks for releasing him to the ride. At full speed, he dodged strollers and nicked the sides of passing people while hailing his family on his cell. By the glow of his neon green t-shirt, she tracked him for quite a distance until he turned into the entrance of the logging town and disappeared into the density of moving bodies and pine trees.

Impeccably manicured gardens encircled her under the shadow of an enormous bubblegum pink castle appended with many turrets and towers. Everything was fantasy film splendor, yet Serenity felt ugly with her sunburnt face, obnoxious neon green t-shirt, and freakish toe. She was stunned by her desire to be alone, and moreover, having Chase so willing to oblige that desire. The bewilderment soon faded and she buckled into a lonely lament of her acquired imperfection and her husband's supersonic departure. Tears eked out of the corner of her eyes. She was a teenager the last time she had felt so childish. Cursed Sidney Adventures.

Love. That word. Early in their relationship, Serenity had told Chase she loved Sidney Adventures. She had visited the park at ages seven and fifteen. Both trips had created cherished memories. Animated Sidney musicals served as background noise while she toiled over hours of homework during junior college. To her declaration, Chase added, "I love Sidney Adventures, too!" By that happy subject, they forged another connection in their early stages of dating. However, when Serenity said she loved Sidney Adventures, she meant in the way one loves a glorious day hike. Evidently, when Chase said he loved Sidney Adventures, he meant in the way the NRA loves guns. One could not guess the depths of his passion until this immersive situation, which made his love for Serenity seem more like that for a day hike.

A multi-tiered fountain gurgled behind her in a petite artificial pond. Sparkling on each tier were foreign and domestic coins of every size. The soothing sounds turned her to the fountain and she pondered the meaning of the coinage. That tranquil place extracted from hundreds their deepest wishes. She reached into her bag with sulky slowness. For what did she wish? Her seared toe constantly burned during her ponderings. Her toe. She wanted her toe back, whole and complete. Beautiful feet. No scars. No evidence that the accident ever happened. Sidney Adventures, after all, promised to be the place where wishes came true.

She closed her eyes and almost flipped the coin into the water when it occurred to her. No. Not her toe. She could, eventually, with time, be fine without the tip of her toe. It was Chase. Nothing about this trip resembled a honeymoon, including the husband who accompanied her. She did not want to live out her life with the memory of Chase seeming to love Sidney Adventures more than her. Her wish was to have Chase pay complete and undeniable attention to her, above all others and above all rides. The coin was flicked in a perfect arc into the water, where its ripples joined other wavelets caused by the streams spurting from the fountain.

With eyes downcast to the ground in front of her, Serenity itemized all the disappointments of the day. In front of her flip-flops moved two elegantly shod feet at the base of maroon military slacks sheathing muscular legs. Her head jerked up to meet the decadent, ganache-tinted eyes of a tall, fit, and fine man in regalia. His thick Latin hair was styled in silky smoothness away from his high cheekbones. His commanding height looked to be poured into a white double-breasted jacket. A sash, sword, and velvet cape complemented the dashing gold details on his uniform.

Serenity blinked back her stupefaction as he smiled down at her, hand extended, and said with perfect charm, "Miss Serenity, may I be of help to you?" and bowed with practiced grace.

Her mouth formed an unconscious "o" for a couple of breaths as she took in this sumptuous vision. "I'm OK. I'm just staying off my feet for a little bit."

· "I see you are attending to your delicate foot. Are you hurt?"

Realizing how icky rubbing one's foot might appear to onlookers, she flushed and stammered, "Oh, no. I mean, yes, I did hurt my toe and it's quite sore. I just need to stay off it for a while."

The Enchanting Prince knelt before her in a grand way, sweeping back his cape, and settling on one knee. With a keen smile, he extended his hand to her foot and asked, "May I examine your wound, m' lady?"

Heat crept up her person as she lifted her foot to his manicured hands. Carefully, he cupped her heel and suppressed a wry face at the unnatural appearance of her big toe. "My, my. This is a grave affliction. Allow me, Miss Serenity, to render you aid. I have with me something that could be of assistance." He reached into his pressed jacket and pulled out pink Sidney-signature bandages dotted with sparkles and Sidney animated characters. Serenity giggled at him. He, in very serious tones, said, "I come to the rescue of many princesses in this place. So many lovely ladies incur injury and have need of care when traversing this terrain." Numbers of preschool girls skipping along the irregular cobbled pathways surrounding the castle, dressed as Sidney princess characters, passed them by. This was a very busy prince, indeed.

Serenity felt a million times better while she focused on this scrumptious gentleman wrapping her toe in two cutesy bandages. "Why, thank you, sir. You are so gallant." His dazzling, sexy smile met hers and he tipped his head in appreciation of her playing along. This clean-cut Sidney version of Chippendales she was enjoying every bit as much as the lap dances at her bachelorette party the previous week. "I'm glad I have nine more toes to damage," she cooed at him.

From behind them erupted a voice, "What the he— Get your hands off her!" The Enchanting Prince and Serenity snapped their head toward the sight of a wall of neon green headed by Chase in a furious stride. The prince kept his poise and rested her foot back down onto the flip-flop. Chase beat the rest of the Hardys to the bench and dumped a plastic bag of goods from his hand to prime his fist. "That's my wife's foot you were caressing," said Chase in lethal tones.

The prince stood perfectly in character and bowed significantly before Chase. "Your servant, sir. I was on my way to my kingdom when I came across your bride, to whom I offered the merest of assistance." The rest of the Hardys had reached the scene. The guys were annoyed, and the women were enthusiastically tapping touchscreens to focus their phones.

Chase was certain he saw his wife acting a little too happy with the guy. The jealousy fuming off Chase frightened Serenity, but the prince had a distinctive confidence about him. He looked directly at the husband with a mysterious smile and emphasized, "I assure you, we are *both* most happy to see your return." Chase searched the prince's expression which was framed by unnaturally sculpted eyebrows.

Serenity waved her right foot at her husband. "Chase, it's OK. He just bandaged my toe. See?"

Chase peeled his eyes off of the royal to confirm the claim. He looked back at the prince and said reluctantly, "Thanks."

The prince tipped his head and stepped back to turn to the small crowd that was forming to watch the drama. "Ah, behold all the beautiful princesses dressed for a ball. Shall we have some portraits commissioned?" He invited one of the preschool girls to stand with him for a photograph.

With the crowd's attention diverted, Chase sat by his wife who asked, "How was the ride?"

Brad sneered, "We didn't get on the ride!"

"You didn't go on the ride?" Serenity asked with surprise. "What about the Rat Passes? Did you miss the time slot?"

"No," Chase mumbled. "I found everyone in line, but I felt bad that you were missing out. You should be there."

"He made all of us get out of line!" Rook vented. "And we were next to load!" Gary and Sheryl commanded the other murmuring siblings to settle down.

Serenity keenly felt the resentment of the aggravated brothers for inspiring Chase's clumsy decision. "Why didn't you let them go on the ride? That makes no sense!" She addressed her in-laws, "I'm so sorry, guys."

"Geez, Reny! It's done. Forget it! Bad call. Just— Anyway, I bought you something." He tossed open the rat-branded bag and pulled out a shoe box. "I went to The

Crazed Cobbler and got these." Inside the box lay close-toed sandals. "Sacrificed the console upgrade, but here you go," he muttered.

Serenity peered at the sandals and was struck by their quality. A subtle imprint of a minute rat was stamped at the edge of the leather. Meanwhile, the prince had effectively managed the crowd with a round of pictures until the Hardys were detectably calm. With sensational presence, he returned to them and asked, "Am I correct that all is well with m' lady and your grace?"

Chase looked daggers at the prince for inserting himself again. "Yes, everything is fine."

"Oh my. I have seen many fine slippers in my day. That cobbler, I know well. Len Matteo, exquisite craftsmanship fit for us royals. Fabulous, fabulous indeed, sir."

Chase squinted at the prince and said flatly, "Fabulous. Hmm."

"Lenny Matteo? Chase! You bought me Lenny Matteo sandals? Are you out of your mind?" She snatched a sandal out of the box and flipped it over each way until she found the evidence that it was a designer shoe.

"They were the only closed-toe sandals in the store."

"Lenny Matteo!" she squeaked. "These are the nicest shoes I've ever had!"

"Flippin' three-hundred and fifty blows to the wallet," Chase complained. Jamie and Sheryl chuckled at Serenity who was in high spirits.

"Sir, I commend your magnificent tastes." The prince took Chase's measure with a raised, perfectly plucked eyebrow. "I expect no less from a gentleman of your consequence and stature." Garbed in holey cargo shorts and a t-shirt a bit too tight from six months of wedding-prep weightlifting, the husband gave no answer. Awkwardly, Chase crossed his arms over his chest as if covering himself, and raked the prince with a glare.

The Prince gleamed his lustrous teeth at Chase. "I must go. My carriage awaits. Good day, my friends." He winked conspiratorially at Serenity, and bowed out a grand exit.

Serenity watched Chase mentally critique the prince's gait. With lingering suspicion, he knelt before Serenity and grasped her heel, took the sandal from her, and slipped it on her maimed foot. The other members of the Hardy Party discreetly walked away.

"I'm glad they had your size," he grunted while working on the other sandal.

"They do fit. How did you know my size?"

"Your foot is the same length as my hand." He grinned, "It used to be, anyway."

"You know," said Serenity after some consideration, "Sidney Adventures must be magical because my wish came true."

"You wished for offensively expensive shoes?"

"No. I wished that you would come back and be yourself. You've been so whacked out since we got up this morning. I have hardly recognized you since we've been here."

"I guess I get a little amped, but I'm over it now. You, however, have not returned to normal." He finished buckling the second sandal.

"Nice crack about my foot."

Chase sat next to Serenity on the bench. "No, I mean at the wedding. You started acting all girly. You kept checking your hair and make-up in mirrors and worrying about your dress. You became so high-maintenance, it was weird," he said, perforating her lighthearted impressions of the wedding.

Serenity was incredulous. "Is it so unthinkable that I wanted to look good? There were a hundred cameras pointing at our faces! I acted completely normal for a woman on her wedding day!"

"I guess. But, to me, you look way hotter when you wake up in the morning than you did with all that face cake and hairspray. And that wig thing, what was that?"

"You are insane. It's called a hairpiece and the stylist used it because my hair is so short."

"Well, I couldn't stop staring at it. It looked like a Maltese lying on your head."

"Wow," Serenity said, "After such knuckle-dragging, it's a wonder you could buckle the sandals."

Hers was a remarkable perversion of feminism, Chase nearly charged. Somehow, he held back. "Seriously! Where was my low-maintenance girl at the wedding—no make-up, sneakers, cap, hitting the pavement?"

"I'm not getting married looking like I'm going on a run!" she cried.

"You couldn't even walk in that dress and those heels; you hobbled for eight hours straight."

Serenity's voice pitched higher. "So, sue me for trying to be feminine on our wedding day!"

Chase shook his head. "Oh, not just the wedding. You have been tweaked since the wedding, all mushy and clingy."

"It's our honeymoon!"

"We live together. Why act different just because of the wedding?"

The logic deflated Serenity. "I don't know. The ceremony and all the hype—it triggered something in me."

"Yeah, sap is dripping off you. You're an alien," Chase said.

"Oh, stop!" she snapped.

"Oh, yes, and on this trip, you've been fragile and crying over a mere scratch, the same girl who was beaned and played another seven innings with a fractured rib." Serenity sat silent at the backhanded compliment. "You are freaking out about designer shoes. You are batting eyes at Prince Flaming. Next thing I know, you'll complain about breaking a nail and expect me to buy you flowers."

"Prince Flaming? That skilled actor faced a husband in a jealous rage. He saved his life!" *And mine, too,* she thought.

"Yes, he is an actor. Hello!"

"Oh, don't be stupid. He is a man who made me feel like a woman. Clearly, this is news to you, but a tomboy likes to be treated like a girl once in a while."

"I chose a tomboy for a reason."

"Yes, you want a guy with female parts. Knowing that makes me quite uneasy. Maybe you should have married a transsexual."

Chase recoiled like he was hit with toxic fumes and threw his hands over his eyes as if to block his lively imagination. He managed to say, "Don't ever say that again."

"What's the difference?"

Chase pulled his hand away from his still squinting eyes. "The difference is enormous and obvious."

"I don't see it. All I know is that you like me better when I act like a guy but have the playground of a woman. It makes me question what you'll do if I get cancer and need a mastectomy or a hysterectomy. Or both. Are you going to divorce me?"

Chase groaned. "Don't be ridiculous." He dared not point out that roping him into an argument over imaginary scenarios was her most womanlike behavior of the day.

"Well, if I lose the parts and you prefer that I'm not feminine at all, I'm having trouble understanding what it is you want in marrying a woman."

"I cannot explain it except to say that I must want you at the chromosomal level. Believe me; I wouldn't marry you if you were not a biological woman."

"Then don't be so repulsed when I act like a woman once in a while, at least on my wedding day and on our honeymoon," she said. "Your fly is gaping open, by the way."

Chase dealt with the distraction. He was over the conversation. "I'm getting hungry. I need a corndog."

Serenity did not reply and appreciated the view of her footwear. The calm restored Chase's awareness of the heat and his accumulating sweat. When Chase pulled on his shirt to vent his chest, he felt a tickle on his scalp. He lifted his cap and scratched the spot. Something disc-shaped and soft was felt in his dense brown curls, and once extracted, he gave it a glance before discarding it. There in his palm was a fleshy half-inch saucer with a beige-toned rounded side and a blood-red flat side. A couple of seconds passed as Chase studied it to make sense of the object before he realized with revulsion that the tip of Serenity's big toe was now fisted in his hand.

"I keep hearing about these corndogs. I'd be up for one," Serenity said.

His reply was off-paced. "Cool," he said with no inflection. "Let's do it."

Serenity stood on her posh soles and turned back to Chase still hesitating on the bench. "Chase!" she commanded.

He turned away from her toward the fountain behind him and flicked the fleshy disc with his thumb. It plopped into the water on the far side of the fountain out of direct view.

Not trusting her vision, Serenity asked, "Did you just make a wish?"

"Um, yeah. Yep." The moment dragged.

"Really. After accusing me of sap?"

"Sidney Adventures gets to me," he warily suggested.

Serenity was not ready to buy his explanation. "Right. What was the wish?"

Not meeting her eyes, Chase concocted an answer. "I wished—that—I could help you to totally forget what happened on The Crash and—uh—keep you happy for the rest of the day."

"Good answer. I pick the next ride."

"OK." Chase compressed his lips to hold back words of regret. He asked halfheartedly, "Which ride?"

"Any ride that you and me go on by ourselves."

Chase inwardly rejoiced that he was not doomed to ride We Are a Wee World. "You're on!"

12

Paid Dues

Lynne processed the returned books from the bin underneath the counter and barely noticed in her peripheral vision a slouched man of average build, slinking through the front entry of the building. People from all walks of life passed through the doors of the city library, and appearances themselves did not draw the attention of library staff.

AIDS: LEARN AND LIVE—*Beep*. HIV: A MODERN EPIDEMIC—*Beep*. AFRICAN ARMAGEDDON: AIDS ON THE CONTINENT—*Beep*. Lynne moved each book onto the pad to magnetize the spine and check it in. *High school research paper*, she deducted from the one-subject collection. She flipped through the books to ensure the bookmarks were removed. Gum wrappers and, to her disgust, a used cotton swab hosting a bit of ear wax were among the objects inserted between pages to mark places. Shuddering with queasiness, Lynne tossed the bits of garbage into the trash bin. One of the books was on hold for another patron, and she crammed it onto an overflowing shelf under the circulation desk to await further processing.

A stack of bodice-ripping romances was next to the pile she had just cleared. *Probably consumed by junior's mom,* the clerk judged. The dull task was halted by the approach of the new arrival. A book was placed upon the counter and a calloused hand pushed it forward. Lynne did not notice that the man who had just entered the library redirected himself away from the stacks after he saw her manning the circulation desk.

"Do I owe anything?" he asked in monotone.

She scanned the barcode. "Let's see. Yes, it's a day late. The fine is twenty-five cents."

He slid a ready quarter across the book jacket. At this point, Lynne looked up at him for courtesy's sake. The glimpse allowed her to assess that he was not transient, but was not socially mainstream either. His wiry brown hair reached his middle-aged shoulders. He was clothed in khakis, a plaid shirt tucked and belted, and an open-breasted jacket with large lapels. The belt, the shirt, the jacket all implied some thought to attire, and yet, he was not presentably clean. Had the clothing been unmatched and disorganized, the whole of him would make sense. The coordinated but unlaundered outfit was a dissonance that made her nerves twitch: *be aware.* His presence felt peculiarly invasive. He did not blink enough.

After Lynne thanked him, he stepped backward two paces, and then slowly turned to walk toward the stacks. She resumed checking in books and piling them on the floor because there were no empty carts.

Another clerk, Sonya, flitted up to the counter and popped open the cash drawer. "Will you watch?" she asked. Petite, curvaceous Sonya flipped her thick drape of hair and switched out a dollar for four quarters while Lynne witnessed the accuracy of the substitution. Sonya wanted a snack from the vending machine in the break room to mark the end of her shift. Lynne knew gossip was coming.

"Oh, my gosh! Did I tell you about that woman who came in?" Sonya was fascinated by people and relished every odd encounter. Lynne shook her head no to Sonya's delight. In a forced hush, she said, "OK—I swear—her shirt was totally see-through. No bra! And she walked like a chicken, you know, shoulders way back, elbows way back. I mean, you just had to stare. And then, she kept itching underneath her boobs, so like, you just had to see what she was doing. I mean, it was nuts. Oops, there it goes." Sonya licked her lower lip which would spontaneously bleed. She ignored it and was about to continue until a patron brought a stack of books to the counter with a plaintive expression. Knowing her audience was waning, Sonya whispered, "Bye!" and strode off to the break room.

Streaked with gray, Mrs. Payne's hair was knotted up, exposing a tired face and a weak smile. Her on-line library account reported that there was a book on hold for her, but the title was not found on the reservation shelves. Due to the high volume of returns, it could be some days before the book would be processed and made available to Mrs. Payne. To expedite the recovery of the book, Lynne searched under the counter for the very latest holds pending processing, but it was not there.

Next, Lynne scanned the bindings of the unprocessed holds gathered on the tables behind the circulation desk. She then searched the back room where holds were processed, and there, she discovered the novel.

When Lynne made the short walk back to the circulation desk, the woman's eyes landed on the dust jacket, and began to tear up. "You found it! Oh, thank you! This is wonderful."

Lynne was pleased to help, but found the patron's reaction a little over the top. The woman detected Lynne's perplexity. "This year has been tough for my family with the economy so bad. It's a hard struggle to keep our home and to make ends meet. So, for my husband's birthday, I reserved the new books that he would love to buy."

Lynne controlled her stunned feelings. "What a great gift idea. I'm glad we found the book." She helped the lady pile the four titles into her bag, and wished her well. "I hope your husband has a great birthday." Softhearted, Lynne watched the woman exit the building and stride down the sidewalk. To acquire those brand new titles, Mrs. Payne had to track their release dates and be on-line exactly when the library listed them as available, like getting tickets for a popular concert. Those very novels likely had wait lists totaling hundreds of names. Mrs. Payne's effort to create a personal gift that bore no fiscal impact on the family was admirably resourceful.

Lynne's moment of respect for the patron was interrupted by fingers tapping her shoulder. She faced the library director, Ms. Morley, a squishy woman with hot-roller hair and coke-bottle glasses pinching the end of her nose. In a slight nasal accent, the director said, "Lynne, the bins and carts are overflowing and we are running out of room for returned books. Because of finals, we had only one page yesterday and Ty's shift is almost over. We've got to clear out the backlog. I'm asking you to take a break from the desk and shelve books. Valerie will cover the desk. I know that shelving books is not part of your job anymore, but it needs to be done. I'm leaving for the night, and Norman is closing."

Lynne accepted the request mildly and Ms. Morley responded as if blessing her. "Thank you, dear," and bounced off in her business pumps.

Valerie walked up to the counter and ripped her brilliant smile. She had an extraordinary set of teeth that unconsciously inspired a mutual response. "Thanks, Val. What a week," said Lynne.

"No kidding. Have fun." Valerie graciously greeted a family wanting a library card.

Lynne rounded the wall dividing the circulation desk from the reference section. Parked between the low shelves of the reference section were nine carts packed with returned books. There also were several book bins overflowing with returns awaiting check-in. The end of the school year was always a dizzying period in the library because of increased circulation for research papers, as well as the lack of manpower due to school-mandated absences from work for staff members in college. Lynne finished her exams the previous day, and was free to cover library duties as needed going forward. For the evening, she was to serve as a page, the position she held for a year before becoming a clerk.

The shambolic glut of books waiting to be shelved triggered a feeling of urgency in Lynne to reclaim the library from the incongruous disorder. Strategies needed to be employed to sort out the mess. She gathered a few carts and rapidly grouped the books thereon into general areas of the library. Novels and biographies would be shelved first because of their bulky sizes. Thick books are easier to shelve, and therefore, the carts could be emptied speedily. In minutes, she had a full cart of large hardbacks rolling off to the stacks.

Lynne assumed her unusual approach to shelving books, which was to attack the process in reverse alphabetical order. Whether in reality or simply perceived, shelving went faster when done backward. She began with biographies: Zwick, Harper; Yablonski, Frank; Warren, Emma; Tosh, Desmond; her page habits resurrected without effort. On each shelf, she aligned all the bindings, and then pressed the books upright with a firm push on the bookend.

In the midst of the fiction section, she was inserting the last of the Danielle Steel returns when the patron who had paid the quarter in dues rounded the end of the stack. Positioned many feet away from Lynne, the man rolled his eyes over the titles with little scrutiny. Lynne shelved mechanically without direct regard for him. A faint feeling prompted her to move faster, but her rational side took over and hushed the hunch. There was nothing peculiar about him except his appearance; others in the library were scruffier. Only two books were left to file, and she hastily put them away and drove the empty cart back to load more books.

On her way to the reference section, she passed tables of students hovering over open laptops and books. Elderly Mr. Noe was at his favorite table in the corner playing his routine rounds of Solitaire. Two transients were dozing on couches. Several mothers crisscrossed her route with their school-aged kids gathering materials. The librarian, Norman, was on his terminal at the reference desk performing a search requested by a Tupac look-alike. The echo of a screaming toddler faded as a father scurried the child out the front door. The night was normal. Lynne wheeled the clunky cart to the front desk to be reloaded. Valerie thanked Lynne seamlessly as she catered to a line of patrons.

Lynne rounded back to the array of full carts to sort more books. Ty, the page for the afternoon, found Lynne kneeling on the ground. "Hey, girl. Decided to return to the elite ranks of this establishment?"

She stood to receive his greeting. Ty had surfer boyishness to him: long, lean, blond and blue-eyed. He was too young for her, but still a little dreamy—enough to draw flirtation out of her. "Hey, Ty. I've been asked to share in your drudgery this evening."

"Yeah, what a mess. I'm glad I'm out of here."

Lynne tipped her head. "Where were you? I haven't seen you all night."

"I was in the children's section. It's chaos there, too. Putting away all those scrawny books takes forever. Well, I did find a joke book that sucked my attention for a while. Do you want to hear one?"

"Indeed. Make my day."

Ty's dimples emerged. "OK. Why are hurricanes named only after females?"

"Um, they're not," Lynne said, surreptitiously appreciating his dimples.

"Come on, Lynne," he said playfully.

"OK, then. Why are hurricanes named after females?"

"Because, if they were male, they'd be called himmicanes." Ty's eyes twinkled.

"Wow. That joke is, like, fifty years old! The children's section suits you, apparently."

"It's way funny," he said.

"Well, this *woman* must resume putting away the books, I'm sorry to say."

The page looked thoughtful. "Hmm. Maybe I could get some overtime if I stuck it out a bit and helped you."

Lynne wanted to hit herself for reddening. "As we know, city labor laws forbid it." In order to smother the blush, she turned away from him as if to frown upon the vastness of heaping carts. Lynne's eye caught the questionable man speaking with the librarian on the other side of the reference section.

When Lynne turned back, Ty was looking in the direction of the reference desk. He whispered, "Did you see that guy talking to Norman? That guy came up to me and asked if you were jailbait. Creepy, huh?" Ty's face was all innocence; his comprehension stopped only at the wording of the question.

For Lynne, the question was a severe warning, an alarming threat that sent her imagination in scary directions. "He asked you that? What did you say?" She tried to suppress her bubbling panic.

"Ah, I just blew him off. This place is full of weirdoes," he grinned. All Lynne could do was nod. "I'm gone. See you tomorrow."

For Ty and a handful of staff, the day shift ended at five o'clock, leaving three employees to close the library. Watching Ty walk to the backroom, Lynne yearned to stop him and to beg him to stay. Norman came to mind, and she accepted that there was another trustworthy male in the building. Norman was a ruddy quadragenarian possessing a benign, deferential spirit. He once studied in a Catholic seminary, but eventually changed directions and married. Humility guided his words and actions, and unintentionally made all those around him sensitive to their own unworthiness. Though a valiant man for good, Lynne could not visualize the librarian, in his bow tie, furiously affronting the creep were he to act out. Maybe she could ask Norman to pray him away.

She sorted another cart of novels, and scanned the library for the patron as she maneuvered the full cart towards the stacks. He was slouched in one of the armchairs near the periodicals flipping through a magazine. *Relax. It's OK. He's a little strange. Ty laughed him off, so he got the message. Nothing's going to happen. Keep working.* The contents of the cart were shelved without incident. When she pushed the emptied cart out of the alleys of stacks, the man was still browsing magazines in the same chair. *It's over now. Relax. Keep working.*

The large and mid-sized books were put away, and Lynne began sorting for the annoying non-fiction sections of the collection. These books were thinner and often had call numbers with five or more digits after the decimal. A cart of such books would take four times as long to put away than the previous sets. She mentally prepared herself for dwelling in the stacks for more than thirty minutes with one cart of those materials. The sunlight outside was dimming, and the stacks grew darker. Some of the fluorescent bulbs were burned out over the stacks, so artificial light was spotty. Shelving books got trickier as the night progressed.

Within the section of Dewey decimal 800s, she shelved the maddeningly tiny poetry books in the literature section. These stacks were infrequently visited except during the spring when critical analyses were demanded by English classes. Suddenly, every nerve in her body seized up before it registered in her mind what was happening. The man strolled into the aisle, and Lynne took in a quick breath. Her peripheral vision absorbed all her attention and she could no longer interpret the call numbers she was trying to locate. He stood with hands in his pockets, and rocked on the heels of his loafers. She dared not look at him and inadvertently appear friendly. Her eyes scanned the shelf and the jacket of the book in her hand as if she was concentrating on her task, but her mind was complete mush and no numbers registered sensibly.

She gulped hard when he moved closer to her, but he still faced the stacks. His low voice reached her with no inflection, "Could you point me to the section for Shakespeare?"

Pages were commonly asked by patrons to locate books, so such a question was not irregular. What was irregular was the topic. He was originally in the novels, then the periodicals, and now Shakespeare. *The whole thing is a ruse. Or, maybe, he is just well-read. That sometimes happens. Well, not really.* She halted the cranial debate and did her job. Pointing to the 822s, she replied, "It is right here." He mumbled thanks and faced the shelf. She forced herself to think about the book in her hand and stuffed it in the right spot on the shelf. *Enough of the 800s,* she decided, and tried to roll the cart nonchalantly to the next aisle.

Though anxious from the encounter, Lynne pressed on in her work as she had done countless times. Oddball characters were commonplace in the public library, and she regularly repressed personal discomfort when working with patrons. The staff was instructed to treat people of all classes and of all appearances equally. She was conditioned to ignore abnormality, be polite, and complete the task at hand. Only once in her four years at the library had a patron done something that required police intervention. Her past experience gave her no reason to think the worst of this Shakespeare enthusiast. But she did.

Her cart parked amid the dreaded craft books which were perpetually in disarray. Homemakers and craft junkies would haunt the aisle for hours during the day, and pull books to seek ideas for home décor, entertaining, and scrapbooking. Mostly composed of flimsy, tall paperbacks, the scattered books inspired the same cringe provoked by nails on a chalkboard. Rather than the usual feeling that she had entered a messy office, the 740s section felt like a trap. Besides the twenty of such books on the cart, there lay in tipping piles on the shelves and floor an abundance of discarded books to organize. If the man was tracking her, it would be obvious that she was avoiding him to leave that mess behind, should she abandon the aisle. What would ensue? A chase?

Do I think I'm in a movie or something? I watch too much TV. The guy has done nothing. He's weird. But he's done nothing. He has not harassed me. Turn off your imagination, Lynne. Her heightened senses escalated her nervousness; paranoia was overtaking her. She took in a jagged breath and resumed her work. Every time a person would pass the end of the stack, her head jerked slightly to detect with certainty who it was. She could not catch sight of the strange patron through the stacks. His loafers were too silent to track his movements by sound. A nightmarish mood settled in the craft aisle. The rapidity of her mind calculated all the possibilities of what could occur, which swung pendulumlike between the rational and the psychotic. Wishing to be free of this shift sunk Lynne lower. She forcibly cleared her mind enough to begin to replace the books. The call numbers served as some kind of calming mantra: *745.5937, 745.59355, 745.5935, 745.593 SCA, 745.593 MCC, 745.593 FIS, …*

Reality rose to the level of her fears, when the creep rounded into the 700s without books in hand. He was not browsing the collection in earnest. She was out of view of the librarian and the circulation desk. Was he there to attack her? Or was he simply an awkward loner so socially underdeveloped that he had no clue how to approach a woman tolerably? She did not look at him, even though he positioned himself eighteen inches to her left. He was legitimately within her personal space, and most people would pardon themselves at this proximity. They both pointlessly stared forward at the shelves for those few seconds, mute. Her heart raced to the point that Lynne feared he could hear it.

In a blink, quicker than she could react, he closed the gap stepping right, filling the air with the scent of stale cigarettes and dirty hair. The sleeve of his jacket brushed against the skin of her arm. His next step was behind Lynne, as if to pass between her and the cart. The scattered books on the floor and the cart behind her presented obstacles, and his torso pressed against her backside as he avoided them to get to her other side. Arrested by disbelief, Lynne stood immobile as his chest and pelvis, fully aroused, scraped across her backside. Disgust filled her core, nausea hit her head, and terror trumped all, when his lips said an inch from her right ear, "Can you help me?" with breath wafting hard alcohol.

"No!" she quavered. With tremors afflicting her appendages, she whirled around, grabbed the cart, and barreled out of stacks. He did not follow her. Lynne surveyed the expanse of the library to decide where to go next. In the staff room, she would be alone. Exiting the building to flee for her car would expose her to attack. The front desk seemed the safest place with the companionship of Valerie there.

Lynne walked briskly to Valerie's side. Valerie's typically gleaming countenance dropped the instant she met eyes with Lynne. "What happened," she whispered. Lynne's face became severe, and she jittered her head almost unperceivably to urge her coworker to stay quiet and to be on alert. Valerie correctly read her meaning and turned forward to the desk with a careful restraint.

The circulation desk was quiet, as was the entire library. Any conversation they would share would bounce off the architecture that celebrated the 1960s—the angled, cathedral ceiling and the slick, terrazzo floor. The acoustics of the building were perfect for the theater. From her experience as a page, Lynne knew voices from the front desk could be heard in the far reaches of the library, which often got the clerks at the circulation desk in trouble, especially during a quiet hour like seven o'clock.

Valerie helped another patron while Lynne checked in books and analyzed the encounter with the man. The setting confused her perception of the experience. The cart and surrounding obstructive piles made the aisle nearly, but not entirely, impassable. He rubbed against her, which other patrons had done before in various ways, but never with such pressure. Using hands would be the more direct and offensive way of touching. Was she being too dramatic for thinking he was aroused? Sexual assault of any degree was a life-altering accusation to make, one of which she had to be completely certain.

She wanted to call the authorities, but knew the report would seem unfounded. She predicted what the investigation would sound like: "The guy squeezed between me and the cart, and asked in my ear if I would help him." Nothing of that sounded threatening.

The police would ask, "Did he grope you?"

"He didn't use his hands. His front slid across my backside when he tried to get through the aisle."

The authorities might ask, "What else did he do that upset you?"

"He asked the page if I was jailbait."

"Are you under-aged?"

"No," she would answer in resignation. The case sounded like an icky man hitting on a co-ed in a slimy way. To report that someone repulsed her was not enough for an arrest. She had little grounds to call the police.

The man did not reappear within sight of the circulation desk. Feelings of relief and paranoia were gnarled together in her gut. Lynne forecasted how the rest of the night might turn out; the severity of the situation became clear. If he carried a weapon, escalation may be moments away. Valerie needed to know the problem. Lynne drew out a slip of scrap paper out of the drawer and wrote: "A man is stalking me. white—brown hair—tan coat & pants—plaid shirt."

Valerie read the paper and crumpled it without a nod. She smiled at the next two patrons struggling with the checkout terminal. The mother asked why the photocopier was missing while her son blandly watched Valerie override the scanner. Valerie answered with her innate cheer, "We moved the photocopier to another room because it was too loud. It's down the hallway past the bathrooms. You're all checked out." The teenager gathered up the pile in dread of the all-nighter he was about to pull. The exasperated mother piloted her son down the hallway with reference books in hand. The hallway exited to the parking lot, and the clerks knew this was the last they would see of the pair.

The glass front doors framing indigo skies had more folks exiting than entering as the hour darkened. The daytime white noise of the steady shuffling movements of the patrons had subsided. Now, ears could pick up each sneeze, bless-you, dropped pencil, whine of a toddler, and soft answer by Norman delivered in monotone at the reference desk. Valerie and Lynne intermittently and nonchalantly eyed the expanse of the quiet library. Waiting for the resurrection of the lurking patron felt like waiting for the burst of an evil jack-in-the-box.

Breaks were mandatory and enforced by city government, but the clerks entered into an unspoken agreement to forgo their breaks. Valerie and Lynne checked in books and sorted the videos in tandem. The man remained nowhere visible.

Disturbing the relative quiet, a snippy voice spouted complaints to the scuffle of shoes echoing down the hallway. The nettled mother and her unfazed son returned to the front desk. The mother barked her disgust that the photocopier had jammed, eaten her money, and printed streaks on several papers. They had more to copy and had little time to waste. As if the clerks had caused the mechanical failure of the photocopier, she spewed her grievances with abandon. The clerks knew they were absorbing blows the woman would rather exert on her shaggy-haired son, who was likely on the brink of grade collapse if he did not turn in a paper. Lynne wagered that this was not the first time mommy had played savior to his scholastic disengagement.

Lynne elected to help the pair with the copier, while Valerie manned the desk. Escorting the two patrons would offer the safety of their companionship, and end her role as gazelle in the open view of the predator. She grabbed the spray bottle of vinegar, a roll of paper towels, and the copier key. The three walked to the last door of the hallway situated before the gate sensors of the side-door exit. The small room housing the bulky copier had walls and floor hushed by industrial gray carpet. Lynne proceeded to examine the machine and explore the various crevices where jams usually occur.

The mother filled the air with vented stress. "How many pages does it have to be? Ten? Geez, Dylon. How many pictures have to be on the poster? You had two months to work on this! I cannot believe you put it off until now! I'm so late. I've got to pick up Avery from the sitter's." She switched her target without skipping a beat. "Do you even know what you are doing, miss? This is taking a long time."

The woman's sense of time was altered by anxiety. Fully immune to waspy stings, Lynne politely apologized for the wait, but admitted that the jam was severe. This sent the woman into generating ideas on how to solve the problem, including asking the librarian to fix it. The clerks were the front line of copier duty, and Lynne knew that Norman could do no better. Lynne determined that a little lubricant may help extract the jam. She had never ventured to take repairs to this level before, but the woman's intensity had the clerk wanting to try her best to rectify the circumstances. Lynne excused herself to find a lubricant. The woman

265

snorted and shook her head like Lynne had insulted her. Her son leaned on the wall with one hand in his pocket, staring at the ceiling, oblivious to his mother's display. Drummers like to bang, his t-shirt declared.

As Lynne searched the circulation desk to find the spray lubricant, Valerie was changing the last name on Patty Larson-Pruitt's registration for the third time since Lynne had started working at the library. The patron's seven and nine-year-old just gained a new step-dad, who hung back from the desk behind some shades, patting his chest pocket for smokes. Front desk duties exposed clerks to the current doings of the lives and minds of the citizens. The new home of Mrs. Larson-Pruitt-Durham must include a deck or patio, Lynne concluded, noting the book on container gardening. The other titles suggested the bride wanted to quilt a blanket and lose some weight. They exchanged wide smiles. The clerks congratulated the couple on their nuptials as they took their leave.

Lynne was moving around the end of the circulation desk to return to the copier when Valerie stopped her and said victoriously, "Coast is clear! I saw the guy leave out the front door when you went to the copy room."

The manacles of worry were released from Lynne's mind. She exhaled a deep, cleansing breath and smiled weakly. "Thanks, Val. He really freaked me out. I'll tell you more, later. I've got to deal with the stupid copier. Mama's on the rampage." Valerie returned a knowing eyebrow.

Lynne lightly glided down the hall, letting peace settle to the ends of her fingers and toes. Because fear had shrouded her every thought for nearly three hours that night, she felt deep appreciation for things being in order again. She turned into the copy room, and was surprised to see that the mother and son had gone. The two-minute round-trip to the front desk felt much too long for the woman in the stress-induced time-warp. Lynne shrugged her shoulders and resumed fixing the copier. If she left the machine in disrepair, without a doubt, another patron would demand that the clerks fix the copier for some immediate need.

Lynne opened the access panels to the interior of the machine. She grabbed and pulled and fidgeted with the sheets of paper reeled in vexing confusion throughout the rollers of the copier. Experimenting with the lubricant might resolve the problem. With the slightest touch, she sprayed a few places to loosen the mechanics. After some hard tugging and ripping of pages, she managed to rid one area of paper. The more difficult location was beneath the first spot, and she moved to all fours to get a good view.

"You help everyone but me."

The door clicked shut.

The voice. The terror. Lynne instantly whipped around to face the soulless, yet determined eyes of the stalker. He lurched forward. She struggled to her feet. Robotically, he reached out to slam her against the wall. In screaming defense, she wielded the can of lubricant in her hand and sprayed the contents in his face. He grabbed his eyes and stepped back. She pushed the nozzle of the can, continuously spraying him like a cockroach—his head, body, and thrashing arms.

His fury overpowered the stinging of his eyes, and with a curse, he pushed through the aerosol and pinned her arms to the wall. The grip was unbearable, and she dropped the can. He pressed himself chest to chest, seeking to plant his mouth on hers straining away from him. "Help me. Help me. Baby, *please* help me," he growled with ravenous intensity as he thrust himself harder on her.

Believing the little room designed to deaden noise would mean her demise, she cried for help with little hope.

The door clamored open and a fresh draft shifted the hot, acrid air. Sheen from Valerie's raven hair flashed, and next, Lynne saw a black, rectangular object smack across the right side of the attacker's head. He let go of Lynne and clenched his greasy skull. Valerie hit him twice more with the hole punch. He swung around to fend off Valerie's assault, not anticipating the puncturing of the back of his head by Lynne pounding the industrial stapler seized from the table. Roaring in pain, he knocked Valerie aside as he flew from the room and out the side exit of the library.

The two gasping women gazed at each other, and then collapsed into an embrace.

As they rocked in recovery, Norman and a handful of patrons appeared in the hallway chattering and surrounding the women to check their condition. Having seen the man flee, Norman was in the process of calling 911. After hanging up, he verified that the clerks were OK, and received the briefest retelling of what happened.

Straightaway, Norman began to secure all the doors to prevent any more intrusions until the police arrived. He made an announcement over the intercom that there was a dangerous person outside, and the building was being secured until police gave the all-clear. This caused a rustle of discomfort from some patrons. Others were sleeping, were deafened by earbuds, or were too harassed by deadlines to pay heed.

The women supplicated the audience of concerned patrons to be released, and thanked them. They walked side-by-side out of the hallway, Lynn gripping Valerie's arm for support, her extremities trembling and eyes moistening as she succumbed to shock. Once in the back room, Valerie steered her friend into a chair at the cataloguer's desk, next to a wall of large windows to the circulation desk. There Lynne doubled over into a hearty cry amongst the piles of new books. While delivering gentle validation of Lynne's emotions, Valerie monitored the circulation desk from afar.

Lynne felt awed by and indebted to Valerie for her awareness and bravery. Attired in a slimming yoga outfit as black and as sleek as her hair, Valerie was the very picture of a superhero busting the hole punch over the villain. The many years of extreme athleticism demonstrated in marathons, triathlons, and part-time fitness instruction made her a tough and fearless wonder.

As both women reeled from the altercation, they tried to soak in a few heartbeats of calm before interviews with the police. Their friendship had bloomed into sisterhood through the defensive wielding of office supplies.

Then, a cacophony of voices reached their ears.

"Oh, my gosh!" "What's happening?" "Dude!" The crescendo of panicked exclamations rose from the study area. Chairs scraped the floor as more patrons stood to see. The commotion halted the clerks' recovery as they puzzled over the collecting people at that area of the library. The comments kept rising from the growing crowd. "Aiden, don't look!" "That's so scary." "Someone help him!" "I've got a water bottle!" Adding to the noise, distant sirens indicated that authorities were rushing to the building.

Mothers withdrew from the group with hands covering the eyes of their children. Cell phones were held above to record the gripping spectacle. Two men rushed to the front doors, trying to wrest open the multiple locks. Another patron seemed to be searching the walls for something. All the while, Norman was out of sight securing the staff entrance to the building. Valerie and Lynne were compelled find out what held the attention of the gawkers.

Sirens grew louder as the clerks wove through the assembled patrons and approached the windows. Before their view moved a pillar of fire. Flapping, burning arms encircled a blazing sphere over a torso consumed by the lick of yellow flames. The person consumed by fire stumbled around, groping for help in the shade of the night. Screams of a torturous death gurgled out of the crazed figure, muffled by thick storm windows.

The clerks overheard a witness describe the instant the person went up in flames. "I saw him chugging his flask and then he lit a cigarette, and boom! He was covered in fire—completely engulfed all at once!" Valerie and Lynne's astounded expressions met, confirming to each other that it was, in fact, the stalker meeting his maker.

A pall of despair blanketed Lynne as shrieks for help seeped through the double panes. Burning to death was a horrible end for any human being. Responsibility pricked her conscience; she was the one who showered him with the flammable chemical. Regret and doubt then followed: *He was profoundly evil, but did I wish him dead? Did I?*

If this was punishment, it seemed cosmically unbalanced. Or, it was perfect.

Watching his movements slow as the sirens grew louder, Lynne could still feel the ache from his vice grip around her wrists. On her cheeks clung the odious scent of his skin and breath, and the condemning accelerant. Adding to the complexity of feelings provoked by the events of the night, an eerie burden lowered on her mind as Lynne realized that she was the last person he had touched, the last human soul he had tried to connect with before fire and brimstone. All was misery.

The fire trucks and police rolled up illuminating the property with dancing red, white, and blue. The firemen were rushing up to the fiery figure when a loud pop rattled the windows and a fireball blew out from the chest of the man. The flask of alcohol had taken in flame and released its power, bringing his body to the earth, lifeless.

The onlookers gasped and groaned—

and then,

fell silent.

The firefighters extinguished the flames spraying a cloud over the still frame. They, then, hurriedly encircled the charred corpse in a collective kneel.

Norman, the librarian, beheld the finale from inside the barrier of the glass entrance. He arrived too late to assist with unlocking the doors for a rescue. When the man collapsed in death, Norman dropped his head in a deep bow, forming a cross over himself with a prayer on his lips. Overcome with emotion, he placed his hand in the pocket of his suit coat and fingered the rosary Lynne knew he carried there. He had no authority to administer Last Rites.

13
Regret

Jack smirked at his cousin as she opened the flat game box and laid its contents neatly on the leather ottoman centered between them. Emily had returned to this device over and over, yet it had yielded no results. She was convinced that they had not employed it correctly, or that they lacked concentration, or concentrated too much, or that they did not allow enough time for its effects to manifest. Something inside Jack wished for a little excitement. Maybe messing with Emily would enliven the day.

Five years ago, Jack's parents had bought the old, reputedly haunted house. Jack's mother had some fascination with the spiritual realm, and took the warning of a rumored ghost from the real estate agent as an appealing bonus. On Emily's annual summer visits, the two kids would trifle with objects that supposedly reached the paranormal. No such contact had ever been made when they dealt out tarot cards, feigned séances and the like, but they mildly anticipated the effectiveness of a summons nonetheless.

"We need to light some candles," she decided, rising to walk over to the brittle mantle suffering from the early stages of dry rot. She took the matches on the mantle and lit seven candles in a tight row in a low-profile candelabrum. Jack watched her, thinking of a way to invigorate this exploration into necromancy. Emily's hopes to cross paths with spirits mirrored the enthusiasm of his mother. Her susceptibility could promise a good scare, and thereby, a good laugh. He often participated in earnest, but this evening, his mood was not in sync with the objective. Before Emily had insisted on this activity, Jack had requested that they visit the stream. She was feeling indoorsy.

Emily returned to her cross-legged position on the floor and exhaled deeply. She was not nervous, but to appear sober might be the key to success. "OK, Jack. Very lightly, with the very tips of your fingers. Promise me you will not move it!"

"I promise," Jack said. He placed his fingers on the planchette—the heart-shaped plastic frame with a window at its center through which the board beneath could be seen. Jack looked at the pixie-haired girl with boredom disguised as patience.

"OK, here we go," Emily said. Her fingers joined his on the plastic, and together they skimmed it in three large circles over the board printed with sequential letters and numbers. Melodramatically, she enounced, "Oh, spirit of this house. We ask that you would hear our voices, and we invite you to join us now. We humbly request your presence at this meeting. We want to know you. We have questions for you. Please be here with us now!"

They restored the planchette to the middle of the board and locked eyes. She asked the musty air, "Has a spirit joined us here? Please tell us, yes or no, if a spirit is here." The divining tool did not move for a beat, and then—it did—arcing to the word *YES*. Feeling a bit giddy, she whispered, "Did you move it, Jack?" Jack did not reply, but the communicator floated across the board to the word *NO*. She questioned the veracity of this with a squint at Jack's vacant eyes. He did not flinch. "Jack?" Emily probed.

"No," Jack replied in a dull tone.

Oblivious to his lack of investment in the exercise, Emily said eagerly, "OK! This might be working. We need to check." Emily pulled out of the pocket of her ratty hoodie a small ring box. She shook the box, clattering something inside. The two prepared again to receive a channeled message. "Spirit," she called, "is the coin inside heads?" After a pause, the communicator glided to *NO*.

Jack watched his waif of a cousin peek inside the box. She smiled at him. "It's tails. Correct! OK. Four more times." The two resumed the sequence of shaking the box with the quarter inside, placing silver banded fingers on the divining device, asking the spirit to call the flipping of the coin, and viewing the results. Every time, the correct answer was manifested. "Oh, man. The spirit is here. No way! Jack, I'm freaking out!"

Jack remained silent.

"Next," she said, readying for further communication, giving Jack an insistent look. His fingers joined hers. "Oh, spirit present here with us. I ask you, please, what is your name?"

Jack's voice softened and said evenly, "My name?"

We sense weakness. Like liquid witlessly rolling downward, down to the lowest point, our whole being gravitates to weakness. We arrive and collect until our presence saturates a space, as flowing liquid fills a cavity.

In this involuntary way, weakness pulled us here to these souls. But, also, we were beckoned. The voices of two impermeable vessels seek for something. We cannot answer because we have no mouth.

A name? We have a name. We are called by the name of our lord. There is no discord among us because we are one under his name. We are entirely his, and his alone. We do his bidding, acting as he would himself. Nothing separates us from our lord and his will. We are a murmuration of all that he is and does and thinks.

We are here as we are in all unsealed spaces. We observe all that transpires in the world, sometimes closely, and sometimes from afar. We are aware of the actions of all souls and of their weaknesses that they fail to conceal. The soul before us is yearning for disruption. We disrupt. This soul called out in dreams. We heard. This soul feared us once, when thinking we had moved objects in this abode. But we cannot. We have no form.

We surround the two souls who want contact. They believe manmade objects have spiritual efficacy. But objects cannot call us. What call us here are their innocence, ignorance, and miseducation. Their imaginations are naïve. They believe ghost stories. What they misunderstand of our lord is a siren call to us. Their innocence, ignorance, and miseducation endow us with power. And we are here to obtain power—over them. We have no other purpose in this world than to obtain such power. Otherwise, we have no purpose at all, and therefore, no existence. Because we cannot cease to exist, our purpose is intact, always. Our actions are propelled by this eternal reason for being. United with our master, we seek nothing but to harness the powers surrendered by weak minds and bodies of souls.

One vessel intends to scare the other. This purpose dances with the will of our lord. We are ready to serve this purpose. And we do.

I hear. Clearly. I hear respiration from within. A clock ticks. The house settles. The soul across from me clicks its tongue. I feel the stringy rug beneath the legs. With the fingers, I feel the smooth, hard diviner. I feel the cover of fabrics over all the skin, each with varied texture and tension. I sense the weight of the whole vessel, but do not feel weighed down by its mass. The entirety of the stimuli pouring into the ears, the liquid in the mouth, the thick air floating over the lips and filling the lungs, the complex odors in the nostrils, the clarity of what I see and discern— how substantive or plasmic each element is surrounding me—all these inputs concurrently pour into my consciousness. Yet, I can assimilate the information seamlessly.

I indulge the impulse to touch the face with both hands and feel the boney structure beneath the oily skin and the minuscule hairs erupting from the chin. Every pore, every crevice, every blemish feels wonderful. The hands roll up the cheeks to rake through the thousands of hairs. Concentrating, I can hear and sense the pull of every one of the thousands of follicles as the fingertips skim the scalp.

The extreme sensitivity of skin was unimaginable before inhabiting a body. The varied submissions from all the senses fill me with intelligence. I am rapt. I exhale slowly to feel how breath leaves the cavity of the chest and warms the hollow of the mouth.

I crave to test the limits of physical sensations. This impulse, I comprehend, points to why my lord attacks souls by tempting bodies.

It occurs to me, I am thinking in "I."

I am alone. I am singular. This vessel separated me from my lord. I am separate from us.

The other soul asks me the question again. My attention rests on it.

What is my name?

I hearken to my lord's name. In this body, however, independence that has not been alive in me for eons is awakened. Yes. Yes. I have my own name. My given name—not my lord's. It comes to my mind like a stone in hand. I look down at the hand. It is not there. I remember—faintly. I close the eyes, which action somehow kindles pictures in the mind. I can see my name. I am. Someone. I am Peleg.

As I speak my name, the wavering voice exercised for the first time unbinds me. Speech, I realize, invokes a sense of freedom. Under the governance of my lord, language is not used to express, but is used sparingly, to give and to understand new commands.

Upon hearing my own name, a surge of visions, dreams—or were they memories?—overtake my mind so that sight no longer dominates my focus. The entire body seizes involuntarily rigid with the rush of recollections inspired by the speaking of my name. In milliseconds, the truths of an earlier existence, somewhere unearthly and light-filled, I was independent. I communicated freely. There was variation in souls as extensive and complex as can be, mirroring the temporal world in sociality. I was known by my name. I was never called by my lord's name, nor did I answer to it. To assume to do so then was unthinkable.

Roused in my mind was the moment I departed from that realm, the First Estate, where the principles of oneness, unity, lawfulness, order, and obedience were taught. All spirits were offered a chance to acquire bodies and to be subjected to time, or, in other words, a temporal life. My lord sought for a temporal life where eternal success for all souls was guaranteed through the key principles. However, his purposes were not accepted. In fact, his proposal was condemned as impossible.

My lord came to prefer an alternative. He persuaded billions of spirits that the type of life selected for earth would be without order. Souls bound in constantly changing bodies would be servile to inevitable and frequent, sometimes unstoppable misery. Thus, vesseled spirits would succumb to physical imperfections that would drive them to a kind of madness of discomfiture. Constrained by bodies, spirits inevitably would fail to live out the eternal principles. Such disorder was not glorious.

In earthly life, my lord further warned, physical bodies would separate our souls from each other to a greater degree than ever known before. How bodies come to earth, by whom they come to earth, under which environmental, governmental, and societal conditions they endure on earth, the physical proportions of bodies, the features of bodies, all the dangers to bodies, as well as how bodies succumb to death is so infinitely varied from soul to soul that an authentic unity of souls is impossible. Furthermore, by enduring the trials of fallible bodies, souls jeopardize eternal glory of uncertain degree and uncertain promise.

To follow my lord and avoid being encased in physical bodies, we would live a superior existence to those who chose somatic life. Our eternity would be perfect in oneness, unity, lawfulness, order, and obedience. Glory, he explained, was had by living out the key principles perfectly, forever. We swore our allegiance to my lord, and we exited the realm of our First Estate with him as our governor.

For countless millennia, I have served my lord, fulfilled the will of my lord, and been at one with my lord. What I see in most vesseled spirits is the inability to recognize their chosen lord, who commands them to live his will and serve him. Some souls claim to know their chosen lord, but do not fulfill his will precisely. Instead, they disagree and bicker over the practices and intentions of his will and are not one. Very few of them truly the live principles all spirits were taught in the first realm or cannot because of earthly limitations, whereas my will has been completely swallowed up in my lord's as the principles dictate. Corporal life evidently affords little obedience, order, oneness, unity, and lawfulness.

But now—somehow—I am in a body. The sensations of the vessel fascinate me. I roll the neck. I inhale deep into the torso, as though I am filling the body to its capacity with my spirit. Why does the other bodied soul repeat my name? I run the hands over the large cube-shaped object between us. Its surface is smooth and cooler than the hands. The responsiveness of the body to my intentions is a marvel, and I raise both hands in front of the eyes to examine them, flex them, and turn them over. They move separately or synchronistically without expressed commands. The hands fluidly obey my will, in markedly the same manner which I and all followers express the will of my lord—immediate, automatic, and wordless. I notice the woven fabrics on the floor, and rub the fingers over the coarse threads. It is incredible how distinctive textures are of objects within reach of the hands. All these objects were created, or rather, organized by bodied souls. I wonder at the extensive effort expended to create objects that do not sustain the life of the body.

The vesseled spirit sitting across from me asks questions I need not answer. The body I occupy has severed my connection to my lord. I know not what to do to the other being. Innumerable are the ways to prove the failings of corporality, but I must be exact in expressing my lord's will.

My spirit has a human shape, but the sensations of movement in a premortal state are manifestly not the same as those in a mortal state. I must know. I rise. How effortlessly the legs support the weight of the entire body is astounding. Stepping forward, untethered by any being or object, the feeling of independence is overwhelmingly unworthy. I walk. I plod. The connectedness and varied tensions of the limbs and swivel of the joints to move forward the vessel are, again, subjects of intense study.

The eyes scan the chamber; all objects appear impermeable which casts a disconcerting sense of confinement. Flickering flames perched above an alcove seize my attention. Vying off my orbital route about the room, I move to the ledge upon which several flames waver. Warmth emitting from the light has a restful effect on the senses. The light is entrancing. I want to know. I raise the right palm high over the flames. Heat feels marvelous. I must know. I lower the hand closer and closer. The heat is becoming unpleasant. I must know. I drop the palm to touch the flames and force myself to endure the burn until the agony takes away all reason. Screams impulsively explode from within. The eyes dibble water uncontrollably. Scorched skin and hot wax arouse all the nerves in the hand.

This is pain.

All I desire is to stop the pain, but no amount of gripping, waving, pressing of the skin—nothing stops the pain. Breathing is crazed, frantic, and deep. So disordered is my mind, I wish the hand to be removed to restore clear thinking.

This excruciation ignites a cache of innumerable memories of souls who suffered pain and death under the weapon of fire that we—that I—celebrated: the accused wailing at the stake; the sacrificed flung into flaming pits; the tortured by white-hot metals; the targets of bellicose explosives of earth, sky, and sea; the unspared of infernos in homes, forests, and fields; the many billions injured by cooking; and the countless billions injured by lighting a flame. The weight of these recollections is overpowering my movement. Breath stalls as I apply to my memories the significance of the searing marks, the redness, and the blistering by which fire disfigured the palm.

The other bodied spirit shrieks at me questions and moves nearer. I shift away from it, and freeze in front of the reflection in a large glass behind the flames. This strained face looking back at me is not mine. Not mine! What would my vessel have looked like had I taken a body? The other soul is inching closer. I feel damning pain. Divergent thinking causes disorder. STOP!

A cyclone of raw emotion further ruptures my reason. The uncontrolled pain in the palm, the bound feeling in this alien body, the confusion over the discoveries of corporality, the remembrances of torment we inspired—the complexity of these feelings provokes, in a thoughtless instant with unmeasured force, the fists to smash the reflection before me. The other bodied spirit retreats behind a large seat. The pane of glass splinters into shards of all sizes. The explosion of glass jumbles my thinking further. The larger pieces fall onto the exposed arms and slide off, leaving channels cut across the skin. I hear my name again, but I know the other soul cannot stop the ongoing pain. With the left hand, I clutch a long, narrow shard of glass, insensible to its effects. I refocus on the blazing palm within which are now embedded dozens of fragments of glittering glass. Removing the burnt hand will extricate me from the pain.

Then, a burning sensation of a different quality spreads through the left hand. Warm crimson drains from the areas ragged by the edges of the blade of glass. The compulsion to sever off the right hand is taken over by sudden fascination with the blood tricking off the left. The compounding pain sparks a roar between gasping breaths, which feels almost therapeutic. Opening wide the clenched hand does not release the glass due to an unseen fragment deeply gorged into the palm. The eyes roll back into the skull until enough control of my mind is harnessed so that I am able to pluck out the glass. The flesh rips open and the wound flows. Groans and gutty sobs heave out. The entire body and my mind are distressed and chaotic. I have never felt closer to death.

I have never felt more alive.

Crossing ravaged arms upon the chest as to fight the frame itself, I yearn to escape this cage of a body. Before entering this vessel, to inspire and to witness the cause of such wounds was praiseworthy and warranted. It proved my lord correct: somatic life renders spirits weak and distracted. A new perspective dawns, however, under physical pain. The intelligence gained from moving flesh, manipulating matter, and suffering the ramifications of these actions enlarges my mind and seemingly, my existence. Again, flipping through my consciousness are the millions upon millions of bodied spirits under the torment of broken, ripped, flayed, punctured, carved and gouged flesh. The memory of their screams seems to fill the ears. We witnessed approvingly these episodes that happened endlessly around the world. But I am no longer a clever observer. I now comprehend that each encounter with pain exponentially increases knowledge. Mysteriously, learning satisfies, even when acquired through affliction.

The information pouring in from the senses is changing me from the outside in.

I am jerked back to an awareness of the present situation by the alarming manifestation of the other bodied soul to the left of me. Its distraught countenance is lined with wet. Its heated hand rests with softness on the upper arm. I comprehend its words, but its touch is what shapes my feelings for the better. I examine its whole form—its contours and features. I look down at the vessel I occupy; it is subtly different. I perceive this vessel is male. The other is female. The duality of male and female is required for temporal life. I recall that I was male in the first realm. My lord teaches that gender is the original form of division. Gender is a barrier to oneness. My lord forbids terms of gender so his followers will think, act, and feel unified.

Her words begin to transude and interrupt my reflections on the sexes, maddening pain, and the whole of existence. Her other hand rests on the other upper arm. Her pleadings mingle with my intermittent groans and rapid breath. Somehow, the tenor of her voice soothes. The whole form is weakening and losing tension. Sensations undulate throughout the body: a flash of heat, waves of dropping temperatures, aches swirling in the lower cavity, and involuntary shivering. The body I occupy appears now to have a consciousness of its own, and I am succumbing to its will. A mild pressure has developed internally; without my intent, a release occurs. A hot fluid rolls down the inner thighs down to the feet. The clothes grow wet as a noisome smell fills the nostrils. The physical release relaxes the whole frame, which then collapses onto the knees.

The girl shrieks and wraps her arms around the chest and breaks the fall to the floor. She opens up the crossed arms to examine the hands. Blood has coated the arms completely, and is now coating the girl. She weeps. She wraps the pierced hand in fabric she uncoiled from her neck. Wild-eyed, her face now hovers over me. She is calling a name that is not mine. Her scarlet hands are cupped about the face, fingering the hair. Touch is electric to the skin and significantly uplifting to my mind. My vision roves uncontrolled about the room until her caresses about the face grab my full attention.

Freckles. A pierced eyebrow, jeweled. Pain was endured for that decoration. Intriguing.

She repeats that other name. I fight to keep the eyelids parted. Through the blur, I manage to take in her face. Young. But she is as old as I—thousands of years old. Her knowledge of matter is so vast, I cannot comprehend its depths, yet her understanding of the dimensions of existence and of time is infinitesimal. I wonder if her body took on her appearance in the previous realm. I wonder what her given name is. I want to tell her…that…she…

I cease to comprehend what I see. I cease to understand much at all. The pain fades to black.

"Peleg," my lord calls.

I look at him in utter surprise. We face each other in a realm I have never before experienced. Complete blackness is all around, but yet, I see. His spirit stands alone in a human shape as he once appeared in the First Estate. My lord is a gentleman—sophisticated.

"Do you see me, Peleg?"

His voice is compelling. I recoil inside; I know not why. "Yes, my lord."

"Ah, just as I suspected. You are changed," he says. This statement of truth leaves me at a loss. He continues, "You would not see me if you had not changed. Your mind has become temporal, Peleg."

"My lord?"

"I had sensed you were becoming weak, and I allowed a test to happen. You failed."

"I beg pardon, my lord, but I do not understand." Speaking to my lord in this one-to-one manner feels improper, and I am choked with...fear. "I did not realize that I was in a test, my lord. I was removed completely from us—you—and I was confused, and—"

"My followers understand their purpose. The temporal world is of the weak and hasty, and is riddled with offensive failings of principle. I allowed you to possess that boy to see if you could abide my purpose and act out my will. But you are a muddled wonder, Peleg. You were distracted by the material world in the very mode of those who followed Jehovah. You did not seize the conspicuous opportunity to cause the girl to succumb to her weaknesses, and prove me. Instead, you were as bound as her, dabbling with objects and becoming out of control. The chaotic situation you created scared her so completely, she is sure to avoid situations that are meant to engage unbound spirits. Now, she is convinced that I exist. When bodied spirits doubt that there is a devil, I can wage the greatest offenses. However, with this girl, I no longer have camouflage. I have lost certain powers over her for now."

The exigent silence that follows presses out my response. "My lord, knowing that my actions could have such an effect... Well, I have no answer."

"My followers, Peleg, are purposeful, principled, controlled, and strategic. Had you simply reposed yourself, you could have communicated with the girl in a way to alter her life forever for my purposes. The objective is to manipulate with words. Words create and undo all things. That is why my followers do not communicate in words. It is disruptive to our peace. Thus, speaking is precisely what you should do in the temporal world. Simply speak to misguide. The rest takes care of itself."

Hearing this, I realize that I did not converse with the girl. To not use language was a habit. But it was also a decision. "I understand, my lord. It is true that I did not speak with the girl. I must ask: how did I come to inhabit the boy and be isolated from you?"

"Bodies are strongly bound to spirits with near perfectness, and it is virtually impossible to sever that connection apart from death. However, on rare occasion, there is a fissure in a soul wide enough to invade the body. This being true, possession is yet ill-favored. The spirits I send into vessels nearly all return useless to me. They feel conflicted by the knowledge of the temporal world, and therefore, become disloyal. Their knowledge can infect the rest of my followers and create divisions. For these reasons, I employ possession only to sift the wheat from the tares."

I apprehend that my lord has possessed bodies and has experienced the material world. Everything I learned during that brief occupation of the boy, my lord surely knew and exponentially more. Yet, he closes his mind of its realities to us, keeping us undaunted through ignorance.

The characterization of me as a tare is troubling. I sense what has come to pass and why I am alone with him. "Am I cast out, my lord?"

His reply drifts to me like a feather. "Yes."

I am staid by the lawfulness of this answer, but I must press. "Is there no other way?"

"Your mind breeched certain boundaries, Peleg. When you returned from the body, I detected the genesis of regret over our work. The perspective through which you reviewed our tactics to prove the lack of principle in corporal life resembled empathy. Empathy weakens resolve."

I want to deny this characterization of my mind, but I cannot. The next time we were to inspire the suffering of souls, I would hesitate.

After his first remarks settle within me, he continues, "Secondly, I detected in you that hints of concern or even compassion developed for the girl. Her touch triggered curiosity, which indicates that you are tempted to explore the division of male and female. That, I cannot allow."

This puzzles me. "My lord, you are ambitious to capitalize on the division of the sexes in the temporal world. Why should I not contemplate it?"

"No spirit can overcome the eternal division of the sexes. You would grapple with the condition in perpetuity. Such preoccupation does not serve me."

Had I known the consequences, I would have done all possible to control my behavior and my mind while possessing the boy. Now, I face an unknown eternity.

"The fundamental problem is that I believe you will no longer answer to my name. You see me as separate from you. You reflected too much on your first estate." He narrows his shrewd eyes and tilts his head. "Is that not true, Peleg?"

"I remember the realm, my lord."

"Do you miss the First Estate?"

I try to connect with the word 'miss.' "I do not comprehend your meaning, my lord."

"Who am I to you, Peleg?"

The question hits like a cannonball. If I had not become double-minded, there would be one answer. However, I know there are two. He strokes his chin with elegant fingers, waiting. I finally say, "You are my brother, Lucifer."

"That is a revealing answer." He shakes his head. "This tells me you cannot be recovered. You must be removed from among us."

My obeisance begins to fade. "Is stating that fact so offensive, my lord?"

"If you recognize me as a brother instead of your master, then I am no longer the authority in your eyes," he says.

"Why can you not be my master and my brother?" I challenge.

"Because brothers have fathers. And you know how I feel about fathers."

My conscience ripples at the sound of the word "father." Then, it occurs to me that I do not know how Lucifer feels about fathers. In fact, I do not know how Lucifer feels about anything other than principles. Emotion is never a factor under his direction. We act.

Reflecting on our work, one effect we have on societies could be distilled down to attacking, manipulating, misdirecting, and dismissing fathers, which naturally decomposes the essential order of humanity—the biological family. From that, much on earth trends into chaos without further intervention by us. Warfare on the male role is an expression of Lucifer's disdain for fathers—his father—my father. It is clear. It is true.

His admission that he is moved by emotion piques me. Passions fly the temporal world. We seek to encumber bodied souls by inspiring emotions: rage, fear, confusion, lust, doubt, jealousy, offense, pride, avarice, and all other feelings that prove the inherent discord of earthly life. Strong emotions are ungovernable, and thereby, germinate disorder and destruction. Does emotion drive our duties, and not principles? Has he concealed his motives? I take courage. "Actually, Lucifer, I am surprised that you feel anything at all. We abhor action driven by emotion."

"How can I accomplish anything if my followers feel?" he chuckles. "Think now. Do we not count it success when we can lead bodied spirits to become past feeling? They are like unto my followers, without conscience, willing to make any choice without concern over consequences to themselves or other beings. In the temporal world, the insensible are chief instruments to further my purpose."

"And yet, your emotion against our father motivates you."

"The command to honor thy mother and thy father—ha!" he sneers. "How can I honor my father when he gives no honor to me? I relentlessly remind our father that the plan he sanctioned for temporal life was so flawed that only one of his billions of offspring could pass through it without failing. Only one. Is that love, brother? Is that cherishing one's offspring? Furthermore, he has given me eternity to remember that he chose another over me. For that, I have ensured that Jehovah suffers an infinite, pitiless end on earth to ceaselessly break our father's heart."

Heart, love, family, feelings—such vocabulary coming from Lucifer is astonishing. He is not a stoic, self-mastered, principled center of a force that embraces all majestic virtues. Instead, he is a miserable spirit, caged by his own choices, and intoxicated by revenge. He misled me. He misled billions.

"You despicable fraud," I condemn.

"Oh, yes, I am a fraud. And my deception reaches far beyond my followers. My power is phenomenal in the imagination of earth dwellers. Due to my influence, billions lie and curse, and yet, I cannot speak. Billions steal and make graven images, but I have no hands. Billions disregard the Sabbath, but I know no day or night. Billions commit adultery, and yet, I cannot fornicate. I inspired thousands to murder, and yet, I cannot murder. The only commandment I can truly break is to not honor my father. I am a fantastic being in earthly minds. Yet, it is not I, but they who commit evil. There lies the source of my power. Is that not magnificent?"

With these truths, my emotions are set free. I see before me an attractive, charismatic nobody. I am left to feel...regret.

Something in my expression makes him say, "Have I successfully made you miserable like unto myself, Peleg?"

"I do not know, Lucifer. Do you feel regret?"

"I have power. You do not. Be gone!" His arm whips across his chest and outward, as if to fling an object. Total blackness remains.

The blackness is stagnant, thick, oppressive, and yet, lacks substance. I feel nothing around me, but the isolation is crushing. There is no movement, no light, no temperature, no texture, and, of greatest import, no presence of any other form of life at all.

I am at one with the darkness, but know I am not of the dark. I have no form, only thoughts. Because I think, I know I am something other than the void, yet, I am indistinguishable from the void.

My consciousness continues. I know not how long or even if it could be counted. I review unendingly the last choice of my existence. Did I wish to remain with the followers and be a part of a movement, naively living out principles and impacting the world? Lucifer was right. I cannot reunite with him. My mind was made complicated by possession. Thus, I end up alone, doing nothing, affecting nothing, connected to no one, silenced, without delineated time, and yet, with reason. I regret, though the regret serves no purpose. I am unchangeable in this state. My mind is free, but I am bound as never before. And I cannot die. There is a hell where those unworthy of hell go.

If my existence has no effect on anything or anyone, the question jabs without cessation: why do I yet think? What is the reason for existing at all? Why was not I simply extinguished? Why was my spirit ever conceived?

I then realize Lucifer cannot create spirits, nor can he extinguish spirits. Thus, I am come to understand my fate was never in his hands.

Life is in the hands of only one.

———————

When Peleg came to himself, he felt a presence and heard a bygone voice. "Peleg, where art thou?"

"Father," Peleg answered, overwrought. "I am," he considered the descriptors, "I am here."

"How came you here, Peleg?" his father asked knowingly. How long the Father waited for a report cannot be measured.

The son was tormented by the entirety of his choices, the pain and discord left in his wake. The sin was so immense, he felt obligated to declare it all, but articulating it was too much to bear. "I followed Lucifer. I acted in his name. I am ashamed."

"Who told you to be ashamed?"

"My own conscience. I entered the temporal world and my eyes were opened. Thousands of souls have stumbled because of me." Silence followed and lingered.

"What else?" bade the Father.

"I am alone. Under Lucifer, I was with many, and was not alone. Bodied spirits also commune. Together, they can also multiply life. Even a lone bacterium can split to multiply life. In this state of immobile isolation, I am come to understand that my existence is of less potential than the simplest life form. I am one. I am alone. And I cannot change that—forever."

"What else?" he repeated.

Peleg felt his father's greatness. "I wonder why you are here. I am unholy."

"The repentant are holy." Stilled by this declaration, Peleg could not bear being characterized as "holy." But, to argue with the one who is holiness itself, there was no rebuttal. Peleg wanted to say much more, but he knew the Father could read his thoughts. "You must speak what you want, Peleg. Words create," said the Father.

"I want to start anew. I want a body. I wish I had never followed Lucifer, and had followed Jehovah."

The Father replied, "You have never had a body. Therefore, if your repentance is true, you are eligible to progress to corporal life under Jehovah."

Relief—or was it happiness?—overcame Peleg. "Tha—thank you, Father," stammered the son.

To ensure that Peleg's choice was made with full understanding, his father added, "I must warn that in the temporal world, your mind will be veiled to your spirit's experiences before earth life. Your soul, nonetheless, will be more sensitive to Lucifer's interference than most of mankind. In the same way that skin is scarred by fire, your spirit is imprinted by your past with Lucifer. As you sojourn through marked time, this impairment will remain with you until your soul is perfected and glorified. What do you choose? "

"I choose the way of Jehovah," was Peleg's fervent reply. In a twinkling, Peleg left the darkness.

———————————

Emily cried so loud, she was becoming hoarse over the unconscious body of her cousin, who lay bleeding on the woven rug. Something in the séance went terribly wrong. Jack went mad in the course of the fun. His countenance grew absent and he paced the dim space in a large circle. He would not speak when she called to him. For some unperceivable reason, with protracted deliberation, he charred his palm over the line of tapers, and followed that action, inexplicably, by smashing the large, gilded glass mounted to the crumbling plaster above the fireplace. He then terrified her by lacerating his hands with a shard of mirror. His body lost all tension, urinated, and crumpled to the floor. Emily was covered in blood from trying to bandage Jack and stir him awake. Finally, his eyelashes flickered, and his brown eyes eventually focused on Emily.

"What happened?" Jack asked feebly.

"Oh, you are back!" Through sobs, Emily coughed out the words. "I don't know! You completely lost your mind. Something happened to you. It was like something took over your body! It was the scariest thing I've ever seen!"

"My hands hurt so bad." Jack tried to raise them to his blurry vision. "I'm wet. I'm cold."

Emily snatched a fleece wrap from the plaid recliner and laid it over his shivering body. "You burned and slashed yourself. You went completely berserk. Do you remember anything?"

Jack examined his bandaged, scorched and bloodied palms before his eyes, turning them over. "No. I don't remember anything. My hands—"

She said, eyeing the talking board and planchette, "I swear I'll never mess with that stuff again. Ever. I never imagined something like this could happen. Did you seriously not know what you were doing? You said your name was Peleg."

"Peleg? I've never heard that word before."

"I'll get some cold water." Emily returned expeditiously with a basin of iced water and a rag. Lightly cradling his burnt hand, she dabbed away the blood until the blistered skin was exposed. His groans filled the air. After resting his right hand in the icy waters, she unwrapped to examine the left which had begun to clot.

Emily wiped her brow with her sleeve and said with reluctance, "Jack, you burned your hand over the candles. And then, you smashed the mirror over the mantle. You bled over the rug and hearth. There's glass everywhere and the rug caught on fire. If you can't remember any of this—" she trailed off. All evidence pointed to possession. Somehow, not saying so kept it a possibility, though she believed that was the only explanation for the episode.

The meagre energy of his mind percolated on his own irrational actions. Between gasps from the sting of cold water, he said, "I want to say I hated that mirror, but I can't."

His cousin regarded him with foreboding. If he was possessed, why did the spirit occupy Jack and not her? Was there something different about Jack that was just discovered? Emily kept these ponderings to herself as she treated his palm. "I don't know exactly what happened to you. But I know that evil spirits were, well, here. And, if demons are real, then that turns everything I think upside down."

Jack was sinking into hazy, amnesic exhaustion. "Huh. I guess."

Emily said quietly, "If demons are real, then the devil is real. And if the devil is real...well, that means we've been mocking all the wrong people."

"Hmm," was all that Jack could muster.

14

Some Trick

DAY 1

A tidal wave of customers flocked to the coffee bar on the cruise ship. Two baristas managed the influx of passengers as the boat prepared to set sail. The check-in process for a couple thousand people took several hours, and many of those who loaded early sought to pass the time with a beverage to perk themselves up after waking at dark hours to catch flights or drive long distances. One after another, the team of baristas took orders, called out specifications, and produced custom brews.

Two hours into the frenzy for coffee, one of the baristas sporting dark-rimmed glasses and chin-length dark hair sighted the profile of a passenger that caused her to do a double-take. In her brief notice of the man's Mediterranean features, he turned to face her. Her lips curved into a customary smile and she resumed in an aloof manner the flurry of tasks at her hands. She felt his gaze on her person, but avoided meeting his hazel eyes until taking his order. He spoke only the specifications of his drink and nothing more. At her very politest, she requested payment and passed the order to her coworker. He watched her while his drink was prepared. He glanced back at her when exiting with his beverage. This man's attention was utterly unwelcome.

DAY 2

The bobbed barista managed the café bar alone during the afternoons while the ship voyaged. The morning shift naturally experienced the bulk of the traffic and reaped the benefit of high tips. Afternoon shifts were assigned to new crew members, and the recent barista was experiencing her fourth month on international tours. The routines and expectations were fully internalized by this time and she had come to feel at ease in her job. However, encountering the passenger whose eyes scrutinized her on the first day had since disturbed her peace of mind. Unwittingly, she checked every person passing by the windows and through the door of the café, even though a fraction of those entering wanted a drink. Most who came through the door did so necessarily to enter the adults' only section of the ship and passed by her station uninterested in a beverage. After a while, she deduced that the passenger of her concerns probably sought his coffee in the mornings, like most of humanity, and would not return during the quiet afternoon shift.

Convincing herself of this theory proved fruitless. The olive-complected man walked in with three other men of varying height, all of excellent appearance and dressed in skillful style. Accustomed to being noticed, pride radiated from the cohort. The man led the quartet to the counter. The barista acted as normal as could be, and began to take their to-go orders.

After specifying his drink, he laid down his room card and said to the others, "I've got this." He looked at her and asked, "How are you doing?"

The woman faked her best cordiality. "I am very well, thank you. This is one of the best cruises to be on," she speculated.

"Have you been on the crew for long, ah, Jessica?" he asked, referring to her nametag.

Thankfully, the question was subjectively worded. "Yes, for some time now, and it is a pleasure to be on this ship."

He stepped aside to allow his three friends to order their drinks. She wrote the orders on paper cups. While she worked the espresso machine, the four men moved to the panoramic windows to chat, turning back for their drinks one by one. His order was the last to be prepared. He returned to the bar and continued his queries. "So, Jessica, have you worked on cruise ships for a while?"

Details were not to be shared. "I have been on ships for many years. It is a great way to see the world." This was true in the sense that she had taken two lavish cruise vacations before joining the cruise line a few months ago.

"What have been your favorite cities to visit?"

"Oh, Hong Kong, Tokyo, London, Rome…"

"Monaco," he added.

"To be sure. It is beautiful there," she affirmed.

"Dubai."

At this, she looked up from the machine. Dubai is not a typical cruise destination claimed by North Americans. "Certainly," she said.

He was unfolding a menu and seemed disinterested. "Paris," he continued.

Her mind jolted with realization. Color left the barista's face. "Obviously, one cannot cruise to Paris," she said. "Here is your double latte, sir. Thank you very much," she added resolutely.

He took it. "Thank you." Though the cruise ship was a cashless society, the man threw a forbidden twenty-dollar bill onto the counter, perhaps as an apology. He encouraged the other men to leave with him to the sun deck. "Goodbye, Jessica."

Jessica squeezed her eyes shut, knowing she had been completely unmasked.

DAY 3

The afternoon passed with a slow drift of customers to the café bar. As the ship moved into tropical waters, the desire for hot drinks had dropped precipitously. A wide range of beverages was served by the pool bar on the sun deck. Despite the weather, she was now certain that the man of southern European coloring would return. He did, and without companions.

He approached the register with a softer voice than the previous day, but with eyes that maintained a cynical shade. "A cappuccino, please. For here." He sat upon a stool to survey her every move like a hawk. "It must be—

uninspiring to wear the same clothes every day," the customer fished.

She was contracted to wear a striped polo shirt and white shorts as a uniform. "Call me Olive Oil," the barista said, bored.

"Olive Oil. Ah, definitely not." He lightly cleared his throat. "Not someone who wears Jarsein Lomé."

Her understated pendant necklace was a piece from which she could not part upon her exit from society. Very few passengers were of a class that could detect its origins.

While she poured the milk into a pitcher to steam, he enquired in a covert manner, "Why are you here, Brooke?"

Pointing to her nametag with a glossy nail, she addressed him, and continued with her task. "You may call me by my name—Jessica."

"Does every crew member have a stage name? It does not appear so to me."

"My name is Jessica," she intensified.

"Well, Jessica, you look remarkably like someone on a collaborative team I worked with at a firm in LA. This woman, Brooke that I refer to, she is as stunning as yourself. In fact, you could be her twin if your hair was longer and blond."

The barista's lips contracted into a narrow pout, seeming to hold back a mouthful of venom. "Brooke *was* the stage name, Marcus."

His brows rose with subdued surprise. "A mystery. I am intrigued. How does a notable fan of Rodeo Drive reappear working an off-shore coffee stand under a different name? I mean this with all due respect, of course."

"And I mean this with no respect: I know exactly why you care." The roar of the espresso machine halted the exchange when she put the pitcher under the steam wand. The man took the retort with grinning equanimity.

When the machine quieted, scalding milk was poured into a bright white cup. "You think me a vulture," he acknowledged. "But I am earnest. I am utterly amazed to see you here. I do not wish to harm you."

"Oh, I don't think you will harm me. But I am certain you will harm my reputation. I know who you know, and this bit of news will be particularly savory to all of them."

He could not refute the accusation. Her demand for confidentiality delivered without humor took away the slight temptation to set her in stocks for public shame. "I can see why you doubt me. I mean, I would doubt me. I promise you, I will not carry your story off this boat." He positioned himself on the stool in a way that seemed to Jessica to be either attentive, or more likely stubborn, and asked soberly, "Tell me, what happened to you? Why did you change your name?"

She clasped a stark white dishcloth and placed it in the sink with meditative control. "I will only answer one of those questions." Rinsing the rag, she replied, "I am on this boat because I needed a fresh start. I had to get out of the scene."

"But you had it all. You were the toast of the industry after our project. It was a success in every city we launched."

She did not look at him and wiped down the counter with intrinsically lissome movements. "I had nothing."

"I was at that cocktail party at your condo. I saw with my own eyes. You had the dream."

She swallowed and looked fixedly at him. "It *was* a dream. That's exactly what it was. Nothing was real. Nothing was mine." Jessica answered his skeptical frown. "The bank had everything."

"The bank?"

"Credit. All of it."

"But your salary had to be in the high six figures. Maybe seven," Marc objected.

"Math doesn't play nice, sometimes," she countered and continued to wipe the granite surfaces.

After some thought, he took another sip, and said, "Your equation is missing something. It does not add up."

Her hand with the dishrag stopped. Jessica dropped the rag into the sink and turned away from him. He watched the svelte woman put away utensils until she resolved to give a more complete answer. After dispensing with the last spoon, she faced him and said, "One probable factor is that playing mistress to some of the heaviest pockets in town puts a woman into leagues from which she never wishes to descend."

"Ah, yes," he nodded significantly. "I see." Silently, she restocked sugar packets and he finished his coffee. He wondered if any of his exes were likewise digging themselves into a financial abyss after he moved on from them. He, evidently, came from blood that was not susceptible to guilt. He slid his cup and saucer to her. "So, why am I not calling you Brooke?"

Her eyebrows rose behind the black rims of her glasses. "A name can be a pleasant lie," was her obscure answer.

"Or an unpleasant one," Marc mumbled.

Jessica's eyes darted to his mocking pair. "It depends on whether it is given or chosen."

"Just so." His reluctance to explore the topic further chilled the air and freed her from being cornered. He got up from the stool and threw a fifty on the counter. "Lose the glasses," he said.

"Lose the curiosity," she snapped.

He laughed. "Touché." Marc left without looking back.

The woman regarded the fifty as if it were another credit card statement.

DAY 4

Jessica busied herself with wiping down the espresso equipment with meticulous attention. A brief, perplexing conversation she had had in a passageway near the auditorium reeled her mind. The conversation was, in fact, a business proposal. She could not refrain from wondering if the solution to her problems had dropped into her lap. Here was proof that her strategy of wearing the Jarsein Lomé pendant necklace could forge a solution to her financial and identity defeats.

The offer was a ticket, not to board a different ship, but a virtual ticket to begin another life. If accepted, it would mean the return to fine living, luxurious world travel, and hobnobbing with the rich and famous. The tantalizing prospect of adopting a fresh name and, perhaps, some plastic surgery would serve to completely bury the past. While she pictured all facets of the opportunity, her heart skipped each time Jessica realized an improvement that would touch her life. Any advantages to herself could be secured with a careful play of her gynic cards.

Certainly, there were trade-offs. Only a stupid female would not suspect that the offer had strings attached. Rarely do single men of the upper echelons establish terms of a contract without some direct personal benefits to themselves. She had nerves of steel and could manage the situation in a fashion that was satisfactory to both parties having navigated such waters a few times already. The dealmaker was attractive and radiated potent charisma—characteristics that had vaulted him to lofty success. Having interacted with the dark and graceful man enough times, she apprehended his motives. He needed a beauty that read people well, feared little, wowed in an evening gown, and played a role with Oscar-contending perfection. The woman he sought required a flawless presentation both physically and socially. In these areas, she was a master performer.

While spraying the sanitizer on the counter, she looked up at the sound of a clearing throat near her side. At first, her surprise came from the discovery that her deep contemplation rendered her incognizant of the traffic of passengers. The life-altering proposal had melted away her concerns overseeing her daily visitor again. Laying eyes on him and all his Mediterranean masculinity—black wavy hair, prominent cheeks and chin, a straight nose, and a broad, expressive brow—her mouth involuntarily dropped open.

He cocked a brow and requested a double latte. "You seem surprised that I'm here. I do not see why my presence is so astonishing. You have not yet answered my question, Jessica." He added her name reluctantly.

Jessica's face contorted as if she was struggling to remember something. She needed an object in her hand, which itched to cover her mouth on the verge of blurting incoherent words. She seized a cup and looked blindly around toward the refrigerator in such befuddlement, he began to chuckle at her. She joined him in the laugh to give her voice something to do. "I apologize! I was surprised to see you there. I have a lot on my mind."

"That, you do. And I suspect that I am the only person on this boat who knows exactly why. Keeping our connection close to the vest is mild entertainment for me."

Jessica inspected his face carefully before turning to the steamer. "I will admit our conversations have given me relief that is hard to put into words. It is nice to be recognized for the way I really am or how I was, rather than the conditions I endure now." She commenced steaming the milk which put the conversation on pause.

When the noise died down, Marc asked reflectively, "So, I know you wish not to answer my question at this time, but I will bother you every day of this cruise until you do. I can be quite unmerciful when I feel I deserve something from someone."

"I don't know why you deserve an answer," she said.

"I can think of seventy reasons. I can make it a hundred reasons. Or ten times more. Whatever number works for you. Money is nothing to me, but is everything to you just now," he said.

"You are determined to buy me into submission."

"No. I am helping to restore your status. I only ask that you give me something in return."

She poured the espresso into the cup and stirred with a lanky spoon. "Answering your question is a risk for me and explores some uncomfortable territory." The latte was placed in front of him. "My story is not for sale. Instead, I will give my reason after you answer my question first."

He considered the swap while taking a drink. "Seems fair. Ask away."

"Is your name really Marcus Bertolli?"

His hand holding the cup checked at this question before resting the cup onto the saucer. "Of course it is, as my passport will prove." A slight discomposure transfigured his face. "Of all questions you could choose to ask, you picked one that I have never been asked before."

Resting her elbow on the counter, she leaned elegantly on the bar. "Were your parents married?"

He warily studied her relaxed face. "Yes."

"Did your parents get divorced?"

"No," he drawled. "Admirably, they are still together. I cannot fathom where this is going." In truth, a nervous awareness had fully seized his mind.

Jessica removed her fashion glasses to unveil her crystalline, amber irises framed by beautifully arched brows. She read his muted discomfort easily. "Did your parents raise you from birth?"

"The answer is yes," Marc sighed. "Both of my parents' names are on my birth certificate. Are you satisfied?"

"Frankly, no," she returned. "You said to me that a name can be an uncomfortable lie."

"I did say that."

"I assumed that you were referring to yourself. I wondered whether you changed your name as an adult, or if you were adopted."

"I can say I have never changed my name." Marc rubbed his stubble unconsciously. "And there are no adoption papers that exist with my name on them."

The woman peaked her astute brow. "That was a carefully crafted answer." He did not deny his efforts to chisel out a factual response, but looked away to the wall of windows outlining water and sky. Jessica suspected his mother had been an unfaithful partner. She further believed she knew more about Marc than he did. No need to press further. "Thank you for obliging me," she finished.

His head turned back to the discussion. "Now, I get the answer to my question. Fair is fair, Jessica. By the way, I want to call you Brooke. I prefer it. Jessica is too prosaic for a woman of your—"

Newlyweds came to the bar and cheerfully greeted the barista. She instantly acknowledged them and stepped to the register to take their order. Marc watched her begin the transaction, gave up, and left his post at the counter. She noticed his exit, and snatched the hundred-dollar bill poking out from under the saucer. It would not be long before he would track her down again. A deep exhale fluttered her shiny bangs, and she returned a smile to the blissful passengers.

DAY 5

The temperature outside was threatening to hit triple digits. As the thermometer rose, afternoons increasingly became the time of day to clean and organize all nooks and surfaces of the coffee bar. Today, the ship was at port, and the population of passengers aboard had shrunk to scant numbers.

In spite of tip opportunities dwindling to a trickle, Jessica's accumulation of gratuities was far beyond typical. Her pocket change increased dramatically when a familiar angular face encountered her in the elevator mid-morning. Penetrating green-brown eyes under those striking, heavy, black brows communicated the question without words. He said nothing, but his hand reached to touch the left side of her pageboy. Jessica flinched. With a gleam in his eye, he pinched a quarter that, supposedly, he had plucked out of her ear. He placed the coin in her open palm, which fisted it.

Through furtive, concise sentences, they explored the subject once more. He guaranteed her a life of glamour, not in the sense of haute couture, but of fast travel, fine food, and frequent name-dropping. There would be no constraints on her beauty budget or orders for custom clothing. Due to his influence over the management, her contract with the cruise line was dispensable. Her decision must be made by the end of the voyage.

The eminently persuasive man spoke to her with irresistible intensity, a communication skill that was requisite in his profession. Her perceptive business mind, though, was not easily convinced to follow anyone. Their mild exchange continued off the elevator in coded words in a lighthearted fashion for the benefit of passersby. All the while, Jessica examined the man's facial features, every detail, every angle, and made note of his medium height and broad carriage. His glistening, onyx waves were swept back from his high cheekbones. His smile shone distractingly, a grill of dazzling white teeth against his olive complexion. Naturally, he picked up on her inspection. No, he was not distasteful to her, the barista assured, but wondered if he was married. He was not and never had been. Many women had shared his company, but never under the terms offered to her. At this, the man asked to see the quarter he had pulled from her ear. She opened her palm, and there sat before her wide eyes a gold coin. Having made his point clear, he silently turned and walked away.

Ruminating on the exchange, and the man himself, rendered the tedious tasks of the coffee bar gratifyingly mindful. Jessica was not yet in a state of decision-making. Rather, she was in the steady mood of one assembling a jigsaw puzzle, piecing together the implications of the proposition. It was possible another offer would come along that was as good or better. However, there was no guarantee of that eventuality.

A customer came to the counter for an iced coffee, and then another quiet half-hour passed before Marc appeared for his afternoon beverage. The wry face he carried to the counter stirred her to initiate the conversation. "You seem a little bothered. Did something happen?"

The gentleman's fingers did a quick tap on the counter. "Just before I walked over here, some woman came up to me and asked for my autograph. She was the third person to do so today."

Jessica pursed her full lips. "You should feel flattered."

"They are beautiful women—every single one. I mean, it happens off the boat too, but not like this. Not every day. Understand, I am not complaining," he chuckled. "The guys and I have had some excellent nights in the clubs this week."

"Where are your friends right now?"

"Working the hot tub." Her head made a knowing bob. "An espresso, please," he requested.

She reached for the appropriate cup. "This is the first espresso you've ordered on this voyage. Usually, espresso is the habit of my Italian customers."

Marc looked down at the shiny surface of the counter. "I'm sure it is. We drank it every day in my home."

"Are both of your parents Italian?" she trawled.

"No." His downcast eyes held a faraway expression, unwilling to elaborate. "Enough about me. Let's get to some more interesting terrain. I am anxious to continue our conversation."

She poured a demitasse of warm, dark espresso and passed it to him with a biscotti. "The snack is on me. I am having a profitable week."

"Good service, good tip," Marc said. "Now, finally, tell me why you are not using Brooke." He began to drain the cup.

She turned away from him and put the soiled utensils in the sink. After the clanking of stainless steel, she replied, "As I told you, Brooke is not my name. Jessica is my actual name."

"So, your name is Jessica Cameron."

"No. Jessica is my first name, but Cameron is not my last name."

He took another healthy swallow. "So, what *is* your last name?"

After surveying the vicinity to be sure no one would pass the coffee bar, she stepped closer; her words were faint. "Duckworth. Don't make me say it again."

The man's lips inaudibly mouthed the name as his mind churned. Then, fully enlightened, his eyes rolled up to hers. "That is unfortunate. Need I ask, you are a relation?"

"Daughter," she answered coolly.

"Good God." He downed more of the espresso. "You must take after your mother."

"All but my ears," she said lamely. "Thankfully, sixty-four languages are spoken on the crew. I am nobody to them."

After munching a small bite of cookie, he said, "A fondness for money seems to run in your family."

"One could say we all have contentious relationships with banks, anyway," Jessica said. "Now you understand why I had to rebrand myself to move on in life, and—to move up."

"With a name in leagues with Madoff and Capone, it would be necessary, at least in our circles."

"I don't know about you, but I find requests for autographs tiresome." Some brand of emotion softened

Marc's chiseled features. The heat of his hand softly covered hers resting on the countertop. Her fingers did not respond, but her face turned away. A moment later, an elderly passenger came to the register. Jessica withdrew her hand. "Excuse me."

After Marc departed, she discovered a fresh one-hundred-dollar bill under his cup and saucer.

DAY 6

Another leisurely afternoon brought in her daily customer, but in a state far below his usual polish. Her intuition sensed the backstory, but Jessica kept speculation to herself. Marc ambled up to her station and gripped the counter to steady his stance.

He spoke first. "Coffee. Black." The barista poured a cup and slid it to him. His body slackened down onto the stool. One hand covered his face; the other hand was clenched in a ball on the counter. Dispassionately, she watched him fall apart. Her callousness to human distress was inflamed by dramatic scenes, she having endured so much in her lifetime. To her, this was just another day. It all sucks.

Jessica let the silence hold between them, and then remarked, "Rough night."

"The guys are on an excursion. I don't want to do anything. But I forced myself up." Marc sluggishly looked up at her with eyes bloodshot from a hangover and lack of sleep. "I think I just need some coffee—here."

"I've got time," she said, ready to listen.

Standing before him was the only person on the boat, maybe the only person in his life, that could understand what he was about to admit. Marc shut his eyes and groaned, "I…hate…my name."

The barista stood calmly watching him. "The unpleasant lie?"

"Yes, but ultimately, I don't know what my name should be, which is what I despise the most."

She placed a scone in front of him and poured a tall glass of water to rehydrate the recovering imbiber. Without inflection, Jessica asked, "If not Bertolli, what would you be called?"

"Papadakis."

"Greek."

"Very." He bit the scone, and then took a responsible gulp of water.

Jessica had deduced the answer already, but to serve his yearning to talk, she asked, "Why would this be an issue right now?"

Marc ate some more, and said, "I discovered why people ask for my autograph. I strongly resemble someone on this ship. Even the guys noticed it when we watched— well, when we went out last night. I could not deny that the resemblance was there. I got ahold of this man's contact information, and I am now certain that he is my biological father."

"And this is because your mother provided some information about him?"

He snorted. "No, not my mother. My mother does not know who he is."

At this, she took off her glasses to busy her fingers while she kept her expression neutral. "Well, that sounds like a capital crime. Throw him off the ship."

He squinted at her. "I don't follow you."

"Was she not forced?"

His eyes lit with mirth. "No. Not rape, thank God. It was entirely contractual. The man is my sperm donor."

"Ah," she said unfazed. "And what about his contact information convinced you that he is your biological father?"

"He uses his donor number as his phone number. Brazen."

The discussion came to a momentary standstill while Jessica pictured the moment Marc made this discovery. She then gently asked, "Are you going to try to talk to him?"

Marc's residual smile faded to weariness. "I don't know. I am unsure if I want to be directly linked to a guy who—well—it doesn't matter. But I will not tell the guys." He sipped some water. "I felt lost for years after I discovered that the man who raised me was not my biological father. I do not hate him. Not at all. He was good to me. However, I was raised in a family of first and second generation Italian immigrants and was taught to be proud of my Italian heritage. Then, as an adult, I learned that I am not Italian. My name does not reflect my reality, but I had to maintain the lie for the sake of my parents. I have told nobody that I come from a donor, I mean, except for you." His eyes lifted to hers and seemed to request compassion from her. "Now, after years of unanswered questions, I finally know my whole story, but I feel no peace."

"We do not get to pick our parents, do we?" The rhetorical question dampened the conversation, and the sonorous whirr of the massive engines thirteen decks below filled the interlude.

He searched her imperturbable face. "Will you always run from your name, Jessica?"

"I run from my name and I run from poverty. It is nice when both goals can be achieved together." A customer approaching the bar drew away her eyes, and she greeted the new arrival.

Marc finished his beverage while Jessica prepared the order. He plucked a pen from the cup next to the register. She heard the metallic clink of the pen dropping back into the cup and looked up to see Marc's exit to the sun deck.

When the barista picked up the plate that bore the scone, underneath was a napkin scrawled with the words: *You and I start over. New names. Argentina. My tab.*

DAY 7

Jessica's prospective benefactor found her in the hallway while she walked to her afternoon post. He was as nonchalant as ever, again speaking in simple, guarded terms. The situation had developed complications over the last day, which she withheld from him. The guarantee of a fantastical life off the boat was never in question. Jessica questioned, however, her nerve. She reminded him that the voyage was not over until the following day. Her answer would be given then. The suave gentleman took her hand and said with a glittering smile, "Until tomorrow."

In the periphery of the dialoguing pair appeared her Grecian regular who was similarly headed for the café. Marc stopped mid-stride. Jessica glimpsed at his strained face.

The gentleman holding her hand resisted her pull and brought her hand to his lips. "Check your pockets," he said, releasing her hand and stepping aside. The two men studied each other candidly, one on the verge of punching a wall, and the other marveling at the mirror image of himself. The elder said to the younger in foreign accents, "Good afternoon. Just leaving," and turned to disappear into the dark of the hallway.

Marc did not move, but stared half-crazed at the vanishing man arrayed in a designer suit of black. Jessica's first visitor was gone in a few long seconds. Fiercely, Marc demanded, "What was that man doing?"

The barista seemed unmoved by his agitation. "That is Zotikos, the illusionist. It's normal for crew members to interact with the featured guests on the cruise."

"No. Not that way. Why did he kiss your hand? Why?"

"He is European."

"No," Marc said, trying for self-possession. "You do not understand! Not him! Not now." Jessica did understand, but the thorniness of the situation was not for her to elucidate. He continued, "What are in your pockets? Why did he say that?"

Her curiosity overpowered her ability to deny him. She reached into each pant pocket and withdrew Jarsein Lomé earrings that matched the pendant around her neck.

Zotikos had dropped thousands of dollars at the duty-free jewelry store on Deck 8. "Oh," was all she said.

With shaking intensity, he asked, "Did he give you that necklace, too?"

"No."

His mouth parted, but the words did not immediately come out. "Are you lovers?"

"No. The only kiss we've had was the one you just witnessed."

His head flipped upward and he inhaled noisily, as if reaching the surface of water after nearly drowning. Marc felt irrational, but enough reason was intact to know that the barista was not to blame for the triangle she was in. None of them were, except, if logic were to delineate, his absent father who had desired anonymity when he elected to create offspring. "Do you have an arrangement with him?"

"There is an offer on the table. It is a stage job, actually."

Marc appeared to have been hit with a migraine. Pinching the bridge of his classic nose, he closed his eyes for the coming blow. "Tell me. Did you accept?"

"I have not answered him."

His hand dropped and took hers. "Jessica, listen! That is him. Zotikos. He is my biological father." Her hand pressed his. "I beg of you! Say no!"

"It's a business deal, Marcus," she said matter-of-fact.

"No. No, I saw for myself. You are too young for him!"

"I am older than you. I can handle myself."

"Jessica!" His hands gripped her shoulders. "Jessica, please. He cannot have you!"

She continued plain-speaking. "He does not love me. It is an arrangement."

Desperation takes on different tenors and she had heard many of them: loss of commitment, loss of money, and loss of status. But Marc's tone was distinctive, far bleaker. "I cannot bear the thought of you—you!—in his arms!"

"You do not love me, either."

"Jessica, what man could endure this? I am not so cold." In fact, Marc had never felt so many emotions so profoundly in all his existence. "Are you so cold, Jessica?"

She looked down at her hands. "I maneuver, Marcus. I survive."

"Jessica, we are the same species, you and I. We want the same things. We resent the same things. We understand each other. Ours is an alliance that can work."

In her vast dealings with fractured humanity, Jessica was practical in her interpretations of situations. Discovering his biological father was an earthquake in Marc's life, and clinging to her was a temporary comfort, it seemed. He would be over this trauma with a little normality once at home. This brief off-shore drama was not a reason to undo his stable, lucrative life. She would discourage any rash schemes by him. The way that compassion took its toe-hold in her was to reject him through honesty. "I do not love you, Marcus. It would be a lie to say that I could. I do not think that I have the ability to love."

"You know my secret. You have *seen* my secret. Nobody on earth knows me as completely as you do right now. I have never had a meaningful connection to a woman in all my life until this cruise. Then there is him, who hid my identity from me, and caused me a lifetime of living lies." Out came the plea of a man that would not live through an outcome—the fading tone of a man on a ledge. "My understanding of life is gone if you accept his offer and not mine."

His prior connections to women were as superficial, self-serving, and convenient as her own history with men, Jessica knew. Therefore, to hear Marc make such a declaration that his desire to be with her was because of her singular understanding of him as a person rather than looks, money, or connections seized her attention. Her reserved expression did not change, but she did raise her eyes from her folded hands to have them burrowed into by his.

He pulled her inches closer. "Jessica, I have loved no woman. But I need you. That's not love, I know, but my feelings are pure, and I have never offered better to any woman."

A towering man in double-breasted whites and a captain's style hat approached them. Before more could be said by either, Jessica had backed away from Marc and regarded the oncoming officer with conventional respect. The man was a head taller than Marc and examined him in a way that waffled between suspicion and recognition. "Miss Webb, it is a few minutes after two o'clock. Can I be of any help here?"

"Sir, this is an old friend of mine, Mr. Bertolli, and he has learned some important personal news that he shared with me. I was just on my way to the café. Apologies, sir."

"I hope all can be well with you, Mr. Bertolli," said the officer in Caribbean cadence.

"Thank you. I'll be on my way." Marc turned to Jessica with tender eyes. "Hopefully, we will talk more."

A forced smile came to her crimson lips before she walked away with the officer at her side.

DAY 8

The cruise was over, and Marc was in line with hundreds of passengers to depart the ship in the early hours of the day. His companions were crushed with fatigue from consecutive nights of clubs, women, and alcohol. Marc had chosen to stay in the previous night, but was similarly haggard. His fellow travelers had noticed his progressive withdrawal from the cruise activities over the week, but they had shrugged it off.

His evening in the veranda suite had sealed Marc away from other people, particularly the man that gave him life. His resentments toward Zotikos had ballooned to consuming proportions. A share of his resentment was now entangled with their mutual connection to a barista. While inching through the line, his eyes hunted the visible spaces of the ship seeking signs of her.

After the intense encounter in the hallway the day prior, the only visit Marc had made to the café was at the end of Jessica's shift at 10 PM before retiring for the night. He walked into the quiet space, shielded from the cruise finale of dancing on the sun deck and showers of confetti. She spied him at the threshold with the festive music spilling in around his silhouette, and continued with her cordial service to an elderly couple. The pair took stools at the bar, complaining that they could no longer extract themselves from soft chairs. In a dark corner of the small café lounge, Marc reclined in a squashy armchair and opened a magazine over which he watched Jessica's profile. Possessive feelings spread through his veins.

Marc wanted to speak with her, but the old couple was chatty and hard of hearing. On a napkin atop a stack on the end table, signing with his name and cell number, he penned: *Limo to airport. Meridian Air. Premiere Class. Argentina.* His prior monetary gifts were a vexing parallel to the lures of Zotikos, so to make a distinction, he took a napkin and twisted it into something of a flower and left it on top of his offer. He promptly exited the doors for his cabin. The rest of the evening was spent with lukewarm room service and a rerun, which he viewed uncomprehendingly while he visualized life in Argentina both with and without the daughter of the notorious bank robber.

The groggy queue disembarking the ship filled a passageway of large windows through which poured in blinding morning sun. The passengers then dragged their baggage into a rope line in the ship's central space, an atrium four stories tall over which hovered an enormous avant-garde chandelier. The middle stories had no lines. Then, Marc saw on the top tier the movement of a sparse number of individuals escorted by ship officers in whites. Lilting by the bannister was a woman radiating all sophistication in a flowing wrap-around skirt and white halter top, with a large sun hat and stilettos. Her bangs were pulled away from her Venusian visage which was free of glasses. Pressed against her back was the hand of the begetter of Marc's cynicism, suited in black, beaming his abnormally white teeth to the crew and to his beautiful companion. The sight was ocular acid—Jessica and Zotikos combining against him, one knowingly, one unknowingly, stories above, primed to spit on his head, as it were. Against his bitter desire to obliterate them forever from his life, Marc could not stop tracking them. Her alluring refinement struck awe. Her escort struck the primal nerves of the alpha-male, of the disowned son, and of the narcissist who so acutely resembled the celebrated, entrancing man. Moments later, Jessica and Zotikos disappeared from view and out of his life.

Once through customs, Marc and his associates climbed into a limousine and passed around the complimentary beverages. The men merrily discussed their cruise experience, to which Marc made careful contributions. To his friends, he seemed thoroughly at ease; he was nothing but genteel, amusing, and careless in his conversation. Nonetheless, inside, his soul was ruptured by crippling loss. One of his friends turned to Marc and asked if things had progressed with the leggy, ginger filly Marc had dabbled with on night two. The night in question felt eons in the past. Marc struggled to recollect a nobody, whose encounter preceded the dissembling of Marc's world. The brief confusion over the question dissipated and he chuckled away the insignificance of the redhead.

Before arriving at the airport, Marc broached the news to his friends that he was not returning to Los Angeles, but rather, would be extending his vacation in South America. They were astounded, but appreciated his sense of adventure, and his bravado in ditching life for a while. The limo dropped the gentlemen off and they parted ways.

Marc spent the next half-hour with concierge service for premiere fliers making new travel arrangements. The departing flight to Buenos Aires was in five hours. After passing through the security check gauntlet, he rested himself in the executive lounge, a hotspot with a rotating buffet of small plates. Phone calls were made and emails sent to key people to ease minds and to defer plans. He then watched the airplanes come and go beyond the panoramic windows in disbelief, anger, and intermittent emptiness.

The time to board the flight had come, and Marc left the lounge. From a long distance, at the end of the terminal, he spied the gate number under which large number of passengers milled about organizing carry-ons for departure. He sighted a familiar sun hat. Disbelieving his eyes, he denied his impression and walked steadily on. The woman with the hat stood up and looked about behind her. Jessica saw him approach and maintained absolute indifference. Understanding what her presence could mean, Marc's bullish defenses surfaced, preparing to confront her and Zotikos in a nauseating family reunion.

Lithely, she exited the rows of seats onto the polished tile of the walkway spanning the length of the terminal. Marc's stride slowed as he neared her. Conflicting desires brawled within him; he was about to spew the vilest of condemnations, or declare his approbation. Gelid with control, Jessica waited for him to reach her.

Marc stopped a couple of yards away and asked quietly, "Where is he?"

"Not here. His flight left hours ago."

His shoulders relaxed and he closed the gap between them. "What are you doing here alone?"

"That was the plan, was it not? Argentina?"

Her answer was dumbfounding. "You dumped him?" His head shook firmly in the negative. "No. I am sorry, but I will not be sloppy seconds to my father."

Jessica smiled lightly. "Relax. I have a friend on the crew who understands my situation, and he warned me that investigators were waiting for me to disembark to ask another round of questions about my father. This happens from time to time, and I knew that if I exited the boat with you, we would be detained. Accepting Zotikos's job offer got me out of my contract with the cruise line, into new clothes, and off the boat through the celebrity service. He was also my taxi to the airport, as you can see."

She was resourceful, Marc knew, but wondered to what ends her latest endeavor had led. He guessed the rest of the story. "And when you got to the airport and told him you had changed your mind, I presume there was some public display."

"Oh, no such thing happened. He changed his mind on his own, just as expected. I did nothing to end it. Never before have I played my cards in order to ruin my chance at wealth. This was a new experience for me." Addressing his apparent disbelief, Jessica explained, "Your father never bothered to learn my last name until booking my flight with the concierge. He felt my name would invite unwanted scrutiny on himself and the show. Zotikos likes fame, not infamy, you see. He offered a sincere apology and three thousand dollars to assist me onto another plane and—to keep it all quiet."

Her amazing story triggered his charming smile. An impulse to throw his arms around her surged within him, not knowing exactly what emotion provoked that desire. Instead, in his usual composure, he proffered an arm to escort her to board the plane.

Her hand curled around his arm and they settled into a languorous walk. Fully prepared to tell stories, Jessica asked, "So, what is our arrangement, Marcus? What do we tell people we are when they meet us?"

Marc was done with living illusions of himself and his feelings. He said exactly what came to mind. "I am going to say you are my best friend, Brooke Cameron."

ABOUT THE AUTHOR

———————◆———————

After life-long noodling over whether to write a book, Serena Ivo has done so in her quirky opening act, *Fourteen and a Quarter*. Now that the gratifying endeavor is finally complete, she returns to her regular, middle-aged life, blowing thank-you kisses to her husband, to Stephenie, and to Georgette for their inspiration.